FUSIØN

Other titles by S. Usher Evans

THE DEMON SPRING TRILOGY
Resurgence
Revival
Redemption

THE MADION WAR TRILOGY
The Island
The Chasm
The Union

THE LEXIE CARRIGAN CHRONICLES
Spells and Sorcery
Magic and Mayhem
Dawn and Devilry
Illusion and Indemnity

THE PRINCESS VIGILANTE SERIES
The City of Veils
The Veil of Ashes
The Veil of Trust
The Queen of Veils

FUSIØN

THE RAZIA SERIES
BØØK 4

S. USHER EVANS

Sun's Golden Ray Publishing
Pensacola, FL

Sun's Golden Ray Publishing
Pensacola, FL
www.sgr-pub.com

For ordering information, please visit
www.sgr-pub.com/orders

THE RAZIA SERIES

Double Life
Alliances
Conviction
Fusion

Beginnings, a Razia Novella
The Razia Short Story Collection

DEDICATION

To Mike and Terry
I love you

CHAPTER ONE

She blinked her eyes open. It was bright—brighter than her ship. The bed was more comfortable, and there was a person curled up next to her, his arm slung across her bare stomach.

And, *shit*, she'd fallen asleep again.

Lyssa Peate threw the hotel blankets and the arm off of her, starting the annoying search for her underwear and bra on the carpeted floor. Twenty-three years old, brown haired with an array of tanlines on her arms and legs, she didn't normally wake up naked in a hotel room. She found her bra hanging from a lampshade, and her underwear flung underneath a table. Memories of how they'd gotten there wafted up and she pushed them back down. If she could just sneak out before he woke up…

"What's the rush?" Sage Teon murmured, propping his head up on his arm and giving her that stupid grin of his. His blond hair was even messier than normal from sleep, sticking up in odd directions. "Why don't you stay? We can get breakfast and—"

"No."

She said it more for herself than for him, as the thought of lounging in bed with him for a little longer was so tempting it hurt. At the same time, it was too much to have stayed with him at all. Too much to have been drawn to his glimmering eyes and that half-smile that insinuated he wanted her. She hated how much she craved the closeness, how easy it was simply to forget how risky and stupid this was and let herself drown with him.

"Lyss," Sage said, climbing out of bed. He obviously had no problem with being naked around her, as he pulled her against him gently. "Don't go."

For a brief, soft moment, she leaned into him, remembering how it felt to be safe in his arms. Her resolve weakened every moment she remained with him.

And yet, if anyone found out about them…

The thought alone was enough to put the brakes on. She shoved him away, and he fell backward onto the bed, overdramatizing the move with a loud sigh. She ignored the way he watched her as she searched the room for her pants, her shirt, her black boots. It was almost like he expected her to change her mind and stay.

It wouldn't be the first time.

She stood up, fully dressed, and faced him. "We're not doing this again."

"You keep saying that." Sage scratched his stomach lazily. "But wasn't this *your* idea last night?"

She sniffed; he was right. She'd been at Eamon's, the top pirate watering hole, hoping to get a glimpse of the new crop of pirates fighting their way to the top of the pirate webs. But when she'd spotted Ganon, Sage's boisterous and obnoxious pilot, walking through the front door, she knew all of her previous plans for the night would fly out the window.

She and Sage had gotten pretty good at pretending to be normal. They idly chatted, bantered a little as per usual, and waited for the crew to become too absorbed in beer to notice them slipping out the back.

They'd made out a little in the private office, and then disappeared to this hotel room for the rest of the evening. Lyssa never planned on spending the night, but after a few hours of sweaty, tangled bliss, the idea of getting out of his warm embrace was hard to justify. Especially last night, when, in-between their more strenuous activities, their conversation had turned to business. Sage offered his opinions on the pirates she was thinking of capturing while placing distracting kisses on her stomach, and she actually considered them, too exhausted for her pride to speak for her.

Those moments, more than the physical, were the most nerve-wracking the next morning. They reminded her that this wasn't just some no-name sex partner, this was Sage, with whom she had nearly a decade of history.

She shook those thoughts from her head. 'We're *not* doing this again."

"I don't get it," Sage said, lying back. "I haven't told anyone. *Ganon* doesn't even know. What's the problem?"

"The problem is that they don't know *now*," she hissed. "But the moment someone does, like Harms or Ganon or someone with a big, fat mouth, everyone's going to…."

"Going to what?"

"Going to think I'm nothing but your bimbo girlfriend," she growled at him and hated the way his mouth twitched at the word 'girlfriend.' "After all the shit I've gone through, I don't want to throw it away because everyone thinks—"

"You worry way too much what others think," Sage said.

Lyssa glowered at him. It was easy for him to say. *He* never struggled as one of the least wanted pirates. *He'd* had his top twenty status handed to him on a silver platter.

"If they don't respect me," she said through clenched teeth, "then they won't put bounties on me. And if they don't put bounties on me…"

"But they have been," Sage said. "You're in a good place now. So why not relax a little? Slow down and enjoy life?'

"Because this isn't going to last," she whispered to herself so Sage wouldn't hear. Nearly every pirate had seen her stand and face Jukin, and many of them continued to add money to her bounty. Harms had even said that Dissident, the runner of her pirate web, had been singing her praises the week before. Far from being at the bottom rung of piracy, she was one of the most well-known and well-respected pirates.

But, a nagging voice reminded her, things were going too well and the Great Creator had a nasty habit of pulling the rug out from under her just when she felt invincible.

"C'mon." Sage kissed her neck, resting his hands on her hips. "Stay a while."

She answered him by shoving him away and rushing out of the hotel room, slamming the door behind her.

***

Razia walked out of the hotel kitchen, hoping it looked like she was hunting a bounty and not coming from Sage Teon. This, whatever it was, sneaking around, had been going on for months now. It had started after they'd busted everyone out of jail—the heat of the moment and a near-death experience had momentarily made her lose her mind and seek comfort in the most unexpected way.

Then it had happened again. And again. And then she asked *him* to meet *her*. They were now meeting at least two or three times a week. And every time she came back to her senses, she hated herself for being so weak.

A loud whistle cut through her thoughts and she searched for the source of the voice. A pirate she'd never seen before, older, chunky, with a smirk on his face, stood across the street from her.

"You're just a flash in the pan, sweetheart," the cat-caller crowed.

"I'm sorry, who are you?" Razia said, placing a hand on her hip.

"Name's Elric Sacrista—"

"Who?" Razia said with the smallest of smirks. "Leveman's are you even in a web, or do you think you'll get Dissident's attention by annoying one of his top twenty pirates?"

The man's smirk soured immediately and he shuffled away. Razia watched him go with a shake of her head. Even though things were better by a long shot, there were still pirates, mostly those without any notoriety, that thought it good sport to flap their jaws at her.

For the most part, Razia wasn't bothered by them. But she was still worried that those small pirates would influence bigger pirates, and, by extension, Dissident, and he would revoke all of the privileges that he'd bestowed on her.

The thought made her ill.

Actually *ill*, she realized, as a queasy, sick feeling rolled up from the pit of her stomach. She pressed a hand to her belly, taking a deep breath until it passed. As the wave dissipated, she chalked it up to low blood sugar—she'd been too busy with Sage to eat anything.

Memories of the night before replaced the sickness, and a blush crept up her neck. A part of her wondered if he was still in bed and ached to return to him. But the other part was quick to remind her that she had work to do.

The pirate city was mostly quiet since most of the rabble-rousers were sleeping off their partying the night before. She forewent the horrible pirate transport shuttle and walked the six blocks to Harms' bar, mostly because her stomach was still churning. She rubbed her midsection gingerly. Low blood sugar was all it was, and she'd order a soda.

Slowing her walk, she yanked out her mini-computer. The screen was still on the previous night's transactions, where she'd left it before Sage had distracted her. She was hoping to ask Harms about two new pirates that she'd...

She paused in the middle of the street, the sickness returning along with a particular need to empty her stomach. It was stronger than it had been before, and she wasn't sure she could resist it for much longer. Plastering a neutral look on her face, she walked into Harms bar, waving to the man in the back.

"I wondered when I'd be seeing you again," Harms said, a wide smile on his bearded face when she slid in across the booth from him. "Saw your capture of Gene McGuffey on the intraweb yesterday."

"Funny how saving Dissident's life was enough to get my captures posted, huh?" She grinned, but it was tinged by the increasingly familiar sickness. She quickly ordered a drink from Harms' tabletop serving program, and a small serving robot brought it out a few moments later. She drank until the nausea lessened and then sat back in relief.

"Everything okay?" Harms asked.

"Yeah," she said with a nod. "Just haven't eaten anything in a while. So I went to Eamon's last night."

"I heard."

She chewed her lip. "Did you hear anything else?"

"Should I have?"

"Nope," she said quickly. "Anyway, I didn't see a lot of pirates I knew. Seems like a lot of guys are bowing out."

"A lot? Try everyone," Harms said. "You heard Stenson retired, yeah?"

Razia whistled. "That's like...half of Dissident's top pirates."

"Not everyone's willing to test the runner's protections," Harms said. "Jukin may be gone, but this Opli guy is...well let's just say he's been too quiet."

"Quiet is...right." After the prison break-out, Jukin had been demoted to an unknown role in the U-POL, although he'd holed himself up in the Manor. The UBU was still trying to determine if he was to be tried for his part in the presidential assassination, but Razia hadn't heard anything about it in a few weeks.

His second in command, Opli, had taken over his elite unite of pirate-catching policemen and the group had had all but disappeared from D-882. No more random inspections, no more haughty requests for identification even though the U-POL could not arrest pirates.

But Razia knew that he was up to something, even if she didn't know what that something was. Her interest in him was compounded when she found out he knew her dual life as Lyssa Peate, something even Harms didn't know about. The thought of Opli sharing her secret made her queasy, or perhaps the bubbles in her soda had worn off.

"Are you sure you're okay?" Harms asked. "You look pale."

"I'm fine. So, what do the runners think about the new pirates?"

"Obviously, they don't like having a bunch of untested kids languishing in their top twenty," Harms said. "These guys don't know anything about hiding or how to use aliases. It's pretty pathetic."

"Just makes my job easier," Razia said, clenching her jaw. "So what do you think? Go after a new kid or go after one of the last remaining guys?"

"Hard to say. Dissident's been giving mixed messages lately. Obviously, he'd like all of Contestant's pirates captured. But he doesn't want Contestant retaliating against him by going after *his* top pirates, present company included."

She didn't miss how Harms beamed when he spoke, but she had to cover her mouth with her hand as it became dry.

"Are you sure you're all right, honey?" Harms asked.

"Nope," she said, flying out of the booth and dashing into the bathroom.

***

A week later, Lyssa couldn't avoid the reality: she'd caught something nasty. She'd vomited her guts out at Harms' bar, and it had taken all her angry bluster to convince him that she could make it back to her ship without an escort. Although she'd promised Harms she would see a doctor, she'd waited a few days to see if it would pass.

It did, at times. But she never quite shook off the constant nausea, and she'd thrown up enough to put her in danger of dehydration. So, she set a course for the Planetary and System Science Academy where she'd find the universe's top doctors to deal with whatever bacterial or viral infection she'd picked up.

She rolled over onto her side and groaned again, wishing she had someone to bring her a glass of water. She reached over to her mini-computer and dialed the number of her best friend, Lizbeth Carter.

"Hey—What's wrong?" Lizbeth said, her smile melting into a concerned glare. Her curly, light brown hair fell around her face. Lizbeth was at work in her glass-enclosed office, visible behind her head. The new space was a perk of her promotion to lead investigator. "You look terrible."

"I'm sick. Going to the Academy."

"Poor baby," Lizbeth cooed. "Do you want me to meet you there? Carry you to the infirmary?"

Lyssa snorted, but another wave of nausea rolled through her. She moaned and covered her eyes, breathing through it.

Lizbeth tutted. "Boy, you really are sick aren't you? What is it? Fever? Cold?"

"Just...sick, throwing up a lot," Lyssa said, picking up the mini-computer and holding it to look at Lizbeth.

Lizbeth opened then closed her mouth, the corners turning up.

"How are your boobs?"

"What?" Lyssa said, giving her a look.

"Your boobs. How are they feeling?"

"I dunno. They hurt, I guess." Lyssa wasn't sure what illness caused sore breasts, but Lizbeth seemed to have an idea, based on the way her eyes sparkled.

"You, uh…you seen Sage lately?" Lizbeth asked, twirling a light brown curl around her finger.

Lyssa glared at the screen. Lizbeth knew the answer to that question. "Do you think he got me sick?"

"Oh, I think it's possible he gave you something," Lizbeth said lightly. "How much longer until you get to the Academy?"

"Few hours," Lyssa said, closing her eyes.

"Try to take it…easy. Get some rest," Lizbeth said. "I have a feeling you're going to need it in a few months."

Lizbeth's confusing conversation aside, Lyssa did get a little rest before she was being called to announce her license number and dock at the Academy's extra-planetary station. She forewent her normal Academy uniform in favor of sweatpants and a sweatshirt, hoping she could avoid all unwanted attention between her ship and the infirmary.

But there was one person waiting for her when she disembarked. And Lyssa was more than happy to see him.

"Hey, Lyss, how are you feeling?" Vel was Lyssa's little brother, although he could no longer be called little by any stretch of the imagination. Nearly eighteen, he towered over Lyssa as he wrapped his arm around her shoulder. He was in his last year at the Academy, and she was going to be rather sorry when he had a real job and couldn't spend as much time with her.

"Like shit," Lyssa responded, leaning into him. "What are you doing here?"

"Lizbeth told me you were on your way."

Lyssa glowered, still not happy with the "Lyssa-Call-Action-Network" that Lizbeth seemed to have established between herself, Vel, and Sage. Though, she supposed she should count herself lucky that Lizbeth had called Vel instead of Sage. She wasn't sure she could handle seeing him while feeling like the inside of a garbage bag. He might want to *take care of her.*

"How's school going?" Lyssa asked as they made their way over to the lift.

"Nearly done," Vel said with a wide grin. "I can see the finish line."

"Then it's off to Dorst's lab?" Lyssa asked with a little jealousy. Dorst was their second eldest brother and also Lyssa's supervisor. He'd taken it upon himself to pull in all of the Peate siblings under his wing to mentor them, including, surprisingly her after her first supervisor "disappeared."

"Maybe." Vel shrugged. "Maybe there's another Peate who would hire me."

She closed her eyes. "Who?"

"You?"

Her eyes snapped open again. "Why'd you want to work for me? I'm barely here."

"I know, and that's…well…maybe if I worked for you, I might get a little…you know." Vel blushed bright red.

"What?"

"Notoriety that's not associated with our last name," Vel said with a slight wince. "I mean, not that you're not notorious but—"

"I get it," Lyssa said, swallowing to brace her stomach. The motion of the lift was making her dizzy again.

"Would you think about it?" Vel asked.

"Nothing to think about. You're welcome to use my name however you wish. Take the lab, too. Take the sensors, take…" She breathed again.

"Which leads me to my next question," Vel said, and she cracked an eye open at the nervousness in his voice. "When are you going to stop being Lyssa?"

"When I die."

"Rephrasing: when are you going to stop coming to the Academy?"

She shrugged. "Haven't decided yet. Don't have to decide yet. But if or when I do, I'll make sure Sostas's lab comes to you."

"That's not why I asked." Their conversation came to a halt when the lift doors opened to the infirmary and they had to navigate the nearly impossible maze of the medical wing, a series of interconnected hallways designed to accommodate the wide breadth of species needing medical assistance. When they reached the right wing, Lyssa signed in and plopped down on a nearby chair, surveying the room for the nearest bathroom or potted plant for her to empty her stomach into.

"This place brings back memories," Vel said. "Hope we don't run into any U-POL here."

Lyssa groaned. Running was the last thing she wanted to do, a true testament to her sickness. Instead, she leaned her head on Vel's shoulder and closed her eyes.

"Wake me up when they call my name."

***

Two hours and three trips to the toilet later, Lyssa and Vel were finally led back to the long hall of examination room doors. She didn't even protest when he joined her in the room, opting to curl up into a ball on top of the paper and whine loudly about how sick she felt. Vel teased her a little about showing weakness and she threatened to vomit on him. This back and forth continued until the doctor arrived, a young woman barely older than Lyssa who didn't lift her eyes from the tablet in her hands.

"Dr. Lyssandra Peate," she read. "Showing signs of nausea and weakness. Have you been to any planets recently?"

Lyssa shook her head. "Only D-8…er…no. I've been at the Academy."

The continued down her checklist. "Any exposure to foreign species or unknown substances?"

"Nope."

"Sexually active?"

Lyssa nearly fell off the table. "What does that have to do with anything?"

The doctor gave her a look, then glanced to Vel before setting down her tablet. "I'm just going to take a quick blood test."

Before Lyssa could react, the doctor pricked her arm with a small needle and sensory machine. The machine beeped while it was processing then chirped loudly, displaying a green light.

"I thought so," the doctor said, turning to smile brightly at Lyssa. "Congratulations, you're pregnant."

CHAPTER TWO

"P...pregnant?"

The word, at first, made no sense in Lyssa's brain. She repeated it in her mind a few times, knowing it meant something truly awful.

"You're just a few weeks along, so you'll need to visit a specialist to make sure. We have some OB/GYN facilities here, but between us, you would be better off finding a personal doctor to monitor you and your baby's progress. If you use the Academy's doctors, you'll be seeing a different physician every time."

Baby. Pregnant. Meaning she was pregnant. As in having a baby. As in...

"*Shit.*"

"Dr. Peate?" The doctor finally noticed the look of sheer terror on Lyssa's face and softened. "I can tell that this is a...surprise."

Lyssa's stomach threatened again and she wrapped her arms around herself. There was a buzzing in her ear as the shock wore off and panic set in.

She was *pregnant,* meaning she was PREGNANT.

The doctor turned to Vel, who had a similarly shocked look on his face. "So you're the father, then?"

"Leveman's, I'm her brother," Vel said with a disgusted look.

Father. Lyssa groaned loudly and placed her head in her hands. Not only was she…Sage was the… This was so far removed from anything she'd ever thought she would be thinking that she couldn't even process it. Didn't want to process it.

"This isn't the end of the world." The doctor was addressing Lyssa again. "The Academy is very accommodating to expectant mothers. I would notify your supervisor as soon as possible so that you can be placed on maternity leave if you choose. I wouldn't recommend doing any more excavations, although some do choose to work until they can no longer do so—"

"I don't want it." Her voice sounded odd coming out of her own mouth. "I can't have a…" She swallowed, closing her eyes. "I don't want it."

"All right then," the doctor said, hoisting her tablet up to type. "I'll make an appointment for—"

"Not here," she croaked. "I don't…I don't want this on my medical record."

The doctor quirked a brow. "These records are sealed from your supervisor."

"Nothing is sealed," Lyssa whispered. Anything associated with her name could be hacked into by pirates. The only safe way to prevent anyone from knowing about this was to create a new alias and to do that, she'd need to go somewhere no one knew either Lyssa or Razia. "I just…I want to go somewhere else."

"Very well." The doctor scribbled on a paper pad, tore the top sheet off, and offered it to Lyssa. "Here are some facilities nearby that perform the procedure."

"Thank you." Lyssa snatched the paper and stuck it in her pocket so she wouldn't have to look at it. If she didn't see it, none of it would be real. Perhaps the doctor had made a mistake. Perhaps she was in some sort of horrible, fever-induced nightmare.

"Look, I know that you....seem pretty sure about this," the doctor said. "I can only assume the father doesn't know."

That 'f' word struck as loudly as the other four-letter one in Lyssa's mind. Fathers and…mothers. Parents. The evil creatures that had made her life miserable and left her to die on pirate ships.

"I'm going to be sick," Lyssa said, pushing herself off of the bed to hurl in a nearby trashcan. When her stomach finished emptying itself (surprising considering she hadn't eaten anything), the doctor helped her lie back down on the bed and fished a bottle and syringe gun out of a drawer.

"This will help with the nausea," the doctor said, pressing the small gun to Lyssa's bare arm. A prick later, the syringe had emptied. Lyssa took a deep breath and knew the medicine wouldn't do much to fix the turmoil in her stomach.

"Before you make any decisions, you should probably talk with him first. You never know...maybe you'll change your mind."

"I won't, trust me."

The doctor nodded, and picked up her tablet. "After it's done, please schedule a follow-up appointment for a psych eval—"

"We're done, thanks." Lyssa cracked one eye open. The medicine had already taken the edge off of her sickness and she felt a bit more like herself. "I don't need a shrink."

"Very well. I'm sorry that I was the bearer of bad news, Dr. Peate." The doctor exited the room and Lyssa was left with her words and news and this new reality hanging in the air.

"So."

Lyssa's eyes shot upward to meet Vel's. She'd forgotten he was even there. Why did he always have to be around in her worst moments?

He looked furious. "When Lizbeth said I should accompany you to the medical wing, she seemed amused about something. Said you'd need some support." He spoke each word as if it were poison. "So she knew?"

"I…She…I didn't… I don't know how she…"

"She knew that you and Sage are together?"

"We're not together," Lyssa stammered.

"You've *been* together. And you didn't tell me. Neither of you did."

"That's because it wasn't… it wasn't…" Lyssa buried her head in her hands. She couldn't handle his angry face, his disappointment in her. She couldn't handle her own disappointment in herself. Her eyes became wet, but she refused to cry. Crying wasn't going to solve anything.

The mattress beside her dipped as Vel sat down next to her. He wrapped his gangly arms around her, pulling her closer to his chest. "It's going to be okay," he said, stroking her back. "You aren't going to go through this alone, I promise. Sage will—"

She lifted her head. "Sage can't know."

"You have to tell him," Vel said gently.

"I can't."

Vel stiffened beside her. "That's unfair to him. He deserves to know."

That was true, but she couldn't even imagine the conversation. Much like she was hoping to wake up from this nightmare, she could get rid of this problem without ever having to see Sage again. Hiding on a deserted planet for the rest of her life sounded tempting.

"You have a choice, Lyssa, either you tell him, or I will," Vel said, his tone harsh, but his embrace still soft. "I'll give you a day. Then I'm telling him for you."

She slumped lower. A day seemed such a short amount of time to gather the courage she needed.

"I'm not... This is your decision," Vel said. "But it's also his kid. And after all you've been through, he deserves a chance to know before...before you do anything."

She knew he was right, but that didn't make it any easier for her to accept.

He stood and walked toward the door. "Let's go find you some seltzer and crackers before you head out, okay?"

***

D-882 had never looked so alien.

As she walked down the dusty orange streets, Razia felt changed, like she no longer belonged there. She'd always had an inkling of otherness, but now it was magnified. As if everyone knew her secret.

It would have been easier to let Vel tell Sage. She could have simply done the thing and moved on before he was the wiser. But that little voice in her head—the one that used to sound like Vel, then like Lizbeth, and had begun to be more like herself—was fairly clear. This was something she had to do.

The message to Sage asking to meet up was queued on her mini-computer, but she hadn't sent it yet. He'd respond immediately—he always did—and then she'd have to talk to him. She'd have to force out the words that she'd been unable to say since receiving the news.

"Bad news, Lyssa?"

Her blood ran cold. She forced her nerves and panic down, plastering on her normal mask of indifference before turning.

Since his promotion, Opli had grown something of a sparse mustache, a dark brown fuzz that gave him an even weirder vibe than usual. He seemed more sadistic now, a little more confident in whatever he was plotting. Jukin had confidence, too, but Opli's was unsettling. Perhaps because Razia didn't understand his mind the way she understood her brother's.

Then again, she didn't understand Jukin's mind at all.

"Captain," she said with a nod. "How's life?"

"I believe I asked you first," Opli said.

"Same ol', same ol'." Razia shrugged. "Nothing to report."

"That face doesn't say there's nothing to report," Opli said with a knowing look.

It took everything in Razia's arsenal not to show the jolt of fear that raced through her veins. Had Opli been checking on her DSE record? Was her record even updated? The medical records were sealed, but…

He couldn't know, she decided. He was fishing for information. And she would give him none.

"Sorry, kiddo," she said, even though they were more or less the same age. "Nothing to see here."

"Mm." He nodded and kept walking by her. "Shame what happened to your friend Stenson, huh?"

"W…what happened?" Razia asked. Harms had said he'd retired.

"Someone found out about that long-standing murder charge from twenty-five years ago," Opli said, and Razia was pretty sure she knew who did. "Nasty business that. Killed an innocent waitress in an attempted robbery." He paused and inhaled deeply. "One down."

In spite of everything weighing on her mind, Razia was interested. "So that's what you've been up to. Digging up dirt on people to scare them into quitting piracy?"

Opli shrugged nonchalantly. "Everyone has secrets. Everyone has their pressure points. Some…are easier to find than others."

"You're going to tell everyone about mine any time soon?" Razia said. "Because I don't care—"

"I don't have to worry about you, my dear," Opli said. "You're too much like Jukin. I could see his implosion from miles away, same as I can see yours. You'll self-destruct, just like he did."

"Uh, he didn't self-destruct. I ruined his career," Razia said with only a hint of pride. "It was my testimony that—"

"Do you really think you were the only person who knew about Jukin's involvement?" Opli asked. "Did you forget about Jos and Harmon? Minister McDougall? Did it ever occur to you that they might testify about Jukin's involvement to save their own asses?"

Razia swallowed. It hadn't.

"That's the problem with you Peates. You're all so absorbed in your own family dramas that you don't see how your spats affect the rest of the universe. You don't look at the big picture until it comes careening into your worldview. Then you make it all about you." He sighed. "It's quite exhausting to have to deal with."

Razia doubted that, but didn't feel like arguing. She had worse things to take care of.

"As usual, this has been just tons of fun, but I have to go," she said, brushing him off as she walked past him.

He grabbed her wrist and spun her back to face him, peering intently into her eyes. "Oh yes, you've got something delicious, I can tell," he said, sounding almost intimate. "I can't wait to find out what it is."

She swallowed before she could stop herself, and he took a step back in victory.

"Until next time, Lyssa," he whispered, releasing her and disappearing around the corner. Razia's heart thudded in her chest, worry and panic and fear, honest *fear* pulsing through her body. She pulled out her mini-computer and pressed the send button, half because she wanted to release herself from the secret, but half because she craved Sage's comforting presence.

***

Lyssa and Sage had been using the same room on the fifth floor of a motel on D-882 for their secret meetings. Neither one of them checked in, however, opting instead to sneak in through the fire escape. Razia made sure no one had followed her to the motel before silently climbing the stairs. The window was already open, and she sucked in a long breath.

She was barely in the room when his hands were on her, his mouth covering hers in a sensual, hungry movement. Her worries evaporated in his safe embrace, and she forgot why she had been so upset. Everything always seemed less terrifying with him.

"Missed you," he whispered in her ear, trailing a long line down her neck as his hands fumbled with her pants. "Where've you been?"

She closed her eyes and moaned when he kissed that shiver-inducing spot. But reality returned as his hardness pressed into her hips. She pushed him away.

"Teasing me today?" he said hungrily, holding her from behind. His hands slid over her hips to join at her lower abdomen and she panicked, yelping and scurrying away.

"No, we're not..." She stammered, unnerved by the intimate touch. "That's not why I called you here."

His shoulders slumped. "That's mean, Lyss. Don't toy with me like that."

"I just said we had to talk," she snapped. "I didn't say—"

"The only time you message me for anything is to meet up, so sorry for assuming," Sage said, sitting on the bed. His body was tense, as if waiting for the go-ahead to take her back into his arms. She wanted to, more than anything. But she also knew she could never let him hold her again.

Her fear must have shown on her face, because a crease appeared between Sage's brow. "Are you all right? Harms said you barfed your face off last week at his bar."

"I...no...I..." Her tongue twisted in her mouth.

"Lyssa, what's wrong?" He nearly leapt off the bed, wrapping his arms around her gently. His hands ran up and down her back, and she closed her eyes, wrapping her arms around him and diving into the solace there. If she just stayed like this forever, she'd never have to tell him. Nothing would ever have to change.

"Whatever it is, it's okay, I can help, I promise," he whispered into her hair.

"I..." She felt sick, the nausea medication must have worn off. "I..."

"Lyssa." He cupped her face in his hands and stared into her eyes. "I promise you, whatever it is, whatever you've done or not done, I'm not going to be angry." His thumb brushed her cheek. "What's wrong?"

"I...I'm pregnant." The words came out before she realized she had spoken them, and her heart leaped to her throat, waiting for his reaction.

"You're...what?" His face turned to stone and her heart sank to the floor.

"P-pregnant."

"Pregnant?" He blinked, his voice raising an octave. "Like...pregnant?"

She felt ill again, turning away from him so she wouldn't throw up.

"I'm—"

He pulled her back to her before she finished, making the oddest sound—laughter? Horrified, she realized he was grinning like an idiot.

"This is *amazing*!" He grabbed her face and kissed her roughly. "You're pregnant! We're gonna have... Shit, we're gonna have a baby!" He let go of her and turned to run his hands through his hair, his smile so huge it might split his face open.

She couldn't believe her ears. He was *happy* about this? Did he not understand? This was a thousand times worse than anything she'd ever imagined. In what universe would he ever be glad that this had happened?

He turned back to her and she was shocked—utterly shocked—at the pure joy written on his face. He walked up to her and pulled her back into his arms. "Lyssa, I can't…wow…just…" He pressed his lips to hers again.

Lyssa blanched and shoved him away. "*What is wrong with you?*"

"Lyssa, we're having a baby!" Sage ignored her panic in favor of his own euphoria. "We're going to be a family, we're—"

"*I'm getting rid of it.*"

Sage's celebrations came to an abrupt halt, and his eyes widened. "You…what?"

"I don't want this, I don't…this was a mistake…it's…I'm getting rid of it." She hated how his face melted into horror, panic. She hated that she'd been the one to do it to him. Perhaps she should never have told him. She'd never considered that he'd be…happy about it.

Who would be happy about it?

"You can't." Sage's voice became strangled. "You can't…Lyssa, it's our baby…"

Our baby. He'd said it so casually like it was a foregone conclusion. Like they were already one big happy family. Like this was some perfect thing that he'd long been hoping for.

It became hard for her to breathe. She sank to the floor, not even realizing she was taking gulping breaths in panic.

"I can't… I can't do this," she whispered. "I can't be p… I can't be. This isn't happening."

"I know it's unexpected but it'll be okay." Sage knelt before her and took her hands into his. "Don't make any hasty decisions. Think about it—"

"What is there to think about? I can't…I can't have…a b…"

"A baby," Sage finished for her with a smile, brushing hair back behind her ear. "And you can. You can do anything. Labor is nothing —"

"Labor?" Lyssa hadn't even considered *that* problem. She recalled her sisters' screams as they had their first babies.

Her father's angry face at Leveman's Vortex.

Her mother saying Lyssa should have never have been born.

If Lyssa were anything like them…the baby *would* be better off not being born. At least then it wouldn't have to hear it.

"I'm getting rid of it," she announced. "I've made up my mind."

"Please don't."

Sage covered her hands in his and she dared to look at him. He looked scared—honestly scared. "Please don't. I'll take care of it. I promise. Just don't..."

"Sage, you can't take care of a b...of this thing," she spat. "And I can't...I don't want to..."

He took her hands and pressed them into his forehead. "I have never asked you for anything in my entire life, but I am asking you. I'm...I'm begging you. Please don't... I want this kid."

A spasm of anger coursed through her. How dare he even ask her to consider another option? She wanted him to be angry about it, to tell her she was careless and stupid. To rage and throw things because they had made a giant mistake together and now things would be different. But his happiness was more terrifying than if he'd put a hole in the wall.

She set her jaw. "I promised Vel I would tell you and I did. But... I'm going through with it."

"Lyssa, don't—"

"*And there's nothing you can do about it.*"

Sage dropped his hands from hers, and his jaw went slack. She pushed herself to stand, leaving him staring at the wall. The part of her that enjoyed the cuddling and comfort that Sage provided was screaming at her to turn around and repair what she'd just done.

But the other half was terrified of the consequences of staying.

Without another word, she walked to the window and left him, slamming the pane shut behind her.

CHAPTER THREE

When Lyssa needed space from people, she usually found a far-flung planet several hours from civilization with room to run long distances and sort through her problems without another person crowding her. But unfortunately, when she arrived on her chosen planet, another bout of sickness cut short her plans for another multi-mile run. And because she was stubbornly trying to ignore the problem in her pelvis, she hadn't picked up any anti-nausea medication.

She settled in the cool green grass next to a mirror-calm pond, the wind whispering quietly to her and filling her lungs with fresh air. She watched the pristine blue sky punctuated with fluffy white clouds and forced herself to think about anything except the parasite that had decided to ruin her life.

She had settled on calling it that on the way to the planet, unable to stomach calling it the "b" word. Parasite seemed fitting—it was a foreign object that made her sick and threatened to ruin her life if it continued to grow unchecked.

Which raised the question, again, why she was sitting on a planet instead of taking care of the problem.

A side of her knew that it was because she couldn't get Sage out of her mind. More specifically, his terrified pleas for her to keep said parasite.

Our baby.

She wasn't sure which part of that phrase horrified her more. *Our* insinuated that she and Sage were anything more than just friends, and it had taken her a long time to accept their friendship. And *baby...*

Why in Leveman's would Sage ever want a baby?

She glanced back at her ship. The list that the Academy doctor had given her was still crumpled up in the back pocket of her dress pants on the floor of her bedroom. It weighed heavily on her mind. She tried to tell herself she'd done her job and told Sage. There was nothing stopping her from simply looking at the list and doing the thing and getting on with her life as best she could.

But she'd come to this planet instead. And she'd been there for at least five sun-up and sun-downs in this spot, turning over the same song and dance in her head. She was no closer to getting back onto her ship and returning to civilization than when she'd first arrived.

She glanced down at the space below her navel.

"Our baby," she muttered. "Our big fat mistake is more like it."

Lyssa should've known better and taken Lizbeth's advice on birth control. But like so many other things, Lyssa had been complicit to walk the line of recklessness. When she was with Sage, reality was suspended. In the dark, her world became his lips on her skin, the way he held her, the way she fell asleep safe and comfortable. But the cold light of morning was always a rude awakening. It was *Sage* who held her like that. *Sage* who kissed her. *Sage.*

As quick as lightening, her mood turned from pensive to angry, and she hated Sage Teon and his stupid kissing and his stupid face and his stupid...everything.

She knew that being with him would end badly. It was all too good—too perfect. Of course it wasn't going to last. Nothing good ever did.

Her anger disappeared as quickly as it had arrived, turning to a sadness that threatened to leak tears down her face. It had been hard to keep them at bay—perhaps the parasite was making her more emotional than usual. But she hadn't cried since Tauron died, and she wasn't about to start because of a little bug in her lower abdomen.

She poked her stomach. "You've ruined everything, you know."

As the words left her mouth, horror washed over her.

"What did I do to you? What could I have possibly done to have—"

"You were born."

Lyssa recalled the conversation with her mother with vivid clarity. She'd gone to Eleonora's birthday party at Vel's request to try and mend fences. But all that trip did was confirm that Eleonora had blamed Lyssa for everything bad that had ever happened in the Manor. Jukin leaving the Academy to become a police officer, Sostas's disappearance. Eleonora had made damned sure that Lyssa understood where she stood in the house, and that she wasn't welcome in it.

Sostas wasn't any better. An aloof father who used his own daughter in his experiments and ignored the rest of his children. Even those who had never met him, like Vel, still bore the scars of his absence. And she could still feel the hollow space in her soul he'd made when he left her behind at eleven years old.

If there were one speck of either of them in Lyssa, the parasite was better off staying as far away from her as possible. As much as it hurt Lyssa to think that, she knew it was for the best.

But to get rid of the parasite completely?

It might never have been a question if she hadn't gone to see Sage. His face had been so…desperate. Sage had never begged for anything in his life, at least not from her. If she returned to him and told him she'd had the procedure, he would be crushed. And if she didn't…

Her mind flashed with a scene from a hypothetical future, where a brown-hared toddler stomped around Sage's ship, getting underfoot with his crew. Ganon would probably be like an uncle, teaching the kid awful things about drinking and women. Sobal would probably get babysitting duty more often than not. And Sage…

Sage would love that kid. He was genuinely decent and mostly kind to everyone on his crew. He made sure they were fed and watered, and they all seemed happy on his ship. He'd risked his life to save theirs without a second thought when Jukin had arrested them.

But taking care of a pirate crew is different than taking care of a baby, one side of her snapped.

But he wants to try, the other retorted.

"Whose side are you on?" Lyssa grumbled to herself.

Her sensors began to beep softly from the pond, and she stood to retrieve them. After wiping it on her pants, she stuck it back in her bag. The results were queued up on her mini-computer, which she'd finally turned off after receiving a series of calls from Lizbeth and Vel. Sage, at least, had been smart enough to give her space.

Or perhaps he was truly hurt and angry at her after what she'd said to him. She had no idea what prompted her to lash out like that, other than that was her default setting.

But she had to admit it was a little…delicious to have the power to make him miserable. To know that with a few simple words, she could ruin his life…

Lyssa felt sick at the thought. That was why her own mother loved to torture her children. That voice, that tendency to rip out hearts and eat them in front of her victims. That evil resided in Lyssa, and it frightened her that she liked it.

"Yet another reason why this is a *terrible idea.*"

***

Lyssa got in her ship, left the atmosphere of the planet, and promptly landed on a different spot half an hour later. She tried to tell herself it was because she wanted to get more geographically diverse samples, but she couldn't even force that thought without smelling her own bullshit.

Which only served to make her sick, considering how sensitive she had become to smells. Even figurative ones.

Having gotten her fair share of sun over the past week, Lyssa was thankful for the thick canopy of trees overhead. Her sensors sat unused in her backpack and her mini-computer was still off. She was now receiving hourly calls from Lizbeth. Based on some of the messages that Lyssa had seen, it might be safer to never answer her mini-computer again. Vel, at least, had stopped calling.

And not a peep from Sage.

It bothered her more than she'd thought possible. She wondered if she'd truly crossed a line and gone too far. Had she maxed out Sage's patience? Usually when she lost her temper with him, he'd bluster and yell back, but he'd always be there when she needed him.

She found herself glaring at the thing in her stomach then stopped, swallowing hard. It was terrifying how much like Eleonora she was becoming. Maybe that was what parasites did—maybe Eleonora had been a decent human before she'd become pregnant twenty-four times.

"Focus," she said to the empty forest and, for the next hour, she did. She used her sensors to test the molecular makeup of trees and bushes and vines. She tested the acidity of a stream. She took photos of the lake it ran into. She even used her fauna sensor on a clump of hair she found. If she hadn't known any better, she would've considered herself a real Deep Space Explorer.

Her amused thoughts ended when she stumbled on a nest of hairy humanoids. Long black hair covered their giant, muscular bodies except for a black face. Black eyes like orbs stared back at her, and they stopped eating and scratching themselves with thick, wrinkled hands.

"Shit," Lyssa swore. If these creatures were sentient, if they understood language and used tools, she'd been in another quagmire where she'd have to run the planet through the UBU inclusionary process. Last time that happened, she was stuck in meetings for three months. "Uh…you guys understand me?"

A faint growling came in response and Lyssa took a step backwards, primed to run back to her ship if need be. She counted the number of black-haired beasts and realized that there were only a few adults and the rest were children. It was a nest of mothers and babies.

"Oh, very funny," Lyssa muttered.

One of the tiniest babies came tumbling towards her and she took a step back, watching the mothers for a reaction. Although they seemed wary, they didn't move to snatch their wayward toddler away from the intruder. Lyssa stood as still as a tree, while the baby played with the laces of her running shoes. It opened one of Lyssa's pockets on her cargo pants, reeling back in surprise when the fasteners made a noise.

Lyssa glanced to the mothers, who didn't move.

The baby returned and played with the pocket a few more times, making a noise that sounded very close to laughter and the corners of

Lyssa's mouth turned upward. She stiffened as it climbed Lyssa's legs and landed in her arms.

"Oof." Lyssa began to laugh as the baby played with her braid, chewing on it before spitting it out with a disgusted face.

She glanced at the mothers, who had returned to their business. One of the smaller babies hung from his mother the same way this little one was in Lyssa's arms, even down to chewing the hair.

This baby considered Lyssa to be its mother. Swallowing hard, Lyssa put the little baby on the ground. "Sorry, I'm not a mother."

The baby tried to climb back up Lyssa and she took a step back. Another faint growl came from the nest of mothers.

"Hey, look, I am the least maternal person in the universe," Lyssa barked at them.

The biggest black-haired creature stood up, towering over Lyssa by at least ten feet. She roared loudly, shaking the forest. There was an answering roar from somewhere far away in response—the father, perhaps?

"Okay, thanks of the fun, goodbye!" Lyssa said, turning on her heel and sprinting to the safety of her ship.

***

Lyssa peered out of her ship, glancing around for any of the people she was actively trying to avoid. She had quickly excavated a different planet, telling herself that it was because she didn't want the Academy to disturb the nest of black-haired creatures and not because she was trying to avoid returning to civilization for as long as possible. But after the second excavation, her meal supplies were running low and she hadn't even *thought* about bounty hunting in weeks, so she forced herself to fly back to the Academy.

That didn't mean she wanted to be seen there though.

She wasn't sure whom she could trust not to put in a call to Vel or Lizbeth, so she hurried quickly to the lift after docking her ship. She had sent a request to Dorst to ask to be put in the planet-selling queue this morning—stating it was urgent that she leave the Academy that day—and was impatiently waiting for a response. Nervously, she checked her medical records to see if there had been any update to her status and was relieved to see there was only a mention of her appointment for nausea.

Next, she switched applications to check on the latest in the pirate web—namely her own bounty. She made a mental note to call Harms to see if anyone had questioned her month-long disappearance from D-882, and prayed he'd say that no one even had mentioned her.

The irony of wanting people to forget about Razia was not lost on her.

The lift doors opened, and she stepped out, eyes glued to her mini-computer as she surveyed the latest news on the intraweb. Most of the names she saw were unfamiliar—which boded well for her since, as Harms had said, most new pirates were stupid and made for easy pickings. Then again, if she went for an easy pirate, it wouldn't be as bounty-worthy as if she went after one of the more established pirates—

She became aware of two people standing in front of her lab. One glance up, and she spun on her heel, running back to the lift.

"Oh, no, you don't!" Lizbeth called, but it was Vel who caught her by the arm, spinning her around to face her fate.

Lizbeth had been angry with her countless times, but the pure fury on Vel's bright red face was new and alarming. He had a vice grip on her arm and dragged her back to the front of her lab to face Lizbeth.

"Where in Leveman's swirling Vortex have you been?" Lizbeth seethed, grabbing her other arm.

"Out."

"Why didn't you answer your mini-computer?" Vel growled.

"Because."

"I'm going to deck her," Lizbeth said to Vel. "I swear to Leveman's Vortex, I am going to *deck you*."

"Did you do it?" Vel asked.

Lyssa swallowed hard and didn't answer.

"Lyssa, you'd better tell me, because I'm going to knock your lights out and I'd feel really bad about hitting a pregnant woman," Lizbeth said.

Lyssa shot her a death glare. "It's none of your business what I do."

"You're right. It's not," Vel said dangerously. "But it is *his*." He pointed into the lab, where a dark figure sat at one of her tables of equipment.

Her heart leaped into her throat.

Lizbeth yanked her closer. "You listen here. You are being a complete and total *bitch* right now—and that's compared to your normal behavior. You drop a bombshell on the guy and then disappear for three weeks?"

"And you don't answer your mini either," Vel added.

"Do you know what we've been doing?" Lizbeth growled. "Babysitting your baby-daddy, who doesn't know if his kid is alive or —"

"Lyssa, he's a mess," Vel said, more gently. "You owe it to him to talk to him."

"It appears I don't have a choice," Lyssa grunted, nodding to the vice grip on her arms.

"You don't," Lizbeth said, as Vel opened the doors. "Now *fix it*."

With a heave, they shoved her into her lab.

The doors closed behind her, blocking out the sound and some of the light from the outside. She didn't move to turn on the lights in the lab—aside from the fact that she'd never bothered to replace the burnt out bulbs. And she always felt a little better talking in the dark.

Sage hadn't moved to look at her. She wanted to ask him why he was waiting at the Academy for her, but her mouth wouldn't work. She couldn't see his face, but he was *truly* a mess. He slumped in the chair, absentmindedly playing with one of her microscopes. His hair was more disheveled than normal, and it was entirely possible he hadn't changed clothes since she'd left him on D-882.

Guilt weighed heavily on her shoulders; she'd made him this way. She had yelled at him then disappeared and she had hurt him.

"So it's done?" he asked, his voice hollow.

She looked at the floor, counting the tiles instead of answering.

"It's okay if you did." His voice was barely above a whisper. "I don't... I know...it's probably for the best anyway."

A vice tightened around her heart, and she turned to run out of the lab. But Lizbeth and Vel stood with their backs to her, guarding the door. She could fight the two of them if needed, but...

She closed her eyes and took a long, deep breath. She was tired of the panic and worry. Of thinking about her own parents and all the horrible things they had done to her. Of worrying if she'd made the right decision. Or if she should change her mind.

"No. I didn't."

The microscope clattered to the ground. "You didn't go through with it?"

She shook her head, still staring at the doors. Footsteps echoed behind her.

"You didn't?"

"I don't…I don't know what to do," she whispered. "I can't…I don't want this baby." He stood behind her, not saying a word and she hated it. She hated that he was deferring to her and allowing her to rip his heart out. She wanted him to yell and scream at her for hurting him like this. He'd never allowed her to do it before, so why were things different now? But even more, she hated that she had thought about hurting him for even a second. Sage was her best friend, and she was destroying him.

"But you do. So I'm going to do it for you."

Sage made a strangled noise behind her and she couldn't look at him. She didn't want to know how happy he was. She was afraid of how that would make her feel.

"Thank you."

His emotion triggered that nasty voice in her mind. The one that enjoyed hurting him. "I want you to understand that I don't want anything to do with this…thing after it's here. I'm just… this is just… You take care of it."

"I will. I promise."

She nodded and took a step forward, but he wrapped his arms around her from behind. For a moment, she let herself lean into him and like before, everything was suspended. She had needed this embrace for weeks, to give her worries to someone else and just be safe.

Angrily, she shoved him away, baring her teeth at him and hating herself for the words that came out of her mouth. *"Don't ever touch me again."*

He took a step back and nodded, and she nearly lost her mind at the hurt on his face.

"You aren't to see me, you aren't to talk to me, you aren't even to *think* about me," she continued. "And you can't tell a *soul*."

He nodded again and it just made her angrier. Why wasn't he fighting back?

"Get lost," she snapped, sitting down at her desk. "I have planets to sell."

He stood behind her for a moment, but she didn't dare look at him. Her heart began to race, wondering if, perhaps, he wasn't going to let her shut him out the way she always did. After an eternity, she heard her laboratory doors open and her heart sank.

"Well?" Vel said.

"I'm gonna be a dad…" Sage was excited, but a bit dampened. It hurt to know that she'd ruined it for him.

Shouts, celebrations, and happy laughter echoed in and it enraged Lyssa. They didn't care how any of this affected her; their only concern was that *Sage* was miserable. They had no idea how the decision weighed on her.

"I can't wait to throw you a baby shower!" Lizbeth said.

Lyssa stiffened in her chair and spun around, marching out into the hall.

"Will you three keep it down?" she hissed, wiping the smiles off of their faces. "This is not to be spread around, do you understand? *No one can know about this.*"

Lizbeth quirked her eyebrow but said nothing.

"I think Dorst is going to notice after a while," Vel said.

"No, he's not, because I'm not going to tell him," Lyssa said. "And if you know what's good for you, you won't tell anyone."

"Understood," Sage said, speaking for the other two who were dumbstruck. "So what do you want me to do now?"

"You heard me," she said flippantly. "Get lost."

She felt the air change then a fist hit her chin. She stumbled backwards into the glass doors and held her stinging cheek, shocked.

"Lizbeth!" Sage cried. "Are you okay, Lyss?"

"Don't help her bitch ass up," Lizbeth seethed, holding her red hand. "She's done nothing but shit all over you and you still defend her?"

"She's pregnant! You can't hit a pregnant lady!" Vel said.

"I can when she deserves it," Lizbeth said.

Lyssa pulled away her hand and saw a little blood. She wiped it on her pants and glared at Lizbeth. "I don't recall asking for your opinion."

"You know," Lizbeth said, approaching Lyssa dangerously, "I have put up with a lot of your shit over the past year because I thought, 'hey, she's had a messed up childhood, maybe I can fix her.' But you can't fix someone who doesn't want fixing."

"I don't *need* fixing."

"Right, you don't, so I'm done!" Lizbeth said, stepping back. "I'm done with you."

"Fine!" Lyssa said. "I didn't want you around anyway!"

Lizbeth gestured rudely before turning on her heel and storming down the hall. Lyssa's heart pounded in her chest as she watched her go.

"Here," Sage said, reaching for Lyssa's face.

"Don't touch me," Lyssa growled, turning and walking into the lab.

CHAPTER FOUR

Planet sold, Lyssa jumped on her ship and shot back to D-882, hoping that bounty hunting would erase everything that had happened—Sage's downtrodden face, Lizbeth's right hook, even Vel's look of disappointment weighed heavily on her. Her mind was too jumbled, too unwilling to focus on the task at hand. So instead of hunting one of the more established pirates, she decided to look for one of the upstarts—Halstead Fiege. He was new to the top twenty, a member of Insurgent's web, and was a fairly decent hijacker. His crew was all newly hired, which meant they were motivated more by money than by friendship, like Sage's crew—

"*Stop*," she barked to the emptiness of her ship. She didn't want to think about him.

In any case, even if Fiege had a good crew, he was still green to a top pirate status. Soon, he'd make some rookie mistakes, and Razia was hoping to capitalize on them.

If she could get rid of the morning sickness. Some days, she could eat normally but others, even the smell of the bland meal bars made her want to hurl. When she stepped into the docking station reeking of ship fuel, she swayed and gagged. Cupping a hand over her nose and mouth, she held her breath until she was on the lift. On the next floor down, someone with terrible body odor stepped onto the lift, and she put her shirt over her nose, earning herself a dirty look from the man.

When she arrived at the shuttle station, the smell of burning trash and smoke welcomed her. And, because she could get no relief, the next shuttle was so far away it wasn't even on the monitor. She had the option to travel back up to her ship and use her Razia C-card to find parking much closer in. As one of Dissident's top pirates, she was now afforded prime parking at discounted rates—provided she use an alias that was publicly linked to Razia. But that also meant that a pirate could see her ship, thus making the shape and model public knowledge. It was stupid to risk it, especially as her mobility was one of her closely guarded secrets. The only people that knew what her ship looked like was Sage—

She groaned loudly and tapped her head against the wall behind her.

The shuttle arrived nearly half an hour after she'd sat on the stone bench, and then promptly broke down near the next station, which meant another hour of breathing through her mouth and trying not to get sick. When she finally reached her stop—Harms' station—she spent a good ten minutes leaning against the railing in the fresh air just to settle her stomach. Harms was pretty quick on the uptake, and would know if something were amiss. She trusted that Sage wouldn't say anything but—

She grimaced again and walked into the bar, plastering a fake smile on her face and waving to Harms.

Harms raised an eyebrow at her as she approached his booth. "What's wrong?"

She nearly tripped over her feet. "W-what?"

"You look too happy. What's going on?"

"N-nothing," she said, her smile falling to a grimace. "Just… whatever."

"There she is." Harms beamed as she sat across from him in the booth. "What's on your mind, Razia?"

"Halstead Fiege. Heard anything about him?"

"A bit," Harms said. "He's the apple of Insurgent's eye since Conboy Conrad got arrested last week."

She furrowed her brow. "Arrested? But I thought we took care of that?"

"Sit back and listen to this," Harms said, and Razia had an inkling that he'd told this story multiple times over the past few days. "You know how you'd always see Conrad and Max Fried together, yeah?" Razia nodded. "Turns out they were more than buddies—they'd been married for a few years."

"Aren't they in different webs?"

"Yep," Harms said with a nod. "Insurgent never quite liked them hanging out together, but when he found out how much time they spent together, he was livid."

Razia was suddenly very glad no one had ever found out about her dalliance with Royden Relleck, a member of Contestant's web. It never escalated to anything more than making out, and he'd been pretty quick to drop her once she left her top pirate status.

Then again, she and Sage—she quashed that thought before it got started.

"As if that weren't bad enough," Harms paused for dramatic effect, "Insurgent found out that Conrad had been feeding information to Fried and Protestor. Pillow talk, as it were. That was his last straw, and he kicked Conrad out of the web." He paused again and clicked his tongue. "But here's the kicker: no one told Conrad. So he's out hijacking a ship, and who should show up but the Universal Police Special Forces."

"Imagine that…" Razia said, but wasn't at all surprised. *Everyone has secrets. Everyone has their pressure points. Some…are easier to find than others.*" At the time, she'd thought Opli was bluffing. After all, pirates had very little shame. How much damage could secrets cause? Then again, if anyone found out about her little parasite problem… She shifted uncomfortably and glanced at Harms. "How did Contestant find out about them anyway?"

Harms shrugged. "I have no idea, to be honest. Contestant had known there was a leak for a few years, but couldn't place the source.

And all of my sources have heard about it from me."

"Your sources at the U-POL?"

"Yeah, Dipzenski and the rest of 'em in booking send their regards," Harms said with a nod. "The boys are wondering when they'll see you again."

Razia smiled, but her wheels were turning. "So if Dipzenski didn't know, that means Opli is using the U-POL outside of the normal process."

"Captain Opli? What do you hear of him? He's been pretty quiet as of late."

"Something he said to me the other day," Razia said, glancing out into the orange street. "Stenson didn't retire, you know. He was scared into hiding."

Harms leaned forward. "Stenson is one of my friends. What do you know?"

"I know he was wanted for murder," Razia said. "That's what Opli said."

"Stenson couldn't have been involved in that." Harms shook his head. "It's not possible. I know him. Do you think Opli was just trying to get under your skin?"

"But see, that's his thing. He's not like Jukin, who's just going to barrel in and arrest people. Opli wants to destroy piracy by exposing secrets, one pirate at a time. I mean, the runners cover a lot of sins, but not all of them."

"No wonder he was so chummy with me." Harms grunted. "He was always floating around here when Jukin was still in charge of things. Speaking of…has anyone heard from our favorite has-been?"

Razia shook her head. "At this point, I'd take Jukin over Opli. At least with Jukin I can mostly predict what he's going to do. With Opli…"

"As long as you're in the pirate web, there's nothing to worry about. Dissident is still grateful. I haven't heard him complain about you in weeks."

She paused, then asked, "Did anyone notice I'd been gone for a while?"

"A few guys wondered, but only because they're hunting you."

She chewed her lip. "Who?"

"I can't tell you, you know that." He grinned proudly. "You wanted to be a top pirate, you gotta get hunted every so often."

She beamed and sucked down some water.

"So, I haven't seen Sage in a while. Hear anything about him?" Harms asked.

She nearly choked. "No? Why?"

"I just usually see him more often than this. I guess that's a good thing, since he's usually here wondering how I can keep your ass out of trouble."

"Yeah," she said, glancing down at the table.

"What? No bluster? No 'I don't need anyone's help'?"

"Not today," she said, feeling a little sick. She hoped that Sage had gotten over her nasty words and was back to normal, but even she wasn't that stupid. A part of her wanted check on him, but she decided against it.

After talking strategy with Harms, and handing over a lot of money to get his information on Fiege, Razia set out in the hot afternoon to look for him. Her fingers danced across the screen of her mini-computer as she walked down the street, searching on the new names that Harms had given her. Fiege had made the unfortunate mistake of using one of his secret aliases when he'd stopped to talk to Harms.

Fiege had recently completed a large hijacking job and Harms mentioned that he had a penchant for gambling, which meant a trip to the casino district for Razia. It was across town from her usual haunts, but she opted against the shuttle system to get there. Even though the city was hot and dusty, the long walk was better than sitting in a shuttle that smelled of body odor. Her nausea was returning, so she stopped in a sundries place to grab a bottle of fizzy water and some crackers.

She reached the casino district by the time the sun was low in the sky, though she couldn't tell if it was night or day from the bright lights of the advertisements and casino signs. Through glass doors that marked the entrance of the betting houses, pirates sat at slot machines, mindlessly pulling levers and grimacing as they lost more of their hard-earned credits. Razia glanced at her mini-computer and grinned; Fiege was, as expected, playing a game of poker.

"I'm so good, I can't even stand it," she said, trotting down to the casino where he'd made his last purchase.

The doors slid open and she was assaulted by smoke and booze. Coughing, she covered her mouth and rushed back out into the night air. Steeling herself, she took in a gulping breath and marched back in.

The room was bright and sonorous from the slot machines, and the contents of Razia's stomach rose in her mouth, especially as a girl approached her with a tray of beers. Razia violently shook her head and waved her off, more to get the alcohol smell away from her than to dismiss the waitress. Razia asked another girl about the location of the poker games, and was directed to a backroom filled with a thick cloud of smoke.

"Ugh." She winced.

She spotted Fiege sitting at a table, grinning with the glow of recent ascension to the top echelon of pirates. Her stomach was a mess, but as usual, her stubbornness won out over the rest of her. She nonchalantly walked into the poker room, keeping her face neutral as she passed Fiege, who ignored her. Razia spotted an empty seat at a nearby table and sat down.

"Deal me in."

"Hey princess!" said a voice to her left. Razia cursed her luck and nodded hello to Ganon, Sage's pilot. Not only did she have the misfortune of sitting at his poker table, but the entire crew was there— Sobal, the seventeen-year-old computer hacker who was attempting to count cards, Keal, Sage's good-natured mechanic, and Sage's three hulking body guards. But, she glanced around several times to make sure, there was no Sage.

"He ain't here," Ganon said. "Gave us the month off."

She nearly fell out of her seat. "Say what?"

"He's been acting real squirrelly lately," Sobal said next to her. "He's not answering calls. Then, he gave us a huge bonus and we got the month off."

Ganon surveyed her. "You know anything about that?"

"Nope. I'm not his babysitter." She tried very hard not to wince at her own choice of words. "What are you playing?"

"Poker, 5-card draw," Ganon said. "You know how to play?"

It had been years, not since her time on Tauron's ship, but this type of poker was a favorite of pirates. She raised her eyebrow at Ganon and turned to the dealer. "Let's play."

With an eye on the table next to her, she played a few games with Sage's crew, winning more credits as Ganon kept buying them rounds of shots. Razia's first one sat untouched next to her, as the mere thought of the whiskey made her want to hurl. After a bit, Ganon noticed her sobriety.

"You're worse than Sage, you know. Won't touch a drop of anything," Ganon slurred, showing off his cards to her. "*Bo-ring.*"

The dealer shared a look with Razia and shook his head. Obviously, this happened a lot.

Ganon, oblivious to the fact that Razia knew he was holding only a pair of aces to her three queens, leaned over to her. "I'm serious, I'm worried about Sage. There's something not right with him—and with all these pirates up and retiring…"

"What do you hear about that?" Razia asked, pulling her cards closer.

"Man, it's bad. Guys are scared," Ganon said. "That's why I'm worried about Sage. It's not like him not to contact us. First, last month, he was telling us to do jobs without him and now he's given us the month off—"

She blinked. "He gave you *this* month off and disappeared?" Which meant he'd gone two months without working. Although Sage wasn't nearly as concerned with piracy as she was, he enjoyed the thrill of hijacking and other nefarious endeavors. For him to have stopped completely… She swallowed nervously. Perhaps it was time for her to call him.

Out of the corner of her eye, she saw Fiege stand and pat a guy on the back. Judging by the way he was walking, he was headed straight for the bathroom.

"Well gents, it's been fun." She stood and put her cards down. "Back to work for me."

Before she got two steps, Ganon grabbed her hand and pulled her close to him. "Please…if you see Sage, can you let me know? I'm really worried about him."

She hesitated, wondering if she should tell Ganon that she knew Sage was all right (at least, she hoped he was), but she was afraid he'd think something was up between the two of them.

With a sneer, she ripped her hand out of his. "I don't know and I don't care."

Ganon glared at her. "I don't know what he sees in you. Bitch."

She turned on her heel and walked away, trying to ignore the way Ganon's barb hit her somewhere deep in her stomach.

***

Razia leaned against the wall of the bathroom door and waited, tapping her fingers on her arms and keeping an eye on Fiege's goons across the room. They hadn't even noticed her yet, or if they did, they didn't want to interrupt their game. Either way, they were too far to come to their boss's aid, which meant this would be one easy capture.

Her eyes drifted down to her midsection, and she snapped her head back up. Now was not the time to be worrying about the parasite.

The door opened and Fiege walked out, wiping his hands on his pants.

"Hi," she said with a knowing grin.

He turned his head to look at her and froze. His eyes darted to his men across the room, who'd finally noticed that he might need them to come to his aid. But, as she'd predicted, they were too far to help. So Fiege took off running—*away* from his bodyguards. Razia sprinted after him, rolling her eyes at his idiot mistake.

He burst through the casino doors and into the dark night, scrambling and clawing at the air as he bolted. She laughed; as if she would lose him so easily.

Then the sickness rolled up inside of her, and she slowed to a jog.

"Not *now*," she hissed to her stomach. With a gulp of air, she sprinted after him as he ducked into an alley. So he wanted to fight, huh? She could do that.

"You're a fast runner," he said, his fists up. "I like that. Bet you ain't fast in bed though."

"Really?" Razia folded her arms over her chest. "You want to start with that? Bet you suck at foreplay, too."

Fiege bared his teeth—he looked a lot older than Razia had thought. Mid-forties perhaps. He must have been working at this piracy thing for a while.

"You'd be a nice prize, you know." He inched forward. "Insurgent's been talking about getting your ass in prison for a while."

"And after I saved his life." Razia tutted, shaking her head. "Well, that's gratitude for you—"

Fiege reared forward with a right hook, which Razia easily ducked. He swung and kicked, and she was content to dodge his blows with a superior smile on her face.

"That's all you got?" She shook her head again. "And here I thought you'd be a challenge."

In slow motion, Fiege's fist flew toward her midsection—and she twisted out of the way so it rammed into her lower back instead. She stepped back from him, trying not to wince as she moved. Fiege smirk told her he knew she was hurt and couldn't fight back.

She pictured him pummeling her stomach and a jolt of fear shot through her. What would that do to the parasite?

On instinct, she spun on her heel and ran away.

It took her four blocks to lose Fiege. Four long blocks filled with self-loathing and wondering why she was running instead of fighting him. When she glanced behind her and saw he wasn't there, she stopped in an alley and leaned against a metal trash bin, clutching her side.

She knew that Fiege would tell everyone that she'd run instead of fighting him…but the more pressing concern was the parasite. Fiege had rammed her hard in the back, but if she hadn't turned in time, if she'd done something to hurt the parasite, she'd never be able to forgive herself. Tears gathered at the corners of her eyes as she imagined the look on Sage's face when she'd told him that she'd ruined everything. Her heart broke when she thought of the parasite no longer inside of her.

She heard footsteps approaching and quickly rubbed her face to keep the emotion off of it. She crouched behind the trash bin, wincing at the bruising on her back, and waited. Fiege had followed her, but his crew had joined up with him now, and they were talking about how cowardly she was to have run away instead of fighting.

And yet, as they loudly besmirched her character, all Razia could think about was getting back to her ship so she could make sure her little parasite was all right.

Fiege and his crew ignored the alley where she hid, but she waited a good long time before painfully standing and heading back.

CHAPTER FIVE

Lyssa glanced around nervously as she left her ship in the docking station and stepped out into the busy street. S-864 was the capital planet of the Universal Beings Union, and one of the most populated in the universe. It also happened to be the home of her supposed-former-best-friend, who had not called her in a few weeks. Lyssa felt odd arriving on the planet and *not* calling Lizbeth, but then again, she didn't want anyone to know what she was up to.

The building before her stretched into the sky, as did all the others. Lyssa took a deep breath and walked into the tile-floor lobby. A lone security guard sat behind a desk, and asked her if she needed help, to which she shook her head. She passed him to step into a gold-plated lift, pressing the button for the seventh floor.

The lift opened into another carpeted hallway lined with doors. She wrapped her arms around herself as she glanced at the nameplates on the door until she stopped at the one she was looking for. She turned the knob and pushed the door open to a room full of expectant women, each with different sized bellies. They all sat uncomfortably, and some with young children they were trying to keep entertained.

One woman, who looked like she was about to explode, gave Lyssa, with no sign of pregnancy whatsoever, a look that could kill.

"Checking in?" The lovely receptionist was perky and obnoxiously happy in the window.

Lyssa ignored the glares and walked to the window. "Y-yeah, name's L—Lauren Dailey." She hoped the new name came out as well as her old one. For only the second time in her life, she'd had to create a new persona in the Universal Bank. Too many people could track her Lyssa Peate account, and she wanted to be able to move in private.

Especially in this place.

"And when is your due date?" the receptionist asked.

"I…I don't know yet," Lyssa whispered, placing a hand on her stomach. "First appointment."

"Congratulations!" She handed Lyssa a tablet and beamed. "We'll just need you to fill out some forms."

Lyssa nodded and took the tablet, settling in a nearby chair. At the Academy, her record was meticulously maintained and she only had to fill out her medical need for that appointment. But since this was unaffiliated—one of the main reasons why Lyssa had chosen it—she had to document her medical history.

She glossed over some of the unimportant injuries and ignored the section on her family's medical history entirely. When she finished, she stood and handed the tablet back to the receptionist and waited. Next to her, a little child with dark brown skin and twisted braids was playing with blocks. She flashed Lyssa a bright smile, and Lyssa smiled weakly back. In the corner, a child with a mop of red hair and porcelain skin squealed as his mother took away his toys then laid on the ground, kicking and screaming.

Lyssa noted it was the same mother who had given her a death look and suddenly felt a rush of pity.

"Miss Dailey? Lauren Dailey?"

It took Lyssa a moment to recognize the name and she scrambled to follow the nurse. Unlike the Academy infirmary with thousands of rooms, this small office had only three, the first of which the nurse led Lyssa into.

"All right, love, now you just settle in and get comfortable. Do you need anything?" the nurse asked. "Crackers?"

Lyssa nodded fervently. "How'd you know?"

"You look a bit green. Don't worry, the morning sickness ends after a few weeks." She pressed a syringe gun to Lyssa's arm and drew blood. "Normally, anyway."

Lyssa gulped. "What do you mean, normally?"

"Some women have the sickness throughout their pregnancy. Poor dears. Sometimes we have to hospitalize them. Oh goodness, your heart rate is quite high."

Lyssa hadn't even noticed the nurse was taking her blood pressure and heart rate. "I'm a bit nervous." Nervous was an understatement. She had spent the past week and a half petrified that she'd done something to the parasite, that her fight with Fiege had caused irreparable damage. Or that something with the parasite was wrong, something unimaginably horrible. She kept picturing herself having to go back to Sage and couldn't wipe his heartbroken face from her mind.

"Don't be." The nurse patted her on the shoulder. "Dr. Bianco will be in shortly. Just make yourself comfortable."

Lyssa watched the door close and kicked her feet against the table legs. Photos of different stages of pregnancies lined the walls, and her eyes landed on a rather grotesque model of a baby coming out of... She blanched and closed her legs tighter. That did not look comfortable.

In an attempt to distract herself, she used her mini-computer to log into the pirate web and check on the latest.

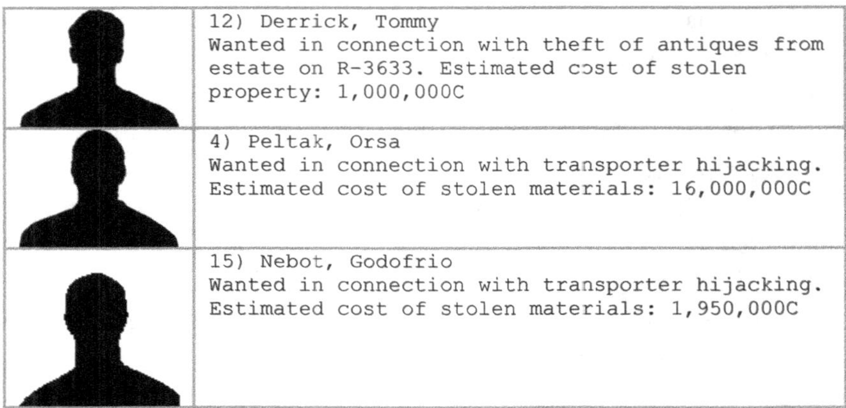

	12) Derrick, Tommy Wanted in connection with theft of antiques from estate on R-3633. Estimated cost of stolen property: 1,000,000C
	4) Peltak, Orsa Wanted in connection with transporter hijacking. Estimated cost of stolen materials: 16,000,000C
	15) Nebot, Godofrio Wanted in connection with transporter hijacking. Estimated cost of stolen materials: 1,950,000C

She frowned, yet again—none of these guys were familiar. She was used to seeing names like Gongago, Hardrict, Stenson, the old guard of pirate who'd been around since Tauron was alive. But Opli was picking them off one by one. Would he keep exposing secrets forever? She thought that would get awfully boring after a while.

On a whim, she searched for her own pirate web history:

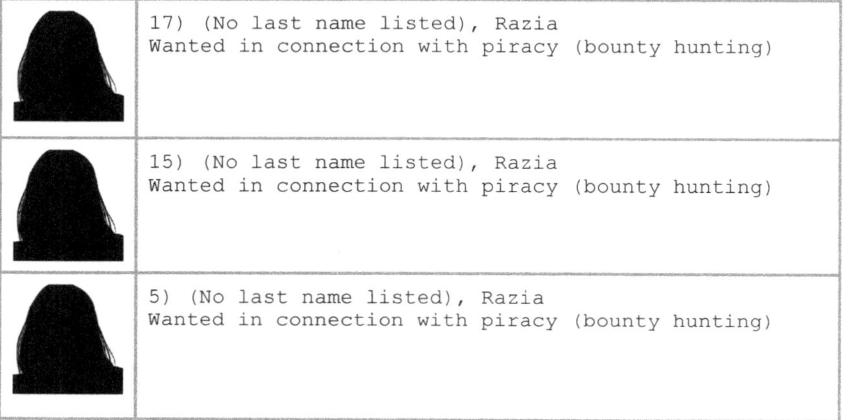

She smiled. Not too long ago, she never would have seen her own activity on the pirate web. A sign that things had changed. Until everyone found out about her parasite problem.

Her train of thought was interrupted by a soft knock at the door. A young, bright-eyed doctor with a wide smile poked her head in. "Hello there!" She crossed the room and took Lyssa's hand in a gentle shake as she introduced herself as Dr. Bianco.

"So," Bianco said, settling onto a chair in front of Lyssa with an excited grin. "This is your first baby, right?" Lyssa nodded. "Any questions for me?"

"I don't even know where to begin," Lyssa said truthfully. "This was...unexpected."

"Would it make you happy to know that nearly every woman who sits there feels exactly the same way?" Bianco squeezed Lyssa's hand, but she didn't feel any better. "So, let's have a look, shall we?"

Despite Lyssa's expectations, the visit was quite painless. Besides one rather invasive exam, everything was fairly routine for a normal check-up.

"Are we going to do that x-ray thing?" Lyssa asked. "Where you look inside and—"

"Ultrasound? Next visit." The doctor smiled as she pulled off her gloves and tossed them in the trash. "Not much to show yet. Your baby's just about this big." She separated her fingers about an inch.

"Really?" Lyssa said, glancing down. She rubbed her stomach. "Anything to help with the nausea?"

Bianco walked to her cabinets against the wall, fishing around for a moment before pulling out a bag and throwing some samples in it. She paused and added some brightly colored pamphlets as well. "Here are some samples that you can try, and I'll write you a script for more if they work for you. Also, here's some material for you to read so you can get a good understanding of what to expect, I find that always helps me to know what I'm getting into."

Lyssa took the bag and glanced at her hands.

"Everything else looks good," Bianco said after a few moments. "Baby is a healthy eight weeks, so just keep doing what you've been doing."

Lyssa winced, remembering her near-miss with the pirate. All of that seemed so far removed from this room of pregnancy photos and white noise. But it was important for her to know just how far she could push herself without hurting the parasite.

"So the para…the…it's okay in there?" she stammered, fairly sure that the doctor wouldn't appreciate her calling it a parasite. "There's nothing wrong with it?"

"It's still too early to know everything," the doctor said gently. "You'll need to come in every few weeks for a checkup, but so far, there's no need to worry."

Lyssa nodded and the knot in her stomach relaxed.

"It's normal to be nervous with your first child. But I'm sure you're doing everything right."

"What kind of exercise can I do?" *And can I still beat up pirates?*

"Plenty of women continue to exercise normally," Bianco replied. "You'll just need to monitor your own comfort level. Don't overdo it and drink plenty of water."

"Right but like…physical…"

"Oh, you mean sex? Go for it." The doctor beamed. "Lots of women—"

"No, I mean…" *Out with it, Lyssa.* "I fight people. Hand-to-hand stuff and I do it…a lot. Is that…?"

"I wouldn't recommend it," the doctor said with a small shake of her head. "But all other exercise is great, in fact, I would recommend walking every day—"

Lyssa didn't hear the rest of her statement. This doctor was a quack. Lyssa couldn't just *not* bounty hunt. That was… She refused to believe that.

She'd just have to be extra careful.

***

Guilt replaced nerves in her stomach when she left the transport shuttle on D-882. The angry voices in her head were a unified chorus —Razia was not supposed to be there. It had been too close a call with Fiege, she was better off just disappearing than risking getting caught or in trouble.

But her stubborn side had won out, as usual, which was why she was hunting Gunnar Bodhi, a member of Protestor's web.

She'd done most of her research on him in the few hours between leaving S-864 and arriving on D-882. A nice distraction from being ten blocks from Lizbeth's apartment and not going to see her.

She'd uncovered three of Bodhi's aliases so far, and was fairly sure she didn't even need to see Harms to get any more information about him. She told herself that she'd quickly get in and get her bounty before she encountered any trouble.

She heard footsteps behind her and stilled.

"Relax, it's just me."

Relaxing was not her first reaction to hearing Sage's voice. But she forced a nonchalant look onto her face and turned to face him. He looked much less desolate since their meeting at the Academy. His face had lost all of its shadow, and actually seemed more tan than usual. He stood tall and confident, much like the Sage she was used to. Especially with the air of anger about him.

"How're you feeling?" he asked.

"Fine."

"Good." He nodded, rubbing the back of his head and reverting back to the nervous idiot she hated. "So you're still... You haven't..."

She narrowed her eyes at him. "Did I not say I was going to go through with this?"

"You did, but you—"

"Do you think I'm a liar, then?"

"No, it's..." He swallowed and balled his fists. "Ganon said you were bounty hunting."

She cursed that stupid pirate. "I was."

"Are you sure you... That's...I mean..." He stammered for a moment, collecting his thoughts. "Are you sure it's smart for you to be out here in your condition?"

Her condition. The condition he'd put her in. Granted, she'd agreed to stay in this position, but still. "Are you suggesting that I stop working entirely?"

"No!" he exclaimed, rushing closer. "No, not at all. I mean, maybe the physical stuff, but that's not what you really like to do in the first place, is it?"

She folded her arms over her chest and wondered how deep Sage would dig himself before she lost her temper.

"You're good at it, but I mean..." He ran his hands through his messy hair. "Are you going to start yelling now?'

"I'm just waiting to see how much more you're going to piss me off so I can be more efficient with my energy."

"Lyssa, I'm trying really hard *not* to piss you off." Sage slouched against the wall, and she felt a little bad for making him so uncomfortable. "I know you don't want this at all, and I'm trying not to...not to get in your business but..." He cursed under his breath.

"Are you done?" she asked. "Because I have a pirate to capture."

Finally, she saw that spark in his eyes, the one that warned her he had reached his limit with her. "And what are you planning to do if you get into a fight, huh? Just let someone beat the shit out of you like Relleck did? Do you even *think* about anyone but yourself?"

She glared at him, already relishing this argument. "I'm not getting in fights. Besides, I already saw a doctor, and she cleared it."

Sage's face lost his fight and he took a step back. "You... you saw a doctor already?"

"Yes."

"Without me?"

"Why in Leveman's would you need to be there?" She tossed her head back. "It was fine. Everything is normal."

"That's…that's good." Sage's voice sounded faraway. "Hey, next time, could you…invite me?"

The thought of Sage at Bianco's office was terrifying, so she folded her arms over her chest and looked away. "I don't need you there."

"I want to be there."

Her palms grew sweaty, and she could practically feel his gaze on her. She hated this intensity between them. It reminded her of nights spent in his arms, exploring his body, being naked in more ways than one. She preferred herself and Sage clothed and with a few star systems between them.

"I *don't* want you there," she snapped. "And I don't want you following me around and telling me what to do. Didn't I tell you to get lost? So *get lost.*"

For a brief moment, rage flashed in his eyes and she hoped, prayed, that he'd return to normal Sage and bark at her. But he said nothing, and let her leave him in the middle of the street.

***

Gunnar Bodhi was one of the better hijackers in Contestant's web, and spent most of his time on his ship or hunting down new transport ships to capture. He was rarely seen on D-882 except for weekend jaunts to Eamon's. Razia walked up to two bouncers whose arms were thicker than Razia's entire body and smiled at them. "Evening boys."

They glanced at each other and parted to allow her entry. She chuckled in amusement; before the prison break-out, she'd had to sneak in a back window or threaten VJ the bartender. But now that she was truly one of Dissident's top pirates, she was afforded the luxury of a front-door entry to the most popular pirate watering hole.

Eamon's had been the site of the Pirate Ball, a hugely expensive gala that had seen the establishment glow with a refinery that rivaled the Manor—and also where Jukin had arrested nearly the entire pirate population. That event had taken place on the beautifully ornate sixth floor, whereas the ground level of Eamon's remained as dingy and disgusting as ever.

Bodhi was nowhere to be seen yet, so she sidled up to the bar and ordered a beer. She had no intention of drinking it—even the smell of the nearby drinks was testing the anti-nausea medication—but she wanted to appear normal. Still, when the waitress placed the sudsy, foaming glass in front of her, it took all her energy not to gag.

Razia surveyed the bar, spying Relleck. She counted her lucky stars she wasn't pregnant with *his* kid. He spotted her staring at him and rudely gestured to her. She snorted; so much for that relationship.

Fiege was in the other corner, looking at Razia and laughing. Probably telling his crew about how she'd turned tail and run. She lifted the beer to her mouth and pretended to drink, holding her breath and the contents of her stomach. She was fairly sure she'd never be able to drink beer again.

"What in Leveman's are you doing?"

She nearly dropped her glass, looking up at Sage, whose eyes were wide with panic.

"You…you can't drink!"

She glanced around, hoping the loud music had drowned him out. Then she narrowed her eyes at him. "*I know that.*"

"Then why did I see you just take a sip?"

"Leave me alone," she growled, pushing herself off the bar. "I don't need you babysitting me—"

"Obviously, you do!"

She grabbed her beer and stormed to the women's bathroom. She checked under all the stalls to make sure she was completely alone before letting out a long, loud breath of anger at Sage. She wasn't sure which was worse—that he yelled at her or that he thought she'd be so careless.

She snorted and leaned over the sink as a wave of nausea washed over her. Holding her breath, she poured her drink down the drain and gagged as the smell wafted into her nose. She pulled out another of her anti-nausea sample packs, tearing the paper and downing the two pills.

The door opened and closed behind her, and she glanced in the mirror. Fiege stood in the doorway, a smirk on his face.

"Hullo lovely."

She rolled her eyes and turned around. "What do you want?"

"Wanted to finish the fight you ran away from."

She grimaced and prayed the pills would work faster. Though he might be less inclined to capture her if she vomited on him.

"I'm not in the mood," she said. "Why don't you run along and play with someone who actually gives a shit?"

Fiege simply smiled and walked forward, cracking his knuckles. "I heard you had a mouth on you. Feel like it should be put to better use, you know?"

She suppressed a bile-filled burp and seriously considered blowing chunks all over him. Instead, she responded with, "Kind of like your face…" She shook her head and pressed a hand to her mouth. "Nope, I got nothing."

"Why don't you be a good girl and beg me to let you go, like you did with Loeb, huh?" He tucked his thumbs into his waistband. "Or maybe I'll make you beg for something else…"

"Ugh. No, thank you." But she had nowhere else to run; Fiege had her trapped against the sinks. Her only escape was a window above the toilets, but that was too far, and she'd have to get through Fiege first. She might've considered fighting him, but her body felt weak and her stomach was not cooperating. "This is really not a good time…"

Fiege was so close she could see the black tartar on his teeth. He grabbed her roughly and went for his handcuffs.

It happened in a flash—the window over the sink opened and a flash of dark green ran by her vision. Then Fiege was on the ground, out cold, and Sage's knuckles were red.

"You okay?" he panted.

"I…" She nodded dumbly. "What…"

"I saw his meatheads guarding the door, and I just assumed," Sage said, walking to the sink and placing his knuckles under the water. "He's been blabbing about how you ran away last week."

She watched her cheeks redden in her reflection. "So you heard about that."

"Everybody heard about that," he said, and she heard the anger in his voice. "I'm just glad there was a window out there." He noticed the empty beer glass on the counter and whirled on her. "Did you drink that?"

"*Of course I didn't!*" she barked back. "I can't even keep down dinner. Do you think I can keep down a damned beer?"

His face shifted from angry to stunned to concerned faster than she could process. "You're…you aren't eating?"

"I'm… Yes, I'm eating, but it's not very fun." She looked at the ground and made a disgusted face. "But I damned well can't drink a beer."

"But you can bounty hunt?" Sage said, angry again. "You can put *my child* in danger by walking down the streets where *everyone* is gunning for you?"

She took a step back and swallowed. So he was more concerned for the parasite than her?

"You know what? I was going to give you your space, but I guess I can't trust you not to make stupid decisions." Sage paced in front of her. "So like it or not, get used to seeing this face whenever you set foot on this planet."

"What if I'm not on this planet?" She lifted her head higher. "I'll just capture Bodhi on a transport station."

"Remember, I can find you *anywhere*." He stepped closer and she swallowed her anger. He looked like he was going to devour her—the same look he'd wear when she entered a room. It made her heart race with memories and anticipation. She wanted him to cover her mouth with his, take her back to her ship and… That was how she'd gotten in this mess in the first place.

She let out a shaky breath. She needed distance between them— preferably a universe—so she could rid herself of these thoughts and get back to hating him like normal.

"So? What's it gonna be?" Sage said.

A smile curled on her face even as his remained angry. She'd had experience with this sort of thing before. Someone who wouldn't leave her alone, someone who insisted on being everywhere she was. She knew just the thing to do.

"Fine," she whispered. "I need more time to find Bodhi anyway."

A lie; she could find him in her sleep. "And I'm due for an excavation."

"One of your planet things?" Sage said, rubbing his red knuckles again. "Sounds safer than you being here anyway." He glanced down at the unconscious body of Fiege on the ground. "Do you want to take him in? I'll help you shove him out the window since his bodyguards are still waiting out front. I know how much it would *pain* you to let anyone know you had any help with anything."

She despised Sage for his words, for his discretion, and later, for his quickness when Fiege awoke at the bounty office and wondered when she'd knocked him out.

CHAPTER SIX

Over the past few years, Lyssa's extra jump seat on her bridge had been occupied by Vel, who sat behind her and helped sort through bounties and her own soul searching. Then Lizbeth had claimed it, bringing with it her femininity and perfume and opinions. Now Sage was the current occupant, and Lyssa didn't like it one bit. He was comfortable already, and she hated how much she didn't hate having him there. Especially considering how strange he'd been acting since they'd left D-882. It was like all of his anger had evaporated in the space between their argument and the trip back to her ship.

Then again, she'd spent most of the rickety shuttle ride with her hand covering her eyes and her mouth, trying not to vomit, so perhaps he just pitied her.

She glanced back at him as he checked his mini-computer soundlessly.

"What's up? Are you feeling sick again?"

"No."

"Are you hungry?"

"No."

"Do you want to look for some bounties?"

"What?" She blinked, not expecting that question.

"You're just staring at nothing. Do you want to do some work while we're going out to the middle of nowhere? I can leave if you want privacy."

She glowered at the screen and didn't care if he saw it. "No."

"Okay then." Silence returned, and Lyssa nearly fell out of her chair. She expected him to come back with some remark about being rude and she'd return fire and they'd go at it. For him to simply acquiesce to her bad behavior was new and strange.

She fidgeted nervously, hating his presence even more. "Go downstairs or something. You're bothering me."

"Okay." He stood robotically and turned to walk away.

"What in Leveman's Vortex is wrong with you?" she barked.

"W-what?" His expression was innocently quizzical, his body tense as if he were awaiting her explosion.

"You're acting…weird." She swallowed the bad taste in her mouth. "What happened to being angry at me?"

"I…shouldn't have been so mean." He struggled to say the words. "I lost my temper. And I shouldn't have yelled at you."

"So you want me to drop you off at D-882, then?"

He cracked a sly smile. "I said I shouldn't have been mean, not that I shouldn't follow your ass everywhere." He laughed at her glowering response. "Besides, all the books I've been reading say you're moody, so I'm trying not to provoke you."

"I'm not *moody*."

The corners of his mouth twitched, but he forced them down. "You're right, you aren't. I'm sorry."

She bolted upright. "Whatever you're doing, stop."

"I'm not doing anything!"

"Yes, you are."

"Okay, I'm going to go downstairs so I don't bother you—"

"*That's what I mean!*" she hissed. "Stop…being…nice."

"You don't want me to be nice?"

"I…I mean…" she stammered. "I don't want anything to change between us," she said, looking down at her hands. "Not anything else, anyway. Everything's already different."

He slid his hands over the top of her chair and spun her around gently. There was a familiar look of hunger and lust swimming behind his eyes. She wanted very much to drown in it. He leaned down and whispered in her ear, "If you want things to go back to the way they were, you should have just said something."

She shivered. A small part of her that missed him—and not just his annoying personality. She missed the physical closeness, too. Her life was such a disaster that comfort would have been welcome. To close her eyes and let him keep everything at bay.

Our baby.

She swallowed hard and clenched her hands around her chair. Distance. She was trying to put distance between them so she'd stop thinking about things like that. But Sage's face hovered near hers, and it would take no effort at all to tilt her head up to capture his lips.

Luckily, a gauge on her dashboard began to beep, pulling Sage's attention away from her. He stood and faced her dashboard.

"What's going on?" he asked.

"Oh, we're just taking a shortcut to the planet," she replied, placing a hand over her pounding heart. In the distance, Leveman's Vortex was just a small speck, but it was rapidly drawing closer.

"Lyss…"

She grinned at the nervousness of his voice. She turned off her engines and the ship continued forward from the momentum and gravitational pull of Leveman's Vortex. Even at this distance, it was enough to draw her toward it. She opened an old application and calculated the weight of the ship and the occupants, the angle to the center of the vortex, the location of other celestial bodies.

"Lyssa, what are you doing?" Sage said, sitting down in his jump seat.

"I told you, we're taking a shortcut."

She was off by a bit, so she restarted her engines to adjust the angle of entry until the dot at the top of the screen turned green. She engaged the autopilot and sat back down, glancing over to Sage who gripped the edge of his seat with a wildly nervous look on his face.

"I'd buckle up," she said easily. As she spoke, her body became heavier, like something was pressing her into her seat. Even her eyelids felt heavy as she kept an eye on both the autopilot and the application —the latter still green.

She heard a yelp of surprise—or panic—when the ship launched forward towards the vortex, now so large it filled the width of her dashboard screens. Space debris zoomed by them on a faster trajectory, and disintegrated in front of them as the pressure became too great.

"Lyssa!" Sage's strangled voice sounded muted as her gaze landed back on the application, still showing green. The pressure shifted to the right, and Lyssa would've flown out of her chair, if not for the straps that kept her in place. Her ship sped up, zooming closer to the white center.

Then the green status blinked red.

Lyssa kicked a button on the dashboard to jumpstart her engines.

As the pressure lessened, she became aware of an odd sound coming from behind her.

Laughter. Sage was laughing. She leaned over the side of her chair to look at him. His face was red with exertion and his eyes bright. But he was laughing, honestly laughing.

"Holy shit! That was *amazing!*"

Amazing was not the word she wanted to hear from him.

"I thought space jumps were a rush but that was… Can we do that again?" He rubbed his face and let out another whoop. "Where'd you learn that one, Lyss?"

She growled and bared her teeth.

***

They reached the planet some hours later. Lyssa found a small clearing near a dense tropical forest that stretched for miles. She made it a habit of avoiding jungles, since that was where she'd usually find things that would eat her. But she was hoping to show Sage the worst parts of Deep Space Exploration.

Which, she realized as she opened the ramp and a wall of moisture hit her, *she'd* also have to suffer through. She wasn't even off the ship and already felt like she needed a bath.

"Ugh," Sage said behind her. "This place feels like the inside of a mouth."

"You wanted to come," she replied, tossing him a haughty look over her shoulder. "So deal with it."

"Not complaining. You sure you up for this?" He joined her on the edge of the wilderness, and she was pleased to see the apprehension on his face. The part of the planet she'd chosen was dense with white-bark trees and long hanging vines, and there was a small swamp-like lake in the middle of the jungle. She was hoping to be in that cesspool for most of the day—or until Sage called it quits.

"Ready to go?" she asked.

"Hold on," Sage said, glancing behind him. "Vel told me to make sure you gave me the bug spray."

She muttered under her breath about traitorous brothers. "In my first aid kit. Lower right cabinet."

His footsteps echoed back onto her ship as he called, "You weren't going to warn me, were you?"

"I might've," she said, turning to watch him dig through her cabinets. "If it was a problem…"

"And is your definition of a problem before or after I picked up some nasty disease?" He glanced up at her from the cabinet.

She searched his face for anger, but all she saw was amusement, somehow making him seem almost…cute.

"You want some, too?" Sage asked, waving the can in front of her face. "Or wait." He leaned in close to her and took a whiff. "You ass, you already used some didn't you?"

"Maybe," she said. He smirked and walked off of the ship, dousing himself in the spray.

"You aren't supposed to use the whole can."

"Just want to be safe. Never know with you."

"Anything else Vel told you?"

"He said not to let you out of my sight," Sage replied. "Said you have a nasty habit of leaving people behind."

"Har har," she snapped, joining him and shoving one of her father's sensors toward him. "Take this." She trudged into the jungle and pointed to a purple-leafed vine hanging from a tree. "Pull off this leaf and stick it in the receiver."

Sage eyed the leaf from a healthy distance. "Shouldn't I be wearing gloves or something? How do you know this thing won't kill me?"

"Because I said it won't."

"And how do you know that?"

She growled at him and fished her gloves out of her back pocket, flinging them at him. "Here, you big baby. Now do the test."

After slipping on the gloves, he did as instructed and she watched her mini-computer for the results to come in. To her surprise, the leaf actually did contain a high level of toxin.

"What?" Sage asked.

"Nothing," she replied. "Enough of that. Let's find some other samples."

She walked through the forest keeping her distance from the purple-leafed vines and most other similar flora. She pointed out white flowers and the low-lying moss, both also poisonous, and had Sage take samples of the tree bark (also poisonous). If she'd been by herself, she would have turned around, gotten back on her ship, and found a more profitable area of the planet to test, feigning ignorance if a purchaser came back and argued that she'd sold him a planet with a deadly forest.

But she wasn't there to make money.

The minutes ticked by and Sage's face grew redder and sweatier with exertion. A few times, she thought he might say something, but he decided against it, glaring at a tree with all the intensity that she was sure he'd rather direct at her. His white shirt stuck to his back, accentuating every muscle move in his back.

Finally, after four long, arduous hours, he broke. "It's hot."

Lyssa couldn't argue with that assessment as sweat dripped down her nose. She wiped it away as she stuffed another leaf into her machine. But she pretended to be unaffected. "So?"

"How much longer we gotta be out here?" Sage asked, turning around and showing off the breadth of his shoulders. "I'm dying."

"It's just as hot on D-882," she said, averting her eyes.

"It's muggy here. Feels worse."

"You wanted to come," she said, wiping her forehead. "So quit bitching and help."

"You've taken a hundred samples. How many more until you're

satisfied?"

She glanced over at him, not quite ready to give up her torture.

"It's not up to me," she said with a shrug. "I've got a quota to adhere to." Technically, it was to capture at least twenty samples in seven different sectors one thousand miles equidistant but…Sage didn't have to know that. This was the hottest point on the planet, square in the center. A little more, and he'd never bother her again.

"Wait a second…" Sage squinted at something ahead of them and disappeared into the bushes. Lyssa followed him, avoiding the purple leaves as much as she could. When she caught up with him, she found him on the banks of a crystal-clear lake.

"Hold it," Lyssa said, as Sage began pulling off his shirt. She stepped forward and dipped her sensor in the water.

"It looks fine to me," Sage said.

"Yeah, so did all those plants back there, but they'd kill you," Lyssa said, waiting for the readings to come back.

"…what?"

She smirked at him, enjoying the horrified look on his face. "This whole jungle is toxic."

He grumbled under his breath, and she was happy that he finally looked angry. But not enough. "Unfortunately, so is this water. I'm afraid—"

He snatched her mini-computer out of her hands and held it above her head. He squinted at the readings and pursed his lips. "Says it's fine."

"You're reading it wrong!" she huffed.

"You're a piece of work, Lyssa," Sage said, shoving her mini-computer back into her hands. He pulled off his wet shirt and tossed it onto the sand, then kicked off his shoes and unbuckled his pants.

"Much better," he said, naked as the day he was born. And with a yell, he ran into the water, splashing and carrying on.

Lyssa stood on the beach, a scowl on her face, as she watched him do laps.

"C'mon Lyssa," he called to her. "Stop trying to make everything terrible. It feels great in here."

It was tempting. So tempting. She was hot and miserable, and the water looked inviting.

"C'moooooooon!" Sage bellowed. "Don't make me drag you in here."

She didn't doubt he would. With a curse, she peeled off her own sweaty clothes, laying them on top of Sage's so they wouldn't get sandy. When she removed her bra, she heard Sage whoop from the water and hated the happy grin on his face.

"Nothing I haven't seen before!"

She removed the rest of her underwear and walked into the water, relishing in the coolness on her hot and stuffy feet. She had to admit, it felt nice to be in the water. She paddled out to where Sage was standing, and treaded water while he stood chest-high.

"There now. See? Isn't this great? Shame we don't have any of Joe's inner tubes, huh?" Sage said, after dunking his head. "We should go back someday. I had so much fun with him."

Lizbeth had asked the same thing.

Lizbeth…

Lyssa hadn't talked to the investigator in over a month. She and Lizbeth would have dustups all the time, but they usually last a week. Going a month without talking to her…

"I'm not sure I'd be invited back there any time soon," Lyssa said, trying to sound nonchalant.

"You two still haven't made up?" Sage said. "You should call her."

"She hit me."

Sage sighed. "She's your best friend, isn't she?"

Lyssa's gaze dropped to the shimmering water between them. Lizbeth was her best friend, but so was Sage. Or at least, he had been before the parasite came between them.

Something slid by the back of her leg and Lyssa screamed, nearly jumping out of the water, but landing in Sage's arms instead.

"What?" he asked.

"Something… A fish I think…" she said, now more concerned that her naked body was pressed against his. His hands slid around her hips to hold her afloat. She sucked in a breath. The parasite. Bad. Holding her like this. Bad. That hunger in his eyes. Bad. Feeling safe. Bad. Putting her arms around his neck. Bad.

"That's better," he whispered, his face close to hers. All bad. Bad, bad, bad. "I'll keep all the evil fish away from you."

The mood shattered when he jumped, clinging to her the same way she'd clung to him. "Shit, something just *bit* me!"

She snorted. "Maybe I'll have to keep the evil fish away."

"Save me, Lyssa," he whined in mock-distress, pulling her closer. She could kiss him right now, she realized. The part of her that was tingling with anticipation wanted her to very much. She recognized the look in his eyes—

Something *big* slid by her legs.

"Sage…"

"You felt it too?"

"We need to get out of the water."

Lyssa spotted something dark behind Sage. Something dark with white, gleaming teeth.

"*Run!*" she screamed, turning and swimming as fast as she could. Sage was by her side as they splashed onto the shore. They stood, panting and gasping, as a giant purple tentacle rose out of the water and slapped back down, sending ripples along the water.

"Shit!" Sage gasped. "What is that?"

"I don't know!" Lyssa replied with a little smile. "I just discovered this planet."

"Never a dull moment with you, is there?" he said, running a hand through his dripping hair. "You okay?"

"I'm fine." Then she noticed where his eyes had landed—her naked stomach. "The parasite is fine, too."

"The p…" Sage's mouth dropped open in shock. "The parasite?"

"What?"

"That's…you're calling it a *parasite*?"

"Why not? That's what it is right now."

"But that's so…awful," he said a little sadly. "Can't you call it something else?"

"What do you call it?"

"The baby."

She stiffened and hated that he saw it. Then again, there wasn't much she could hide at the moment.

"Okay, you're not ready for that yet," Sage said after a breath. "How about bug, then?"

"Bug is better than parasite?"

"Some bugs are cute."

"Like which ones?"

"I don't know, Dr. Peate," Sage said with a grin. He walked over to the pile of clothes and tossed hers over. "Now tell me we don't have to trudge all the way back through the forest of death to get to your ship." He paused and gave her a once over. "Unless…"

She clutched her mini-computer and chewed on her lip. "Sage, when I said I didn't want anything to change between us…"

"Yeah?"

"I meant… I don't want…" she motioned between the two of them, "this."

He smiled, and damn it, half-naked and glistening in the sun, he was even more handsome than usual. "I know. So are we going to head back?"

Her mouth opened in shock. After the whole water, bodies-pressed-against-each-other, nearly kissing her episode…*nothing?* Not even a small comment?

"Problem?" he asked with a knowing smile.

"Nothing," she said, lifting her chin higher. "No, we have to walk back to the ship."

With that, she yanked on her clothes and trudged back through the forest, hating that Sage seemed less annoyed by everything than when they'd started.

CHAPTER SEVEN

Hours later, Lyssa stood in her closet surveying her options for DSE clothing. She'd tried on two pairs of black pants and found them both impossible to button. She ran a hand over her stomach—it didn't seem like it had grown that much in the past week. But her waistlines didn't lie.

She grabbed her largest set and yanked them on, but they didn't button either. She stormed out of her closet, nearly tripping over the spare air mattress that marked Sage's side of her bedroom, and flopped on her own bed. Sucking in her stomach as far as it would go, she latched the button When she exhaled, her pants stretched and then the button flew off.

"*Bitch*!"

The noise drew Sage's attention, who was in the bathroom.

"Wha' er ew dewin?" Sage emerged from the bathroom, toothbrush hanging out of his mouth.

"Trying to clothe myself." She glanced down at her absent button and could not deny it. Her DSE clothes officially did not fit anymore.

A few moments later, Sage reappeared, sans toothbrush, and

quirked his eyebrow at her. "So you need some new clothes?"

"I'm not calling Lizbeth."

"She'd probably love to go shopping with you."

Lyssa snorted. "She'd wrap me up in pink bows, too." Her gaze fell to Sage's shirtless frame and then back up at his face. Every time she closed her eyes, she saw him naked on the banks of the lake, remembered the way his hands had felt on her hips and how he pressed himself against her. It was even worse when they'd both taken a nap after leaving the planet, with him sleeping shirtless just feet away from her. She'd lain awake and fought the urge to crawl into his arms, deciding that she needed to figure out a way to get him *off* her ship before she slipped and ended up in bed with him again.

"Maybe she'd add one bow, for kicks," he said with a charming grin. "She did get you to wear a dress that one time."

She groaned and stood up, kicking off her pants and walking to her closet. Sage gently took her arm and spun her around.

"What?" Was he going to kiss her.

"Just…" He turned his head to the side. "You and Lizbeth are good together. I don't want you to lose that because you're a stubborn ass."

"I'm not stubborn," she insisted, but it was half-hearted. She twisted out of his grip and ducked into the closet, in search of something work-appropriate to wear. Unfortunately, the only pair of pants that fit were some black stretchy pants that Lizbeth had left behind. She combined that with her lab coat and one of her button-down shirts, and her stomach was unnoticeable.

She found Sage adjusting his silver-framed glasses and sporting his authentic Academy badge.

"What do you think you're doing?"

"Oh come now. You're going to deprive me of the full Academy experience?" Sage asked, turning back to look at her. "I did nearly get eaten by a giant tentacled fish-thing."

"The rest of this is quite boring," she said, checking her mini-computer to see if Dorst had answered her message to add her to the planet-selling line up.

To her annoyance, the response was, "*Come to my office and we'll talk about it.*"

***

It was awfully strange, Lyssa thought, to be strolling down the halls of the Planetary and System Science Academy with Sage Teon. Not that he looked out of place. The smart silver frames on his nose, the crisp button-up shirt, dark pants, and clean white lab coat were quite convincing.

"So when we get there, please don't have any extended conversations with my brothers."

Sage laughed. "Why not?"

"I don't like it."

"Why not?"

"Why do you *want* to?" she growled.

"Besides the fact that it pisses you off?" Sage said with a grin. "Because I want to know where my kid comes from. These guys are going to be his or her uncles."

She swallowed hard, hoping she could wipe that panic-inducing image out of her mind. Sage showing up at the Academy with a dark-haired child in tow. Seeing the looks on her brothers' faces, similar to the disgusted ones they'd given her as a little girl. They'd probably hate the kid as much as they hated her.

"I don't think you want to bring the bug around here."

"I didn't say I'd bring him or… When do we find out the gender anyway?" Sage asked. "I'm getting tired of him or her."

"Call it an it."

"No, Lyssa."

The laboratory doors opened to reveal the gargantuan space of Dorst's lab. Unlike Sostas' lab, which was dark and dank, this lab featured multiple levels, visible from the main common room. Scientists in white lab coats stood in front of tables with various sensory machinery, microscopes, separators, and the like.

"Lyssa, so good of you to come," Dorst said, as if he hadn't blackmailed her into coming to see him. His eyes drifted over to Sage and grew even brighter as he extended his hand in greeting. "Al, always a pleasure."

Sage shook his hand mightily. "And you as well, Dorst."

Lyssa watched the exchange with a mix of horror and shock. Seeing Sage in the midst of the Academy with her brothers was akin to seeing Pymus and Relleck having a discussion. Especially as that Dorst already considered them a couple. Not much she could do about that now.

"Vel said you two were working together," Dorst said, ignoring her completely.

"Just a bit," Sage said.

"Did Vel tell you anything else?" Lyssa grumbled.

"No, I didn't." Vel appeared at Dorst's right elbow with a happy grin. He clasped Sage's hand then pulled Lyssa in for a hug. "How ya feeling?"

"Murderous," she whispered back.

"So back to normal, then?" Vel said. "I told Dorst you'd caught a nasty bug a few weeks ago."

Sage snorted and covered it up with a cough.

"Yeah," Lyssa said, unsure whether to thank Vel or not. "What are you doing here? Shouldn't you be in class or something?"

"I don't have class every day," Vel said with a quizzical expression.

"Are you ready to have our counseling session?" Dorst asked her. "It's only a year late."

"Go on," Sage said, pushing her forward. "Vel and I can catch up."

Lyssa didn't like the idea of Sage and Vel alone, but unfortunately, she didn't have a say in the matter. Before she could get two words out, she found herself trapped in Dorst's office, staring at him from the other side of his expansive desk.

She made a huge show of rolling her eyes. "Well, here I am. Career's going fine. Leveman's Vortex still spins. Planets get discovered and sold. No problems."

"How about we forget that I'm your supervisor for a minute and just talk like siblings?" Dorst offered. "I barely know you, Lyssa. You're here for flashes and then you're gone for longer. You don't answer your mini, you don't answer messages, and you don't ever go home—"

"I wonder why that is?" She leaned forward and placed her hands on the desk. "And what about you? Not two years ago, you couldn't stand the sight of me, and now you want to be best friends? Are you sucking up to me to get at Sostas' work, or are you just being a jackass?"

"Neither actually," Dorst said. "If you'd slowed down long enough to have a conversation without rolling your eyes, you might have noticed that I'm trying to…well, I'm trying to apologize for how I used to treat you."

She sat back, shocked into silence.

"Wow, it is possible to shut you up," Dorst said with a catty grin. "Look, for a number of years, you walked around the Academy like you owned it. You'd skip class and tell your professors you were off doing Father's work. You'd taunt us with knowing where he was, but give up no information. Honestly, I'd thought you were just like Mother—selfish and cocky because Sostas *happened* to have chosen you for his assistant."

How was she supposed to respond to that? True, that she'd been a little arrogant in her younger days, but that was when she'd been on Tauron's crew and thought she had an exit. It wasn't until she found herself at Leveman's Vortex that she had started to care about the Academy. And even then, it was…limited.

But what really bothered her was his insinuation she was like Eleonora. She'd begun to see it more and more in herself, especially around Sage. And it made her nervous.

"In all my years of wishing I was in your shoes, I never once considered what it might be like to actually be in them, until Vel and I started talking." Dorst put his hands behind his head. "It reminded me that Sostas really wasn't a great father—Leveman's, he wasn't even a great man. He and Mother barely spoke, and when they did, it was to fight about something." He paused with a sad smile. "Usually you."

She desperately wished for a change of subject. "Why are you talking to Vel about Sostas?"

"I think Vel is trying to find himself. It's very difficult for him to have so many older siblings and still feel like he matters. That's probably why he wants to work for you. I think Vel wants something to prove that he's…different. He's his own person."

"But why Sostas? He can be his own person without having to take on his work?"

Dorst took a long pause before replying, "I think Vel wants to continue work on his research. At least, that's the feeling I get from him."

Her eyes widened and she nearly flew out of the office, intent on ringing her little brother's neck. Dorst didn't know that their father had made it inside the Vortex, that he regularly used Lyssa as a good-soul-shield so he could experiment without incurring the wrath of the Great Creator. He didn't know that Lyssa, Vel, and Dr. Pymus had journeyed there, and that Dr. Pymus had fallen into Plethegon. Dorst thought that "experimentation" was simply tossing satellites into the gravitational pull and seeing what happened.

"That's a terrible idea," Lyssa said. "And why is he talking with you about it? Why not come to me?"

"Rumor has it that you refuse to talk about Father with anyone," Dorst said with a knowing smile. "But we're not here to talk about Vel. We're here to talk about you."

"Can we please talk about Vel?" Lyssa said, glancing out to where Sage had gathered a group of…five of her brothers and cousins. He was, as usual, the center of attention, and the group roared loudly with laughter. Sage could make friends with anyone.

"I mentioned some time ago that you needed to think about what you were doing with your life," Dorst said. "Whether you wanted to be a DSE or if you wanted to do something else. Have you given any more thought to it?"

She wrenched her eyes away from Sage and back to Dorst. "No… yes…I don't know." She huffed. "Can't I just continue to do what I'm doing? Why does *everything* in my life have to change right now?"

"Lyssa, there's so much that goes on at the Academy that you have no idea about," Dorst said. "There's meeting after meeting. I have a weekly call with my supervisor to discuss my subordinates. Do you know who nearly every call is about?" He shook his head. "People want to know, Lyss. They want to know what you're up to. You can't just walk in and flaunt knowledge about Leveman's Vortex and expect them to forget about it."

"So what do you want me to do, then?"

"One briefing," Dorst said. "One briefing, one…just…throw

them a bone or something. Make it up if you have to, but…"

"You want me to give a presentation on Leveman's Vortex?" Lyssa asked.

"I want you to present something so that I can keep people off your back, and, more importantly, mine."

"And what if I don't want to?"

He pursed his lips and sat back. "Don't make me write you up. Please, I don't want to. But I can't…I can't keep fighting your battles here."

She glanced out again at Sage, who had the group (now numbering eight) in stitches.

"Fine. I'll do it. But not now. Later."

"Oh, Lyss…" Dorst stood and rushed around his desk. Before she could stop him, he enveloped her in a bear hug. She'd never been this close to him, not that she could remember anyways, and she didn't like it. He stepped back and beamed at her. "I'll announce it straight away, and I'll put you in the line up to sell your planet today, as well."

"Hooray…"

***

"So, wait…" Vel gawked as they left Dorst's office. "You have to put together a presentation on Leveman's Vortex?"

"Yup."

"I can't wait to see what you come up with."

"Yeah, about that…" She grabbed Vel by the arm and yanked him down to her level. "You are not *allowed* to go to Leveman's Vortex."

He opened his mouth to deny it but no sound came out.

"Do you not remember the fire? What happened to Pymus? What nearly happened to *us*? In what universe would this ever be a good idea?"

"The one where I'm trying to figure out what I'm doing with my life," Vel replied, gently releasing his arm from her vice grip. "I graduate in six months, Lyss, and it's scary. I could jump into an Academy position here but…is that really what I want? And maybe the Great Creator would show me a vision like He showed you—"

"*Leveman's Vortex is not a damned career counselor!*"

"I know, I know." Vel winced as her voice echoed in the hallway.

"But I just feel so lost. Why am I even at the Academy? Mother enrolled me so I never had a choice."

"You sound like Heelin," Lyssa grunted, releasing his arm. "He was being a little bitch about it too."

"And then you used him to get into the pirate jail."

"He figured it out, didn't he?" Lyssa shrugged. "Something about looking at your death puts things in perspective."

"Yeah I know. Which is why I want to go back," Vel said.

"Look why don't…" She took a long breath. It was bad enough she had Sage following her, but she felt she needed to spend more time with Vel. "Why don't you come with me for a few days? We'll go hunt down a bounty like we used to."

His face lit up. "Really?"

"Yeah. Maybe then Sage'll be more bearable to be around."

"Says the woman pregnant with his kid…"

"I'm serious," Lyssa said, adding, "And I don't want you to ever think you can't talk about Sostas with me."

Vel's mouth dropped open in surprise. "Wow, Lyss, that actually sounded…maternal!"

"Get sucked," she snapped.

"Lasted for a second," Vel said with a grin as Lyssa swiped her badge to open the doors to her lab. She paused when she realized Sage wasn't with them.

"Where's Sage?" Lyssa asked. At that moment, he emerged from Dorst's lab with him, a smile on both their faces as they spoke. Sage shook Dorst's hand and walked to join Lyssa and Vel in front of her lab. She stared at him, trying to suss out what they'd been talking about. After a moment, she swiped her badge and led them inside. By habit, she flipped on the lights, and was surprised to find them actually turn on for once.

"I took the liberty of calling in the maintenance team to fix the lighting," Sage replied, passing by her to sit splayed-legged on one of her chairs. "It was too dark in here."

She mumbled her thanks and sat down at the main computer, starting the long process of pulling her data reports into a presentation she could use to sell the planet. But out of the corner of her eye, she saw Sage and Vel strike up an easy conversation.

"Lyssa's going to take me bounty hunting," Vel said to Sage.

"Oh yeah? Tired of me already, Lyssa?"

"I was tired of you ages ago," she muttered under her breath.

"It'll be fun. I haven't been back to D-882 in months," Vel replied. "Ready to get out there and find some pirates."

Sage laughed heartily, and it drew Lyssa's eye. "Slow down there. You can't just walk onto the planet and start fights. Do you even know how to hit?"

"I've been taking boxing lessons at the Academy gym," Vel said, making a right hook then a left.

"So if we run into any punching bags, we're set, huh?" Sage said.

"Lyssa taught me some things," Vel replied as Sage mock-punched at him.

"So if we run into any easy pirates—"

"Get sucked," Lyssa snapped from the computer.

"Actually," Sage said with a cautious tone that piqued her interest, "that isn't such a bad idea. I've got...some business to take care of elsewhere."

Lyssa stopped typing and spun around in her chair. "What? Where? Does it have anything to do with what you were talking to Dorst about?"

"It'd make me feel better if someone else made sure she doesn't get into trouble," Sage said, ignoring Lyssa completely.

"*Sage!*" Lyssa barked. "I thought you said you were going to...to... *be here!*"

His eyebrows shot up in surprise. "I thought you didn't like having me around? You've been doing everything possible to get me to disappear, haven't you?"

Her mouth opened. Was she that obvious? She screwed up her face. "Of course I don't like having you around, but—"

"And I thought you didn't want my help anyway?" Sage said with a half-smile.

"I don't, but—"

"So why is it a problem if I leave for a few weeks?"

"Weeks?" She didn't know which she hated more, that Sage was leaving or the way he was smiling at her outburst. Either way, she felt trapped.

"I promise, I'll just be a little while," Sage said, walking over to her. "Unless, of course, you'd like to come with me?"

"Ugh, no," she said, forcefully typing on the computer. "Go away. What do I care?"

"That's what I thought."

She snorted and continued typing, waiting for him to continue arguing with her. But the only sound that came was him leaving. And the voice in her head telling her that it was, yet again, her fault.

CHAPTER EIGHT

After her planet was presented and sold, Lyssa and Vel left the Academy for D-882. With Vel aboard her ship, she almost didn't notice Sage's absence. But she definitely thought a lot about how she'd told him to go, and for the first time, he had gone.

Vel fit back on her ship as if he'd never left, settling himself onto the bed that Sage had occupied, throwing his bag in the same place it had sat for his six month internship with her. More importantly, with all of the worry about Sage and the bug, it was nice to have someone to ground her in reality and keep her focused on what she was supposed to do.

"So it's a choice between Cree Hardrict or this new guy, Cadman Mead," Lyssa said, showing Vel the wanted posters for the two men. "I've captured Hardrict before, but there aren't a lot of older pirates left that I haven't captured."

"What's happened to them?"

"They keep retiring, or getting arrested for things not covered by the Piracy Act," Lyssa said. She told Vel about Opli, and her suspicions that he'd been behind all of the secrets—and that he had one on her as well. "So there are all these new guys flooding the top twenty."

"Why not go after them?"

She made a face. "They're *boring*. And most of them can't hide for shit."

"So picky with your bounties now. You don't have a big head at all."

"Hardrict it is," she said. "You know, I might still have some of his alias information from when I captured him the…" She trailed off and frowned. She had captured Hardrict the day she'd met Lizbeth.

"What's wrong?" Vel asked.

"Nothing," she said. "Back to Hardrict."

Since her capture, Hardrict had apparently gone to great lengths to create a whole new set of aliases, as the ones she'd discovered hadn't been used in quite some time. She and Vel tried looking for members of his crew to find correlation, but he wasn't a top twenty pirate for nothing; all his crew members had stopped using their old aliases as well. Without any other leads, Razia decided to check in with Harms when they arrived on D-882.

"Do you think I'll get to meet Harms one day?" Vel asked as they walked out of the transport shuttle station across the street from his bar.

Razia, dressed like herself but feeling like Lyssa next to Vel, shrugged. "I don't know. Maybe he already knows about Lyssa. He did have my Academy bag at his house for a while. I left it there after Tauron died."

"And he's never said anything to you about it?"

"Shocking, I know. I guess he doesn't tell everything."

"So…" Vel stopped in front of the bar. "I can't meet him?"

"Not this time, kiddo," Razia said. "I'll only be a second." She made a mock angry face. "Go sit on your bench!"

Vel laughed and sauntered over to the bench where he'd waited for Razia when they'd worked together. Truly, it was pretty amazing that no one had noticed or asked about him. Then again, she realized with a jolt,—back then, though she was in the top twenty, everyone had assumed that she'd just fade away after a while.

She glanced down at her stomach and winced. Stay being a loose term.

Brushing those thoughts aside, she strolled into Harms bar and spotted him in the corner. He was deep in conversation with someone, not a rare occurrence. But what annoyed her was with whom he was meeting: Relleck. Harms' eyes slid over to her long enough for Relleck to turn around and spot her. She swallowed a look of disgust and realized her morning sickness had gone away over the past week or so. Perhaps the planet had been good for her. Or maybe she'd been too distracted by Sage to notice.

Sage, who was gone. Ass.

Relleck rose from the booth and sauntered over to Razia, making a big show of eyeing her up and down. Razia still couldn't believe she'd had a fling with that asshole, especially as he walked by her and said, "Looking a bit chunky, baby. You need to work out some more. Call me if you ever want some real exercise."

"Maybe I'll just capture you right now and save myself the effort," she replied.

She and Relleck locked eyes in a battle of wills before he gave up and left the bar. Her eyes lingered on the way he'd gone. If Relleck noticed that she'd gained weight, she had a problem. Her cargo pants were a bit looser than her DSE attire, but they'd still been tight when she had buttoned them. Her time of walking around D-882 was quickly coming to an end unless she figured out something else, and soon.

She forced an easy look onto her face and sat down at the booth. "Why are you still talking with him?" she asked Harms.

"Because he pays good money," Harms said. "What's the problem? Ex-lovers getting you down?"

She glowered at him. "I hope you aren't spreading that around."

"And risk being on the other end of one of your legendary beat-downs? No, thank you." Harms laughed, and she cracked a smile. "Besides, I know better than to piss off a woman who can stare down a gun and survive. So who's on your mind today, my dear?"

"Hardrict, actually," Razia said.

"Hm," Harms said, rubbing his beard. "You know, Relleck was

just in here to tell me to quit selling out all of Contestant's guys. He said that they've lost ten to retirement in the past month."

"Maybe they shouldn't have so many secrets."

"Everybody's got secrets, including you, I'm sure," Harms said. She resisted the urge to place a hand on her stomach. "But, unfortunately, I'm in the business of selling secrets. And as it so happens, one of my informants told me about a new alias of Hardrict's just yesterday…"

The information Harms gave Razia was, as usual, on point. He had not only one, but two of Hardrict's brand new aliases, and three of his crew members. In any case, it was more than enough to get started building a pattern of transactions so she could corner him. She and Vel walked a few blocks to an out-of-the-way restaurant to start work together.

Yet again, she was thankful for Vel's presence. She was having trouble keeping track of the names between reading them on the Universal Bank ledger of one bar and comparing it to the names on another, so she was calling the names out to Vel as she came across a new one.

"It's pregnancy brain," Vel said after she'd told him about it. "Makes sense. All your energy is being used to grow a tiny human."

"It's annoying," Razia said, rubbing her face. "I can't even think straight. When does it go away?"

"I think it's usually replaced by newborn brain." Vel said with a smile. "Feedings every two hours, diaper changes, not showering…"

"That's Sage's problem, not mine," she muttered. "And change of topic, please? I don't know who's listening."

"Besides the bartender?"

"He talks."

"Fine, fine. Here's a new name." He wrote it on the list with the others to check in the Universal Bank.

They worked in silence for a little longer when Razia had a new thought. "You know, you're pretty good at this bounty hunting stuff," she said, not looking up at him. "Did you ever consider maybe…doing this instead of being a DSE?"

"And break Mother's heart even more?" Vel laughed. "No,

thanks."

"But you wouldn't have to break her heart. You could just say you're working for me and be gone as much as I am," Razia replied. "Here, write this one down too."

Vel scribbled the name down. "But it seems like it's always such an ordeal for you to keep everything straight. Who knows you're Lyssa and who knows you're Razia?"

"Sage, his crew, you...Lizbeth." She pursed her lips in anger.

"Still haven't made up with her, have you?" Vel shook his head. "No wonder you're friends. You're both stubborn."

"I don't understand why I have to be the one to apologize," Razia said, purposefully looking at her mini-computer. "Wackily Paulus, write that down."

"Maybe she's thinking you don't want her to apologize?" Vel said. "You can be awfully hard to read sometimes, especially when you're angry."

"Darrell Kalkstein—"

"Huh?"

"Here," she shoved the mini-computer over to him so he could get the spelling right. "I just...it was really none of her business."

"It was when Sage showed up at her door."

She growled. "They're awfully close, you know. Lizbeth and Sage."

"Lyss, don't do this," Vel had started searching on the list of names in the Universal Bank. "Especially considering that anyone with two eyes and ears within a star system of you two knows he's in love with you."

She flushed pink. "Let's not talk about that."

"You brought it up, not me." He crossed off another name on his list.

"See? Look at you. You're a natural at bounty hunting," Razia said, desperate to change the subject.

Vel laughed. "So you're telling me that you'd actually allow someone else to join you on your 'I-don't-need-anyone' vendetta?"

"Hey now..."

Vel just laughed, the sound so bright even Razia couldn't be sour. "I won't graduate for a few more months. And by then..." He glanced down at her stomach, and his brow furrowed. "Do you think…?" He hesitated, glancing nervously at her hands then back at her face. "It's getting a bit obvious now."

She glanced down at her bulge. "You think?"

"If you really want to keep this a secret."

"What? Give up?" she snapped.

"No, just…maybe let someone else do all the hard work for you?" Vel said. "Like Sage?"

A bucket of cold water washed over her and she scowled darkly. "Well, he's not here, is he?"

"Do I hear a hint of loneliness in your voice?" Vel said, mock-aghast. "Could you actually like having Sage around? Even though you told him to, what was it, get lost?"

She fumed. She didn't want Sage around and she liked having Vel here instead. But she missed Sage. It wasn't just about the bug either.

"At the very least, you should consider buying some new clothes. I'm not sure how much more that poor shirt can handle." He smiled. "Why don't you try calling—"

"Quiet," Razia said as the door to the cafe opened. Opli stood in the light, and she didn't have to guess what had drawn him into the cafe.

"This is so heartwarming, to see the two of you together," Opli said. "I suppose your professors don't know about your extracurricular activities?"

Vel glanced at Razia, but she simply folded her arms over her chest, hoping it would hide her stomach. Opli wouldn't miss the way her shirt hung a little tighter, and he would connect the dots.

"I don't suppose your supervisors know you're the one behind all the retirements, do they?" Razia asked.

"What do they care for political infighting of pirates?" Opli said with a small shrug. "As far as they know, the U-POL is back to the way it was before your brother's vendetta."

Beside her, Vel shifted, but Razia looked unfazed. "If you're just going to yammer pointlessly, you might as well leave."

"Don't see your compatriot around these parts very often," Opli said. "His crew has been awfully active without him."

She narrowed her eyes, deciding to play his game. "I can only assume that's your doing, huh?"

"I wish. Squeaky clean, that one. Though I don't need to worry. I'm sure you'll bring him down with you when you implode."

She gritted her teeth and forced herself to stay seated. But curiosity was burning within her to know what he meant.

"Well, I should be off. I have to check on the status of my latest… investment," Opli said. He nodded at the two of them and left.

"That guy gives me the creeps," Vel said, a full minute after he'd gone.

"You're telling me." Razia unfolded her arms from over her chest and put a hand on her stomach. "I can't imagine if he found out about this thing."

"Are you doing anything about him?"

"Not my problem." She glanced out the door. "Yet. Besides, I can't go around saving piracy every time some Captain of the Special Forces gets a wild hair." She paused and glanced back at Vel. "What do you think he meant about Sage?"

Vel quirked an eyebrow. "Are you planning to implode any time soon?"

"No" She shook her head. "But something he said about Jukin. That he'd hastened his own demise…I just…I hate not knowing what he knows. Especially if it means he's got something on Sage."

"Mm," Vel said with a small shake of his head. "Back to bounty hunting then?"

***

Razia didn't disagree with Vel's assertion that she needed to be more careful about showing her face (or more importantly, her figure) in broad daylight. So they waited until night fell on the pirate city to set out for one of the three bars Hardrict had been frequenting over the past few months. They kept to the alleyways, especially after she'd noticed two young pirates eyeing her hopefully. The last thing she wanted tonight was to have to outrun a pirate with Vel.

They staked out the bar for a few hours until Hardrict showed up with his crew members. Razia counted five of them, too many for her to handle. She'd have to figure out a way to draw him out of the bar by himself.

"I'm going in," she announced, standing up.

Vel grabbed her arm. "No you aren't. You're pregnant!"

"Keep it down!"

"Sage would kill me if I let you go in there alone."

"What Sage doesn't know won't hurt him."

"Lyssa—" She shoved him against the wall and bolted across the street before he could stop her. With one triumphant look back at his irate face, she sauntered into the bar.

Her victory was short-lived, however, because the smell of pirates and booze and sex and dirt brought her ever-present nausea back with a vengeance. She turned and burst out of the door, covering her nose and mouth as she tried not to vomit all over the side of the street.

"So about you going in there…" Vel said behind her.

"Don't be smug. It doesn't suit you."

They crossed the street to their stake-out spot and strategized. Razia's stomach settled enough for her to consider going back in, but one look from Vel and she acquiesced. After a hissing argument where both got in a couple good jabs, Vel disappeared into the bar.

She waited, tapping her foot and sighing loudly every few seconds. Finally, his face lit up her mini-computer and she snarled at him for an update.

"He's in here." She watched him both on the screen and across the street. "So how do you want to handle this?"

"Tell him you're one of Dissident's new guys and you're there to capture him," Razia said.

"What if he laughs in my face?"

"Then fight him," Razia said. "Didn't you listen to anything Sage taught you?"

"He showed me for like an hour!" Vel whined.

"What about all your Academy boxing lessons?"

"Because a fifty pound sandbag is the same as a two hundred pound guy who hits back," Vel grumbled. "Okay, I'm going in. Are you ready?"

She glanced at the window and shook her head. "I should really be in there with you."

"Lyssa…"

"Fine, fine, fine," she said, rubbing her stomach. "Just…be careful, okay?"

"I got this." The screen went dark.

Lyssa paced up and down the alley, nervously thinking about all the different ways that this half-cocked plan could go wrong. She chewed her lip and her thumb and rubbed her arms and her stomach, casting furtive glances at the bar door. She should've gone in with him.

Then the doors to the bar burst open, and Cree Hardrict came flying out with Vel fast on his heels. And he looked…scared, almost. She scurried into position, waiting with a spare piece of wood she'd found lying in the alley. When she heard Hardrict run by, she swung, tripping him and sending him to the ground. Before he knew what had hit him, she'd handcuffed him and tied his feet.

"W-what…you!" Hardrict said, finally looking over his shoulder. "What's… You can't do this. You can't take me in!"

"Of course I can," she said, unhooking her canvas. Vel came trotting up behind her and she motioned for him to stay in the shadows.

"You can't! You don't know what they'll do to me in there!"

She paused before kicking him onto the canvas. "Somebody got a secret on you?"

"Yeah, they're going to take me down, you don't know. Please, just let me go."

She exchanged a look with Vel, who shrugged. Then she kicked Hardrict in the jaw, knocking him out.

"You think he was telling the truth?" Razia asked, resting her hands on her stomach.

Vel's gaze darted to her hands and then back down to Hardrict. "Who knows? Guys will say anything to get out of being arrested."

She rubbed her stomach in thought and noticed Vel watching her do it. "What?"

"You've been doing that a lot," he said with a smile. "It's sweet."

She dropped her hands and made a mental note to be more careful. "Let's just get him to the bounty office."

***

91

Though she would have loved to have kept Vel with her forever, he reminded her that he probably needed to get back to the Academy so he could finish his education. She knew it was better if he had a choice of careers, instead of being forced into one over the other. Tauron had given her the same choice, and for that, she was grateful.

In truth, she was upset that she'd be alone again. Vel reminded her that she could've gone to find Sage if she was really lonely, or call Lizbeth. She could even stay at the Academy. But none of these options were appealing to her.

As she was saying her goodbyes to Vel, her mini-computer buzzed at her hip; Dissident was calling her.

"This isn't good," Lyssa said to Vel. "He never calls me unless I've screwed something up."

"You never know," Vel said. "Maybe it's a good thing this time?"

She steeled herself for the worst and answered. "Y-yes?"

"Razia, my girl, we have to talk," Dissident said heavily. She swallowed hard. "I need you to figure out who in Leveman's Great Vortex is taking down my pirates."

She blinked and shared a look with Vel. "Really?"

"The latest, did you hear? Jeam Bullock was arrested last week," Dissident said. "Arrested! For drug trafficking! Nasty business. I had no idea he was dabbling in that stuff still. He swears he's cleaned up his act, but I just don't know, girlie, I just don't know."

Vel pointed at her stomach and mimed something.

She furrowed her brow and shrugged, not understanding. "One second," she said to Dissident and muted the call. "What?"

"Tell him that if you're hunting down Opli, you can't bounty hunt at the same time."

"I…oh!" She nodded in understanding. "You're brilliant."

"I know."

She turned back to Dissident and plastered on a haughty face. "So, you know if I start hunting down this mystery man, I won't have as much time to hunt other pirates?"

Dissident snorted. "You get one month."

"Fine. I'll be in touch."

The call went dark, and Lyssa hooked her mini-computer back

onto her belt with a satisfied smile. "That buys me a few weeks, at least. Maybe more."

"See? Not everything goes wrong in your life," Vel said with a smile. "Now I think you might need help in finding out some more information on Opli."

"I'll call Harms."

"Not him."

Lyssa took a long breath and glared at him. "No."

"You should call her. You're running out of clothes that fit."

Lyssa scowled. "She did deck me."

"You did deserve it."

She shot him a look, which he returned.

"Call her. For once in your miserable life, don't be stubborn." Vel kissed Lyssa's temple and left her on her ramp.

CHAPTER NINE

"You're progressing quite well," Dr. Bianco said, pressing down on Lyssa's upper stomach. "How are you feeling?"

"Nausea is gone. And everything else is..."

Tricky.

After dropping Vel off, she'd thought she'd head straight back to D-882. Until she got a good look in the mirror. Even with her biggest shirt and loosest pants, it was getting very obvious that her shape was changing. Instead, she'd found cheap parking on S-864 and hung out the a week and a half until her appointment, working on her Opli project.

Unfortunately, she had no idea where to start. Her brain was still full of sludge, and she found herself blankly staring at the Universal Bank search window more than once. To make matters worse, she was running out of clothes that still fit her. When she got dressed for her appointment, her only options were a ratty shirt Sage had left and Lizbeth's stretchy pants.

Bianco gently lifted the shirt. "Are things all right with the father? I didn't see one mentioned in your file."

"It's…complicated. He's…" She winced and took a deep breath. "He's the one who wants it. I don't."

"I can't say that's normal, but it's definitely not unique," Bianco said, squeezing the jelly onto her stomach. "It happens much more often than you think. But why isn't he here?"

"I don't want him here," Lyssa said. "Him being here makes it… real. And I don't want him thinking we're something that we're not. We're just friends and this," she gestured at her stomach, "was a major accident."

"I can understand that," Bianco said with a kind smile.

"Besides, he's off doing something else right now," Lyssa snapped, jumping as Bianco squirted the cold jelly on her stomach.

Bianco made a small sound. "Is he contacting you regularly?"

He was, nearly every day. She refused to take his calls, though, because if he had anything to talk with her about, he could stop whatever he was doing and come find her.

"I don't need him around. Everything's fine. He just complicates things."

"Mm."

"But what in Leveman's Great Vortex could be more important than this?"

"Have you asked?"

"N-no," she huffed and stared at the ceiling. "Because I don't want him around."

"You've said that." Bianco pressed the sensor into Lyssa's skin and turned on the attached screen. "Well, are you ready to see your baby for the first time?"

Lyssa's blood ran cold, and she hesitated. If she looked at that screen, what would she see? A deformed monster? Sage's face? Her face? Some horrible—

She lifted her eyes against her will and took in the scanned 3-D image on the screen. A long cord connected the tiny thing to her, but it looked nothing like a human. A bulbous head, small spindly hands and…the cutest little fingers she'd ever seen. Tiny ears, eyes, nose, mouth…

"Pretty cool, huh?" Bianco said, moving the sensor around to show different sides of the baby.

"Y-yeah," Lyssa breathed. She absorbed every single detail, unsure what she was looking for. "Is it…is it—"

"We won't know the gender for a couple more weeks," Bianco said.

"No, I mean, is it…okay?" Lyssa swallowed. "Is it supposed to look like that?"

Bianco tittered a little. "Yes, Ms. Dailey, it is supposed to look like that." She reached over to the sensor and pressed a button. The machine began humming and spat out a few photographs of the parasitic-looking alien living in Lyssa's lower abdomen.

"Here," Bianco said. "For Dad. If you choose to give it to him. Something tells me he'd like it very much."

***

Lyssa stared at the grainy, orange photograph of the bug growing inside of her. She ran her finger along the head, down the nose and the lips pouting out and smiled to herself. There was something special about the photo, about knowing what exactly the little bug looked like in there.

The only thing that smelled good to her in this coffee shop was warm tea, and she sipped it gingerly while she considered the photo. She should tell Sage. She should have invited him to come to the appointment. At the very least, she should have shown him the ultrasound photo. But she didn't want to hear his joy; it would be too much to take.

Still, she toyed with the idea of asking him for help on her Opli project. She had full-on…what did Vel call it, pregnancy brain? She could barely remember to use the right C-card anymore, let alone find a pirate's alias. She had tried Harms, but the pirate informant didn't know much more about the captain than she did.

There was the other option, but it would require her to eat a lot of crow. And there was no guarantee Lizbeth would even help her. Even so, she had to admit to herself that wanting Lizbeth's help was less about Opli and more that she missed her best friend.

So Lyssa swallowed her pride and trekked across the capital city to the looming Intelligence Agency building. The last time she'd been there she'd also been eating crow after nearly tearing Lizbeth to pieces for spilling her secret. Lyssa considered that it might be easier to not have blow-up fights.

The glass double doors opened to reveal the small lobby with a portly woman sitting at the desk. This woman was Lyssa's nemesis. Although she now worked for a new company—Optimization Security —she had the same unhelpful look on her face.

"ID, please."

"Oh, you know who I am," Lyssa snapped, slamming her ID down. "I'm here to see Lizbeth Carter."

The woman glanced down at Lyssa's protruding stomach and Sage's grungy shirt and snorted. Lyssa folded her arms over her chest and waited as the security guard took an exceedingly long time to type in Lyssa's credentials. She then reached forward and picked up her phone, mumbling into it. Lyssa rolled her eyes as the security guard laughed into the phone and sat back, having a conversation.

"When you're quite finished," Lyssa snapped.

The guard gave her another once over and turned around continuing her conversation.

Lyssa waited and toyed with her hands. What if Lizbeth didn't come down? What if she was truly so upset that she'd never speak to Lyssa again? The thought churned in her mind as the moments ticked by and the security guard continued to talk on her phone.

"Well, well. I wondered when I'd be hearing from you."

Lyssa turned to the source of the voice and half-smiled. Lizbeth wore a very stylish dark purple suit with a pink button-up, complete with a pair of killer heels. Her normally untamed curly hair was pulled back behind her head as she surveyed Lyssa with a steely expression.

"Hey," Lyssa said, her own voice small and insignificant.

"Let's see, it's been how long? Two months?" Lizbeth stalked closer, like a predator about to destroy its prey. "And you just show up here out of the blue."

"I'm not...I wanted to—"

"And you just expect me to what? Forgive you for being such a total bitch? Not calling? Making me clean up *your* messes?"

Lyssa's heart began to race. "I haven't... I need your help with something…and I—"

"Well, it is a *damned* good thing you did, because what in Leveman's Vortex are you wearing?" Lizbeth's stern face broke into a smile and she pulled Lyssa into her arms.

Lyssa couldn't help the sigh of relief that left her body as she slumped into her best friend's arms. "You scared the shit out of me," Lyssa said, before tightening the hug. "I missed you and…and I'm sorry."

Lizbeth returned it with gusto. "I missed you and I'm sorry, too." She stepped back and looked down, unabashed glee crossing her face. "Look at your belly!" She pressed her hand to Lyssa's midsection and grinned. "Are you feeling better?"

"Why don't we have this conversation in your office?" Lyssa looked at the security guard, who was eyeing their interaction with curiosity.

Lizbeth led Lyssa back through all the detectors and the screeners into the room of dark blue cubicles where Lizbeth worked. But instead of heading into the bullpen, Lizbeth led Lyssa into an expansive office at the far end of the room. A fine desk made of dark, shiny wood centered the office, and Lizbeth's awards and diplomas hung on the wall. A photo of Joe and Billie, Lizbeth's parents, stood on the corner of her desk. Lyssa sat in one of the chairs facing the desk while Lizbeth settled into her side, leaning back with a smug expression.

"Well?"

"I am impressed," Lyssa said with a hearty laugh. "I even hear work going on out there."

"Had to fire half these assholes to do it," Lizbeth said with a shake of her head. "So what's up?"

"I need your help," Lyssa said, placing her hands on her stomach. When Lizbeth noticed the movement, Lyssa quickly removed them. "Captain Opli is taking down pirates, and Dissident wants it to stop."

"That little kid?" Lizbeth snorted. "He's about as dimwitted as your brother."

"Except he's not. He's exposing the pirates' dirty laundry and getting them either kicked out of the Pirate Web or arrested on charges that are outside the scope of the Piracy Act," Lyssa said. "I need to dig up some dirt on him. How much have you interacted with him?"

"Actually, even less than I had with Jukin," Lizbeth said. "Since the prison fiasco, that whole organization's budget got cut by two-thirds. Opli's got maybe ten guys now, and they're definitely not the same caliber of guys Jukin had. I saw one of them sporting a pirate-paid-for gold watch when I met with them a few weeks ago." She paused and tapped her fingers on the table. "But I don't get it. Pirates are shady bastards regardless. Everything they do is illegal. What's the big deal?"

"Not everything is covered under the Piracy Act. Hijacking, bounty hunting, some limited assault charges and such. But things like murder? Rape? Drug trafficking? The kind of stuff that's coming out about pirates is pretty serious."

"I wonder what Opli's secret is, then," Lizbeth said, tapping her chin.

"What do you mean?"

"People usually want to hit others where they, themselves, are weak. Opli's probably harboring some not-so-great things about himself, and that's why he's going after them in this way."

"Hm. Good point."

"Let's see what I can find on our good captain," Lizbeth said. "Make yourself comfy, preggo."

"Don't call me that."

Lizbeth ignored her. "So where do you want to look first?"

"Can you get into the UBU vital records and look up a birth certificate?" Lyssa said. "I want to know if Gelbard Opli is who he says he is."

Lizbeth began typing when there was a small knock on the door. A mousy man came walking into the room with two cups of coffee.

"Ms. Carter, here's your cup," he said, placing them on the desk. "And decaf for you, ma'am."

Lyssa took one sniff of the coffee and gagged.

"Oh, what?" Lizbeth said with a smile. "You love coffee."

"I haven't had a sip in months," Lyssa said sadly. "I can't stand the smell of it."

Lizbeth sat back from her computer and grinned. "What other

weird pregnancy shit have you had? Any cravings yet?"

Lyssa snorted. "Only the craving to bounty hunt."

"Yeah, I wanted to ask about that. How did you manage to take down Cree Hardrict?"

"How'd you know?"

"I'm head of the Piracy Branch, remember?" She nodded at a large screen to Lyssa's left, displaying the latest from the pirate web news feed. "But I have to ask, *you* didn't fight him, did you?"

"I'm not allowed to. Vel did." She paused. "Kind of. He drew him out. It was teamwork."

"Good girl," Lizbeth said, turning back to her computer. "Hm. I don't have a birth certificate record for Gelbard Opli. What do you think that means?"

"See if there's a record of him at the U-POL Academy."

A few moments later. "He is definitely in there."

"Hm," Lyssa said, rubbing her stomach and pulling up his Universal Bank accounts on her mini-computer. Opli was using one account for all his transactions. "So somewhere between birth and the U-POL academy, Opli changed his name."

"What do you need to change your name in the Universal Bank?" Lizbeth asked, adding, "If you aren't a pirate."

"You can't unless you get married or something. You get the name you get," Lyssa said. "Because it's not just a name—it's fingerprints, your photo, your entire identity. That's why it's such a big deal when pirates have more than one. Flies against the whole," she tossed her hands in the air, "authoritative data source idea."

"Opli's fingerprints don't even register," Lizbeth said. She furrowed her brow. "There aren't any fingerprints in the system, actually."

"Which means that Opli is an alias," Lyssa said. "A pirate-given alias."

"The plot thickens," Lizbeth said, leaning across the table. "And it also makes sense. I mean, that guy hates pirates. You don't get that way by growing up on a residential planet. At least, I'd hope not."

"Jukin did," Lyssa said.

"No, if he's making this much effort to tear down pirates, it's personal," Lizbeth said. "Speaking of, you heard from your brother lately?"

"No one has," Lyssa said. "Dorst said he hasn't left his room in weeks. The servants just bring him food that he barely eats."

"I'd feel bad, but he's a dick," Lizbeth said, pushing herself up from her desk. "Well, this has been fun, but let's be honest. We know why you really came out here."

"To find dirt on Opli?"

"Oh, you're funny," Lizbeth said, pulling out her wallet. "I have been dying to take you to this great maternity store around the corner from my apartment…"

***

Lizbeth wasn't kidding; she had a list of four stores within a six block radius where she dragged Lyssa. Some were maternity stores, others were baby furniture, where Lizbeth oohed and aahed over strollers and tiny shoes and teddy bears while Lyssa tried to not feel moved by how tiny and adorable everything was. Especially when she saw a pair of tiny black boots.

"So if you had to choose, which crib do you like more?" Lizbeth asked, standing in front of a dark mahogany crib with pink dressing and a white wooden crib with gray dressing.

"I don't know…the gray one, I guess?" Lyssa shrugged. "It's not really my call, you know."

"Oh, yes, but just for laughs," Lizbeth said, taking a photo of the tag with her mini-computer.

"So what do you think I should do about Opli?" Lyssa said, eager to talk about something other than the small teddy bears embroidered on a onesie.

"Look at this," Lizbeth said, holding up a bright pink shirt. "I could see you from space."

"Thanks. So Opli?" Lyssa said, making a beeline for shirts that were decidedly darker. "I'm actually kind of thankful that Dissident told me to work on this. I can't be seen on D-882 anymore."

"Really, Lyssa? More boring black shirts? You're pregnant. At least you could look a little cute." Lizbeth grabbed Lyssa by the arm and pulled her back to the brighter maternity clothes.

"You really aren't going to help me with this investigation?" Lyssa asked.

"Oh, what? I got you started." She picked up a blue polkadot dress that Lyssa vetoed with a shake of her head.

"I don't know. I've been off my game. Vel says I have pregnancy brain or something like that. It's like…I feel just *dumb* lately. Is this how everyone else goes through life?"

Lizbeth snorted when Lyssa grinned at her. "Glad to know you haven't lost your sense of humor." She picked up a teddy bear and squeezed it to her chest. "Why don't you ask Sage to come help?"

Lyssa shrugged, and couldn't wipe the frown off her face. "He said he was working on something. Haven't seen him in a few weeks."

"Did you say something to scare him off?"

"No!" Lyssa said, a little too quickly. "I mean, I…" She considered the planet, the Academy, and all the trouble she'd put him through just to make him miserable. He hadn't seemed too affected by it, but what if he had been? What if he'd finally had enough of her?

"I'm sure it's fine," Lizbeth said, coming to rest a hand on her shoulder.

"I know it's fine," Lyssa barked, angry that she'd let her emotion show on her face. "He's…whatever. I don't care what he does. Or where he goes. Or how long he's gone."

Lizbeth laughed and picked up a baby blanket. "Okay, Lyss."

Lyssa paused and glared at her. "Have *you* heard from him?"

"Hm?" she said, not meeting Lyssa's eyes.

Lyssa picked at the seam of the shirt she was holding. "Did he… mention anything?"

"Only that you made his life miserable on a planet excavation, which I can only assume is an initiation in your mind," Lizbeth said. She crossed the room and put both hands on Lyssa's shoulders. "He's not angry with you, I promise. But have you ever thought, perhaps, that he might be waiting for *you* to come to *him* for once? You do tell him to go away a lot. Maybe he's finally listening to you."

"No, he—" She felt something akin to a bubble popping in the center of her stomach. Her hands flew to the bulge and she gasped loudly.

"What is it?" Lizbeth asked. "Are you okay?"

"I..." She felt it again, the thump against her hand. It was small, almost like a tiny flick. "Holy shit."

"Is the baby kicking?" Lizbeth gasped. Lyssa placed Lizbeth's hand where her own had been and they waited. After a few breathless seconds, the *pop* happened again and Lizbeth squealed.

"That's the first I've ever felt it," Lyssa said with a grin. "It's...alive in there."

"I really hate to ask this, but...you have been seeing a doctor, right?" Lizbeth asked.

Lyssa nodded, mesmerized by the fluttering movements. She reached into her pocket and handed Lizbeth the ultrasound photo.

"Wow," Lizbeth breathed. "Look at that. You've got a baby inside you, don't you?"

"Don't tell Sage I have a photo," Lyssa whispered.

"Why not?"

"Because...I don't...I don't want..."

Lizbeth sighed loudly, drawing the attention of two other expectant mothers in the shop. "You know, one of these days, he's not going to put up with your bullshit. And then where are you going to be?" She wrapped her arm around Lyssa's shoulder. "You know the price of my silence is you trying on *at least* four dresses of my choosing, and buying *at least* two of them..."

They shopped until Lyssa's feet hurt and then Lizbeth invited Lyssa over to her fancy apartment for a glass of wine. Or rather, Lizbeth drank while Lyssa nursed a water. But the conversation was the same, and Lyssa was glad for it. Being with Lizbeth and talking about everything *but* the bug was the first time Lyssa had felt normal in months.

"I really meant it, Lyss, I missed you," Lizbeth said, swirling her wine around in her glass. "Guess we can't have any more adventures for a while, huh?"

"This bug is going to come and I'm going to go back to normal," Lyssa said, rubbing her stomach. "Nothing's going to change."

"Except everything," Lizbeth said. "Like it or not, that 'bug' is your baby. And you've got to accept that sooner or later."

"I don't have to accept anything because I'm not going to be..." She swallowed. "I'm giving it to him, and that's that." She couldn't help but add, "Besides, it's not as if anyone would miss me anyway."

"Oh, I see." Lizbeth nodded, leaning against her hand. "Jealous, are we?"

"Of what?"

"You're such an open book, it's hilarious," Lizbeth cackled. "Listen to me, please. And please listen with both ears and no sass." She glared pointedly at Lyssa. "Sage Teon could literally have a baby with any female in the universe. Leveman's, I'd have a baby with him."

Lyssa stiffened and looked forward.

"He's kind, he's thoughtful, he's funny. He's great in bed, if your judgment is any measure." Lizbeth grinned slyly. "And he's obviously ready to settle down and commit. Who wouldn't want that?"

Me, Lyssa thought.

"But here's the thing, babe, you're the one knocked up," Lizbeth said. "Accident or not, Sage wouldn't have been so careless if he didn't want this on some level. And I think...maybe, deep down... you're the same way."

"I don't want this."

"If you're going to be stubborn, just promise me one thing," Lizbeth turned to look at her. "Promise me that you will be very careful with him. He's...I'm not saying he's delicate, but you can do an awful lot of damage to him right now." She took another sip of wine. "Just be aware that he cares a lot for you. And if your plan is really just to pop out a kid, leave it with him, and never see him again..."

"Never see him again?"

"He's going to have his hands full for a while. Years probably," Lizbeth drawled, swirling her wine in her glass. "So unless you want your kid knowing you, you're going to have to say your goodbyes to Sage now." She took one long swig and winked. "If that's your plan."

That was her plan, wasn't it? That's what she had been saying but somehow she had't quite realized or understood the consequences. She'd never see Sage again, never spy him poking around where he wasn't welcome. He'd never come swooping in to save her ass when she didn't need it.

"Well, some of us have to work in the morning," Lizbeth said, pulling herself to stand. She leaned down and pressed a kiss to Lyssa's forehead. "Let me know if you need any pillows. Wouldn't want you to be in a foul mood or anything."

"Night, Liz," Lyssa said with a smile. Lizbeth waved at her before disappearing behind her bedroom door.

Almost as soon as Lizbeth's light went off, Lyssa's mini-computer was lighting up with Sage's face. Snarling, Lyssa reached forward and ended the call.

A few seconds later, a message came in.

Hope you had fun with Lizbeth. Call me when you get a chance.

She glared at the offending message and rolled over onto her side, angry that she was being watched and he wasn't there.

CHAPTER TEN

"Twenty weeks. Halfway there," Bianco said as she shook Lyssa's hand in greeting. "How are you feeling?"

"My hips hurt," Lyssa said, rubbing the spot under her protruding belly. "I can't sleep on my back anymore."

"All normal," Bianco said, stepping over to her cabinet and digging for her machines. "You might experience the round ligament pain until you deliver, so you'll want to take it easy."

"I don't know how much more I can fit in there." Already she felt stretched to the limit, and she still had another twenty weeks to grow.

"Your body will adjust," Bianco said, sliding over on her rolling chair. "Has the baby been moving at all?"

Lyssa nodded and couldn't help but smile. "It felt like a pop, but now I can feel more movement."

"That's excellent," Bianco said. "Now, today we can maybe find out the gender of the baby. Do you want to know?"

Lyssa squirmed. "No."

"Do you want me to put it in an envelope for later then?" Bianco asked gently. "You can give it to the father. How are things with him?"

She glanced at Bianco then back down. She almost regretted sharing the details of their relationship to the doctor. At the same time, it was nice to be able to talk freely about what she was going through without judgment.

"Weird," she said. "Just…weird."

"Are you still thinking you'll give him the baby?" Bianco rolled over the ultrasound machine and lifted Lyssa's shirt. She squirted a cold gel onto Lyssa's stomach and glanced up; Lyssa still hadn't answered.

"Yeah, probably," Lyssa said after a moment. "I'm the least qualified person to be…"

"A mother?"

"Yeah, that."

"I've heard that before. But you know, things change. Just keep an open mind." Bianco smiled and pressed the sensor to Lyssa's belly. "Well, let's check on the little…bug, do you call it?"

Lyssa glanced down and chuckled. She watched the sensor go over her skin and the screen light up out of the corner of her eye. But she was never ready to look right away.

"Let's see. Oh my…" Bianco gasped and Lyssa's heart dropped. Was something wrong with the bug? Had she screwed it up? Was there…

Her words died in her throat and something between a coo and a chuckle came out. She saw the bug, face, eyes, lips…and a little toe stuck in its mouth. She coughed, trying to cover up the intense need to both cry and reach out and touch the face.

"I've never seen that before," Bianco said with a laugh.

"Does the… Is everything normal?" Lyssa whispered, watching the arms and hands move in the ultrasound.

Bianco nodded. "So far, so good."

The scan took twenty minutes as Bianco checked everything from the baby's face to the spine. Lyssa's heart stopped in the breath between when Bianco announced the next examination and when she gave the all clear.

"You are looking great, Lauren," Bianco replied, wiping the gel from Lyssa's stomach. "Any questions for me?"

"Did you find out the gender?" Lyssa asked quietly.

"I did," Bianco said with a nod. "Do you want to know?"

Should she find out? It would be good to give the bug a name instead of just…bug. But she didn't trust that she could keep that information from Sage—or that she'd want to.

"N-no."

***

"Honestly, Razia, I'm getting a little offended. You haven't come to see me in weeks!" Harms was joking, but Razia winced. It had been over a month since she and Vel had turned in Hardrict, and there was no way she could possibly show her face on D-882. It was a good thing she'd gone shopping with Lizbeth because she had definitely "popped" in the past two weeks. Now all her black tanks sported much more room in the middle, though she was able to keep her mini-computer camera above the bump to keep it away from prying eyes.

But the bigger problem was that if Harms had noticed her absence, so had others.

"Dissident has asked me to dig up some dirt on Opli to get him to quit targeting pirates," she said. "It's keeping me busy."

"You'd better get a move on. The latest is Waslow Needler. He was wanted on S-864 for beating up women, and now he's really on the run. Cree Hardrict just flat-out retired, so I don't know the story there."

"Hardrict retired?" Razia said, pausing the gentle stroking on her stomach. "I just turned him in a few weeks ago."

"And he promptly announced his retirement after that," Harms said.

Razia bit her lip. "I thought all that crying about 'they were gunning for me' was just him trying to get out of being captured."

"He's gone," Harms said. "Now *Contestant* is starting to wonder when you're going to make headway on your investigation."

She snorted and shook her head. "Him and me both."

"So it's going that well, huh?" Harms asked.

"That's an understatement." She'd had Lizbeth pull a list of all babies born on a three year period on D-882, with Opli's given birthdate in the U-POL Academy as the mid-point. But that list numbered in the four hundreds, and with her fuzzy brain, she was going much slower than usual, which only served to frustrate her, which, in turn, made her work even slower. Three weeks had gone by, and she was only through a fifth of the list.

What was worse was that Sage kept calling—daily now—and when she didn't answer, he'd send her a message wondering if she was feeling all right, asking if she needed anything. Once, when she was feeling particularly lonely, she almost asked him to come find her. But her pride got the better of her, and she simply ignored the message.

"You know, I wouldn't believe half of the stuff that's come out if it weren't for everyone dropping like flies. It's creepy how many guys are spooked now. Reminds me of after Tauron died." He shook his head. "We had a wave of retirements after that fiasco too. But now it's like… I don't even know anybody in the top twenty anymore."

"Who's left?"

"Protestor's got a few guys. Contestant's still got Relleck."

Razia snorted. Relleck's ego was so big and his compass so skewed, it would take a very big secret indeed to have him run for cover.

"Insurgent is hurting. The only guy he's got left who's worth his salt is…well…" Harms shrugged. "VJ."

"He's worthless," Razia said with a roll of her eyes. "After that fluke with Eamon's, he hasn't done jack."

"And Dissident has you and Sage, though Sage… man, Sage has been a ghost lately. First, he just flat-out disappears for weeks, and now he's giving you his crew to manage? I'm a little worried. I wonder if the whole prison incident spooked him. Or if Opli's gotten to him."

"I'm sure he's fine—*wait, what do you mean he gave me his crew to manage?*"

"Ganon stopped by and said he was now detailed to you for some indeterminate amount of time," Harms said, leaning closer to the screen. "News to you?"

"I mean…" She pursed her lips. "I didn't realize that Sage was… I'm not… I don't need…" She banged her hand on the chair. "*Asshole.*"

"You really got nothing else going on?" Harms asked, pressing his chin onto his hand. "Nothing else you want to share?"

"Nope." A pause. "Gotta run."

She barely let the call end with Harms before she was angrily dialing Sage's mini-computer.

"Yeeees?" The son of a bitch looked smug, like he knew why she was calling him. It just infuriated her more.

"What in Leveman's Vortex are you telling people? And where are you? And where have you been? And—"

"Slow down, Lyss," Sage said with a laugh. He was much more tan than usual, and the tops of his nose and cheeks were red with sunburn. A wind was blowing, and she heard voices and hammering behind him. "First of all, if you were so concerned about me, why haven't you returned any of my calls?"

She scowled.

"Second of all, Lizbeth told me you were too big to be seen on D-882 anymore, so I made a contingency plan. I told Dissident you had an idea who was taking down the pirates, which meant he didn't expect you to bounty hunt for a while. And now, I told Ganon and the guys to help you out while you're off saving piracy again."

She realized her mouth was open and closed it quickly.

"Ganon is expecting your call any day now. Until I get back, they're yours." Sage smiled. "It'll be good for them to have something to do again. They've gotten lazy."

"I didn't ask you to—"

"I told you I'd take care of you while you're pregnant, and I meant it." The sincerity on his face was nerve-wracking, and she had to look away. "I'm sorry I can't be there, but I hope that this is a suitable alternative until I can be."

She glanced at the screen behind him. Nothing but blue sky.

"Unless, of course, you want to come visit me here?" Sage asked. "I'd love to see you."

She desperately wanted to ask where he was, and what he was doing that was more important than her, but said, "I'll call Ganon. Bye."

***

"So, we get to work for you now?" Ganon sounded none-too-pleased about this relationship. "Joy."

"Don't think I like this any more than you do," Lyssa snapped. "But Sage went blabbing to Harms, which means that Dissident will find out soon, and I don't want to hear a whole bunch of bullshit from him. So you're going to go take care of a few pirates for me to keep him off my back."

Ganon snorted. "Listen here, I'm only doing this until Sage gives me the go-ahead, then he says this ship and her crew are mine."

"What?"

"Yeah, he said that if I suffered through a few months of you, he'd step aside and let me take over for him."

Lyssa sat back, stunned. Now he was giving up his ship and his crew? She shook her head and plastered a disinterested look on her face.

"I need you to go after Zolet Obalone." She'd tried to capture Obalone a few years back, but Relleck had gotten in the way. It had taken the kid a few years to rise back to prominence, and he seemed a bit wiser than before, focusing more on hijacking ships than on bounty hunting and bragging into D-882. She had found him by sheer luck; she'd been refueling her ship at G-279 and saw him and his crew. When she traced his alias information, it showed he'd been spending time on the transport station between jobs.

"So where am I supposed to find him on G-279?" Ganon drawled after she explained her plan. "It's kind of a large station. And what if he doesn't come back? And—"

"Did Sage not say you were working for me?" she snapped. "This is what I need you to do!"

Ganon leaned into the screen and glared at her. "Don't misunderstand. I am helping you as a favor to *Sage*. Because, for some reason, he thinks you're worth helping, whereas I think you're just an immature little brat."

"Are you done?" Razia said. "Get to G-279. And if you backtalk again—"

"Calm down, princess. It's not like we got a whole lot of other shit to do."

She paused. "So you really have no idea what Sage is up to? And he really promised you his ship?"

"He's got a special project he keeps going on and on about. If you ask me, I think Opli's got hold of him and he's trying to mitigate the damage before the secret comes out."

She rubbed her stomach. Opli said he didn't have anything on Sage, but what if he did? Still, Sage hadn't looked worried about anything. Though she'd been too angry with his long-distance puppet-mastering to really pay attention.

"How bad is it there? With Opli?" she asked.

"Bad. Good thing I'm an open book. I have no secrets I'm ashamed of. Not like somebody who's Jukin Peate's sister."

She furrowed her brow. Ganon brought up a good point. Opli could very easily make life worse for her with one simple announcement, and yet…six months had passed since the break-out and not a peep. Why hadn't Opli ruined her life the same way he was ruining the others?

"Well?" Ganon drawled. "Is there anything else you would like to share?"

"Just get going."

Pregnant or not, Razia was never one to sit back and let others do her work for her. She wanted to be nearby to make sure Ganon didn't screw up. Besides, her eyes were starting to cross from the list of names for the Opli investigation.

She parked her ship at G-247 and waited, marking Obalone and his crew for a few hours until Ganon and the crew showed up. The transport station was heavily populated, so she was in no danger of being spotted. Even so, she'd bought a hat and sunglasses at one of the small sundries shops while she waited.

When she saw Sage's ship had requested access to dock, she left Obalone eating lunch and ventured down a few levels to the docking station. Sage's ship was in the back. The hatch was open and Ganon, Sobal, Keal, and the three meatheads milled out front talking to the dock hands.

She scowled when Ganon waved goodbye to the crew, obviously intending to take on Obalone by himself. She hissed and yanked out her mini-computer, trying to figure out how she could direct him without him knowing. After a moment, she yanked off her hat and sunglasses, trying to look nonchalant as she called him.

"What?" he drawled, looking bored.

"What's your plan?" she asked.

"Oh, I was thinking I might just arrest him. Wasn't sure, only did this a few hundred times before."

She cleared her throat. "How many guys are you taking with you?"

"Five," Ganon said. Razia glanced behind him; the rest of the crew was still on the ship. "Are you gonna babysit me the whole time or can I do the job your boyfriend is paying me to do?"

The line went dark, and Razia angrily redialed the number.

"You'll need more than one guy," Razia said. "And don't lie to me. I know you're going by yourself. You'll get your ass handed to you."

"And how, pray tell, do you know that I'm going by myself?" Ganon drawled.

"Because I know. So go get the rest of them, and I'll message you the coordinates." She paused and scowled. "*And he's not my boyfriend.*"

She ended the call and watched Ganon curse something filthy at her. But he turned and barked for the rest of Sage's bodyguards and Sobal, the youngest on the crew, to come with him for back-up. She yanked her cap and sunglasses back on as they passed, and she heard him complaining about her.

"*Because I know.* That little bitch. I can't believe we have to work for her," Ganon was saying to Sobal.

"Yeah, but Sage asked," Sobal said. "You think he's okay? He's been acting odd lately."

"I don't give a shit. I'm about done with both their asses," Ganon said, and their conversation died as they blended into the crowd. Razia kept her distance but followed close enough to keep Nalton's dark scraggly hair in view.

Her mini-computer buzzed again and she answered it.

"He's not here, O Great Bounty Hunter."

Razia cursed and glanced up—Obalone and his crew had finished eating and left. She murmured a quick goodbye to Ganon then pulled on her hat and sunglasses, sauntering up to another patron of the diner.

"Hey, did you see a group of pirates walking by here?" she asked.

"Small, scrawny kid with a bunch of thick guys?"

The man pointed to the right and Razia quickly thanked him, rushing in that direction. She spotted Obalone at a small shop, deciding which of the icing-covered desserts he wanted to take with them. She called Ganon back.

"Okay, he's down the hall," Razia said. "At a dessert shop. Hurry up."

Ganon rolled his eyes and ended the call. She sat down at a nearby table and waited, chewing her lip. She dipped her hat lower in an attempt to avoid their attention as Ganon and the crew walked by, jawing loudly and scanning the room for Obalone.

She glanced down the hall again—Obalone had moved on, which Ganon told her when he called her a moment later.

Ganon clicked his tongue against his teeth. "I'm having so much fun wandering around this station to your wildly inaccurate directions."

"Then move faster and you'll catch him," she snapped. "Give me a second." She ended the call and glanced around. Ganon and the crew were still standing in front of the shop, and Sobal was salivating while he stared at the cupcakes. While they were distracted, she pulled the lid of her hat lower and breezed by them, praying neither of them would see her. When she passed, she hurried forward, coming to the large terminal where most of the shuttles came and went.

In the distance, she spotted Obalone walking toward the lift. She sent a message to Ganon without any further explanation, then sat down on one of the terminal seats to wait for the fireworks. Not a moment later, Ganon and Sage's crew sauntered by her. Sobal pointed and waved to the rest of them, running forward.

Sage's crew approached Obalone's and Razia compared Sage's five to Obalone's four. Obalone's might have won on size alone, but Razia wouldn't bet against Ganon. Too far away to hear the repartee between Ganon and Obalone, she read the latter's face as Ganon presumably told him he was there on behalf of her. Obalone's face darkened, and his bodyguards moved forward to begin their fight.

She watched the melee with mixed emotions. On the one hand, she rather missed fighting her own fights and taking down her own people. But on the other—she winced as Sobal took the brunt of a fist in his jaw—it wasn't completely terrible to have someone else get all the bruises.

After a few moments, it became clear that Obalone was in a losing battle and he held his hands up in surrender. Nalton slapped on the cuffs and began chatting with the rest of the crew, who grinned as they wiped their bloody noses. In fact, if Razia hadn't witnessed their brawl mere seconds before, she would have assumed they were all old friends.

She shook her head. "Pirates."

CHAPTER ELEVEN

With Ganon and crew taking care of her dirty work, Lyssa was able to take out four pirates in four weeks. Since most of the pirates were on D-882, she forced herself to stay away from the action, although she called Ganon every few seconds to check on his progress.

After the fifth pirate, she received the following message from Sage:

Stop micromanaging my guys.

Then,

And call me. I want to show you something.

She was most assuredly *not* going to call him, nor was she going to answer when he called her at the same time every day.

After several weeks of painstaking, distracted work, she had nearly gone through the entire list of names Lizbeth had given her as she tried to figure out why Opli was so concerned with eradicating piracy. The birth certificate data included all the identifying information—height, weight, fingerprints, blood type, even a newborn photo. Lyssa was having to open and sort through the files one by one. Once she reached the end of her search, she figured she'd dive deeper into the fifty or so that had piqued her interest, searching for patterns or transactions that would clue her into who they really were.

She opened the list and scrolled through until she found the next profile.

Sage Alejandro Teon

There were his tiny fingerprints, his height and weight (eight pounds, seven ounces, twenty inches), and the photo of him at birth.

She stared at the squalling bald baby, and imagined it as Sage today. Against her better judgment, she bent down and unlocked the hatch of the secret compartment under her dashboard where she kept her most prized possessions. A half-empty bottle of whiskey Tauron had given her and that she and Lizbeth had partaken of one night during their first investigation; a black, leather-bound journal that contained the formula for entry and exit into Leveman's Vortex; and her ultrasounds. She pulled out the latest one, the one where Bianco had given her a full view of the little face. Her heart twisted every time she laid eyes on it.

Curious, she placed it next to the photo of Sage. She cocked her head to the side and compared the two, deciding that the bug had his nose and maybe his chin, but it was hard to tell—

"What am I doing?" she said, nearly dropping the ultrasound photo.

Quickly, she stashed it away and locked her hidden compartment, sitting back in her chair and rubbing her stomach to soothe herself. She glanced up at Sage's birth certificate again and was about to close it, when she noticed the line denoting his mother.

Isabel Teon

Sage, of course, had a mother. And a father, too, perhaps. She'd never asked.

"That's the problem with you Peates. You're all so absorbed in your own family dramas that you don't see how your spats affect the rest of the universe. You don't look at the big picture until it comes careening into your worldview. Then you make it all about you."

Opli was right, at least, about that. But perhaps now that she was aware of it, she might be able to change it. She could ask about Sage's mother, which might give her insight into why he was so eager to—

Another thought popped into her head.

"The mothers…"

She pulled up her list of fifty babies that had piqued her interest and opened the first one, again, displaying the fingerprints, height, weight, and photo. But this time, her eyes drew to the mother field. If she were to search on the *mothers*, they would theoretically be active with their UBU-given names. And through the mothers, she would be able to find the sons.

Including Opli.

***

Rejuvenated by her new direction, she breezed through the final names on her original list of four hundred. Once that task was complete, she put together the names of all the mothers and their last known locations and transactions. Forty of those names she sent over to Ganon with orders to split them amongst the crew and report their findings back to her, in-between hunting down her bounties, that was.

But the ten she kept for herself were the ones that had tingled her bounty hunter senses. Not that it meant a whole lot, but she wanted to pretend it did. More than anything, she wanted to be the one to make the big discovery about Opli, if only to prove to herself that she was still herself.

Herself plus six months of pregnancy.

Even with the black tank top and black jacket, she looked big. She was taking a huge risk by going to D-882; not only could her pregnancy secret be discovered, but she could also run into someone with an inkling to capture her. She was having a hard time even walking fast—fleeing was out of the question.

But damn, she missed the thrill of it.

As if on cue, the now-familiar fluttering sensation rumbled from the bulge, and she placed her hand over the spot.

"Quiet down in there," she muttered. Under her palm, she felt the smallest of thumps against the inside of her stomach. The bug had become quite active in the past few days, especially when she had been focused most intently on pairing vital records with Universal Bank aliases.

The bug moved again, and she smiled even though she poked at her stomach. "What do you want to do, Bug?" Another thump against her hand meant nothing to her.

She tapped her feet against the metal floor of her bedroom and considered her options. It was night in the pirate city. Most pirates would be in a bar or already drunk. If anyone said they'd seen her, she could simply tell Harms that it was the alcohol, that she was actually far away, hunting down leads on S-864 or something.

Bianco did say that more walking might ease some of her hip pain.

She stood and marched out of her bedroom. The baby seemingly agreed with this movement, as it thumped against her ribcage.

"Okay, I am not your punching bag!" Lyssa bellowed. She immediately felt guilty for yelling at the bug and rubbed the side of her belly. "Sorry, Bug. I hear you in there. We should go investigate. After all, this is *my* thing."

She waited for confirmation from the bug and felt none.

"Well, that's it then. We're going."

***

Using her Lauren Daily credentials and waiting until after the sun had gone down on D-882, Razia parked her ship in one of the far-out parking stations. She felt a twinge of guilt when Sage had called her, and his message was a reminder that he wanted to know how she was feeling, and to take care of herself.

But her guilt disappeared as soon as she was off her ship. Everything was beautiful to Razia, even the grimy and disgusting shuttle system. She rode around at the back end of the transport shuttle for a while until she found a station that was both isolated and had a working lift so she wouldn't have to walk up several stories' worth of broken escalators. Her sense of smell was still overactive, but the trash and dust smell was welcome instead of nauseating. She placed a hand on her stomach and kept to the shadows between the streetlights, ears alert for the sound of footsteps approaching.

Most of the women she was looking for were still working in the main pirate city—which might explain how they ended up pregnant in the first place, though Razia couldn't very well talk. She had mapped out a walking path that would take her from one end of the city to the next, and just hoped her lower back wouldn't protest all the time on her feet.

Her first stop was a bar in the middle of the city. Bypassing the front door, she slipped in through the backroom and cracked the door into the main barroom. She checked the few patrons—most of them were old and grizzled, their shirts too grimy to be pirates. She stepped away from the door and pulled her hair back into a bun. She considered adding her glasses as well, but decided against it.

Adjusting her jacket over her stomach, she slipped through the door as quietly as possible, keeping to the wall until she reached the bar. The bartender was Razia's intended target, an older woman with graying red hair and a cigarette dangling from her lip. Razia tried not to cough at the smell, and slouched when she sat down on the barstool.

"What'll it be?" the woman asked.

"I actually have some questions to ask you," Razia replied quietly. "Did you have a son about twenty-four years ago?"

She nodded. "Yeah. What about it?"

"Do you keep in touch with him?"

"A bit."

Razia wished Lizbeth was here; she was always better at these interrogations than Razia. "So…tell me about him?"

"Why? You know 'im."

"I do?"

"Yeah, ol' Roy's a good boy. Bit big on the ego. Gets that from me, you know."

Razia blinked and realized she was, in fact, looking at a female version of Royden Relleck—complete with mustache. She slouched a little more, hoping to hide the bulge. "I didn't mean…sorry. Was looking for someone else."

She snorted. "Don't know why he was all smitten with you. Ain't nothing special about you. Too small for him."

"Right, well, this has been great."

Thanking her lucky stars, yet again, that she was *not* pregnant with Relleck's kid, Razia made a quick escape out the same back door.

Her goal had been to try to speak with all ten women that first night, but after riding around in the shuttle for way too long, she found herself tired so she returned to her ship. She hadn't realized how much actually moving about was exhausting now that she was carrying around an extra few pounds.

Not only that, but trying to keep hidden from a city teeming with pirates was another challenge itself.

The second night, she chose a docking station a little closer in and found the head maid at one of the cheesy hotels. But that was a dead-end in more ways than one—the woman said her son had died from illness when he was ten.

The next night, Razia met with a lovely woman who owned a coffee shop, though the woman's swollen ankles prevented her from working too much. She had invited Razia inside and made her the best cup of tea Razia had ever tasted ("I drank it all the time when I was pregnant"). The woman told Razia that her son had gone on to enjoy a great life as a lawyer for a large corporation, and showed Razia a photo of a handsome man with gleaming teeth. The mother had been able to secure him a new alias since most law schools in the capital system didn't accept children from D-882. They spoke more about Razia's pregnancy, and the woman gave Razia a big bag of loose-leaf tea to take with her.

Razia couldn't even make herself leave her ship for another three days after that; the exhaustion of walking and moving was too much. Besides, she was fast approaching another visit with Bianco, and she had to leave her investigation for a week while she tended to that.

When she returned to D-882, she was even more worn down than usual. Bianco said that she was now in her third trimester. Razia knew that if she wanted to get Opli out of the way, she'd have to do it soon before she was too big to climb her ladder and fly her own ship.

She hurried through two quick meetings with women on her first night back on D-882, and was going back to lie down on her ship when she heard voices.

"I swear to you, Sage, she ain't here."

"Well, I have no idea where she is, and I wouldn't put it past her to show up to help out. Are you sure that you checked both her accounts?"

With a gasp, Razia dove into an alley and flattened herself against the wall. Ganon and Sobal walked by her, talking to Sage on the mini-computer.

"I've been watching her accounts," Sobal said. "She hasn't made a transaction in two and a half weeks."

"I bet she created a new alias, then. Damn her."

"Why are you so worried about her anyway?" Ganon asked. "She's not worried about you at all."

Lyssa furrowed her brow and swallowed the need to refute that statement.

"I'm nearly finished here, and then I'll take over. There's just a few more things to do. Just, please, if you see her, don't..." She waited to see if he'd say anything about the bug, but he didn't. *"Just tell her to consider what she's doing."*

"Consider it? I am considering it, you jackass," she muttered under her breath. The bug moved in agreement. "Yeah, see? We're being careful."

To her horror, her mini-computer lit up with Sage's face. She jumped and the device popped out of her hands, vibrating loudly as she tried to grab it.

"I think I hear something," Sobal said.

She gasped and pulled the mini-computer to her chest, covering her mouth with her free hand.

"Nah, don't worry about it," Ganon said. "We've got to go through this list. Never thought I'd want to know who anybody's *mother* was before."

Their voices died and Lyssa breathed out a sigh of relief. She looked to her phone and saw the frantic messages from Sage piling up as the ones before went unanswered.

Where are you

Why haven't you made a transaction

Are you all right

Lyssa, please answer me

I'm getting pissed off now

Tell me where you are

She tapped out a message. *I'm busy, leave me alone.* She winced and added, *And I'm not doing anything stupid.*

"Lies, Lyssa. Pure lies," she muttered to herself as she slid her mini-computer back in her pocket and hurried down the street. She needed to get this list of names finished *that night.*

***

The sky was pink when she reached the tenth and final name on her list. She arched her back and groaned, promising herself a long, hot shower when she got back to her ship. She'd had a few close calls, even running into a very drunk Silas Brendler, who said she needed to lay off the desserts for a while. Hopefully, if anyone asked about it, she could pass it off as a hallucination.

Her last name was a woman living in the not-so-great part of the pirate city. Which, for a pirate city, was saying something. This section was where the poorest of the poor lived, where all the waitresses, barkeeps, and bouncers rested their heads when not dealing with the top pirates in the universe. Based on the trash piling up in the alleys and the long walk to get there, she knew the pirate runners didn't care much for this side of town and the services extending this far were meager at best. She placed a hand on her stomach, a twinge of worry eating at her for all the kids born there who'd never get out. No small wonder so many pirates came from this planet; it was the only way they could escape the cycle of poverty.

She craned her head at the building. The woman's account was sparingly used, which was why it had piqued Lyssa's interest more than the others. She rarely paid for rent, which meant someone else was paying it for her. What money she did receive from a few odd jobs was spent on booze.

Razia pushed open the broken doors and gagged from the smell of half-cooked food and overflowing trash. The floor was sticky with orange dirt and mud, and when she reached the old elevator, a few presses of the button showed it was out of order.

The bug was moving again, perhaps feeding on Razia's unease, and she pressed a hand to the spot. "Ssh, it'll be fine, I'm sure." She spied an open door and a set of stairs, and plodded over. The woman was on the fifth floor, if her receipts were any indication, and so Razia began to climb slowly, listening for footsteps behind her.

The fifth floor smelled as putrid as the rest of them, and Razia had to pull her shirt over her mouth to breathe. The hallway was lined with wooden doors with askew numbers, and when she passed by the garbage chute, it was overflowing. At the end of the hall, one of two doors marked the apartment she was looking for.

She reached the door and knocked softly. "Hello? Anyone home?"

She waited a few minutes then set to work on the lock. She wasn't an expert pick, but the lock was so flimsy she was able to get through it in no time. The door swung open to more darkness, and she groped for a light switch. Flipping it on and off did nothing.

"Hello?" she called again and listened for the sounds of lift. She walked in a few feet and nearly tripped over a glass bottle. Using the light from the hallway, she gingerly picked up the bottle. Whiskey. The apartment was littered with trash.

A snort drew her attention to a dark shape in the corner. She shuffled forward, kicking away more bottles and trash, and could make out the form of a woman sleeping on the couch, her mouth open and another bottle in her hand.

"Huh," Razia said, stepping back. She poked the woman with her boot, but the woman simply snorted and turned around. The bottle fell from her hand and landed with a thud on the ground, brown liquid pouring onto the stained carpet.

Razia looked around the dark apartment. She wasn't going to get any information from this woman tonight. Even if she had light, there was nothing but trash and old food in this place. Finding a birth certificates or signs of Opli would be be nearly impossible.

She paused by the woman once more, feeling a twinge of pity. This was someone's mother. Razia rubbed her own stomach for a moment, reminding herself that she was doing the right thing letting Sage take the bug.

"What in Leveman's Great Vortex are you doing here?"

A smile curled on her face. "Jackpot."

Opli stepped into the apartment, looking more livid than she'd ever seen him. Razia kept to the shadows, thankful he couldn't see her shape, as she braced herself for whatever he might do.

When he spoke next, he seemed to have recovered from his shock. "I wondered where you'd been all this time."

"Been busy doing a little research on you," she replied, forcing her hand to stay at her side, instead of to the bug, who was moving like crazy. "Not very much fun when the shoe is on the other foot, is it?" She glanced at the woman on the couch and swallowed her pity. That was what had got all of the pirates arrested by Jukin. She wouldn't make that mistake again. "I take it this is your mother, huh?"

He said nothing.

"Why the pirate vendetta, then?" Razia asked. "What's this all about, really?"

Opli's eyes flashed for a moment, but he recovered. "You sure you want to continue down this path, Lyssa? It's very dangerous to expose secrets when you have your own to protect."

She narrowed her eyes defiantly. "Do your worst."

He slowly approached her, and she backed up, accidentally stepping into the light. Horrified, she glanced up at Opli, whose mouth had opened and was slowly forming a pleased smile.

"Very stupid of you indeed, Lyssa," he said with a soft laugh. "No wonder you've been so absent. And Teon! Well, when's the wedding?"

She swallowed her nerves. "Don't think this changes anything."

"I don't think it will at all," Opli said. "Except now your self-destruction will be *oh so much* more fun to watch." The woman on the couch murmured, and Opli's attention shifted her, concern on his face. "Run along, Lyssa. And do me a favor, please be a better mother to your child than mine was to me." He glanced at her. "If that's even possible for you."

Heart pounding, Razia scurried out of the apartment and down the stairs, not stopping until she was three blocks away. The bug was kicking and thrashing, and she had to stop in an alley to calm both of them down.

"Sssh, sssh," Razia whispered, wishing she had someone to calm her own nerves the way she was calming the bug's. After a good few minutes, the movement quieted and Razia gently held herself until it ceased and the bug went back to sleep. "Good bug."

She leaned against the brick wall in the alley and let out a long, loud breath. She was furious with herself for making such a dumb decision—so what if she'd found Opli's mother? Now Opli had even more dirt on her, which he could exploit at any time. Should she even continue her investigation?

She looked at her mini-computer; Sage had sent her a few more messages.

Call me when you get a chance

She closed her eyes and called him, not even caring if he knew where she was.

When his face appeared on the screen, his bright smile dampened into an annoyed scowl. "I knew you were on '882."

"Congratulations, you know me too well," she said quietly.

"What's wrong?"

She snorted. "See?"

"What's wrong?" he repeated.

"I just…I need to get away for a while." *And I miss you.* "You were right, I shouldn't have come here."

"You're in luck, because I was just about to ask you to come see me," Sage said. "I want to show you something."

"What?"

"I'm done with my project."

CHAPTER TWELVE

Sage had given her his exact coordinates in a system six hours out from D-882. There were a few populated planets, but Lyssa's destination was a moon circling one of the gas planets.

She double-checked the numbers. She was headed straight for the middle of the ocean on the moon. But as she drew closer to the spot, she saw one speck of land. It grew into an island with a single structure on it and a very visible dock with a small ship already resting on a large concrete pad.

"Since when did he buy another ship?" Lyssa muttered. "And a house?"

She landed hers next to his and waddled back to the ladder. It was getting to the point where she could barely grasp the rungs without hitting her stomach. She'd just marked thirty weeks on the calendar; ten more to go.

Which meant she hadn't seen Sage—actually *seen* him in person—for nearly three months. Despite herself, she was a little excited. The bug danced in her stomach; this, for once, was a good kind of anxious.

She paused before walking out of her bridge and picked up the ultrasound photo that now seemed to have a permanent spot on her dashboard. She fingered the edges and stuffed it in her back pocket before rushing to the back of her ship and down the ladder.

Her heart fluttered madly as her ramp lowered.

There he stood, and she'd never seen anything so beautiful. His skin was golden, his hair even lighter than normal. He wore a simple white shirt and khaki shorts. But more than anything, the smile on his face sent her jitters into overdrive. He looked happy—genuinely, unbelievably *happy* to see her.

"Whoa! You're so big!" He stretched out his hands as if he wanted to grab her belly, but he kept his distance.

"What is this place?" Lyssa asked, coming to join him on the wooden dock that connected the house with the concrete pad.

"My new house," Sage said, turning to look behind him. "I bought this moon."

She nearly tripped over a slat of wood on the dock. "You *bought* this whole moon?"

"Yeah," he said, rubbing the back of his head.

"When did you do that?"

"I bought it from Dorst at the Academy after our planet excavation. He said he'd been unable to sell it because it wasn't suited for agriculture or anything like that. I was really lucky to find this island—took me a few days of circling."

She glanced over at his new ship. "And when did you buy the ship?"

"Around the same time, since I didn't want to leave the guys stranded on '882." He looked out at the ocean, blue and green and white churning in front of him. "I'm sorry I didn't come back sooner, but building a house was a lot harder than I thought. We just finished it a few days ago. Let me tell you, trying to get materials and equipment here was a pain—"

"So why didn't you just buy a plot of land on a residential planet?" Lyssa asked. "Sage, you should have asked me before you made such an idiotic decision. Supplying a whole planet is way more difficult than you'd think." She'd thought about doing it herself, one day in the distant future when she wanted to retire. But the sheer difficulty of basic things like food and supplies made her less inclined to do it.

"Oh, I got the lecture from Dorst, don't worry," he said with a small smile. "But it's worth it, to me, to be alone out here. This island is nearly ten miles around—that'd be quite a way to run, you know?"

She sighed longingly; she hadn't run in ages.

"Come inside."

She followed him up a wooden staircase and through a set of glass doors into an expansive living room. Rustic wood covered the floors, and white, gleaming cabinets sparkled from the kitchen. The living room furniture was soft leather couches and a coffee table that looked made of driftwood. She spotted a small room off to the left and strolled over, opening the double doors to reveal an office of sorts.

"This is nice," she said, running her hands along the computer setup.

"So predictable," Sage said, leaning against the doorframe. "Six bedrooms and you head straight for the office."

She sat down in the black leather chair, running her hands along the three monitors. "Definitely a level up from that pathetic system you had on your ship." She tapped on the keyboard and chewed on her lip—the pirate web was already logged in on the far left, the middle was dedicated to the Universal Bank search screen, and the right was an open notepad.

"I didn't take you for a bounty hunter, Sage," she drawled, turning to look at him.

"I wanted you to make yourself at home," he replied with a smirk.

She opened her mouth to retort and get up at the same time, but couldn't find the momentum. After she struggled valiantly for a few moments, Sage reached down and pulled her upright.

"You are *so…*" He trailed off, turning his head to the side.

"If you call me fat, I'll deck you."

"I was going to say, pregnant, but I think that's the same thing."

He showed her the rest of the downstairs, another bathroom and the laundry room, before they walked up to the second floor. Four bedrooms and one bathroom made up this floor, though the bedrooms were devoid of any bedroom furniture.

"Lizbeth's got them ordered, but they haven't arrived yet," he said.

"Lizbeth?" Lyssa stopped in the middle of the hall.

"Yeah, you think I could do all this?"

Lyssa frowned and folded her arms over her chest. "So she's been here?"

"Not yet," Sage said, adjusting a photo of the ocean on the hallway wall. "I wanted you to see it first."

Lyssa let out a quiet "oh" and followed him up the final set of stairs. There were only two doors on this level, and Sage led her into the closer one.

She sucked in a harsh breath. Gray walls accentuated a white, wooden dresser with a pad on top of it, a white rocking chair, and matching white crib—the same crib she'd picked out when she was on S-864 with Lizbeth.

"That crafty bitch," Lyssa said, running her hands along the painted wood.

She glanced around the small space, imagining it occupied by a little dark haired child. There were children's books in a basket in the corner, and, to her amusement, the tiny pair of black boots from the maternity store, hanging against the wall like decoration. Her eyes lingered on them, and her mind drifted to the ultrasound photo of the bug, sitting in her back pocket.

"This is really cool," she whispered, running her hand along the edge of the crib. "Lizbeth did a good job."

"One last room to see," Sage said from the doorway.

She didn't quite want to leave the small stuffed bears and tiny blankets, but she followed Sage across the hallway into the last room.

"Whoa." Floor-to-ceiling windows welcomed her into the master bedroom, providing a panoramic view of the ocean. A wrap-around balcony lay beyond a pair of open glass doors, where white sheer curtains fluttered in the breeze. A bed sat in the center of the room, with two nightstands. She strolled to the far side of the room, where an open door led her into a hall flanked by two large closets—one filled with Sage's clothes, absent the usual pile of dirty laundry on the floor. She wondered where he was hiding his porn. The hall ended in a large bathroom with two sinks, separate shower and tub, and a small water closet.

"This is way too nice for you, Sage," she called, running her hands along the white porcelain of the double sink. "It must've have cost you a fortune."

"I had a lot of money saved up," he said with a shrug. "I mean, I didn't expect to blow it so soon, but..." His gaze fell to her stomach. "It's worth it."

She followed him back out into the master bedroom and ventured onto the porch, breathing in the crisp air of the sea. She leaned against the railing and stretched her back, which was starting to ache from standing for so long.

"How's it all going?" Sage asked, coming to stand next to her. "The pregnancy?"

"Well, my hips hurt, I have massive heartburn when I eat, and I don't even know how I'm going to fit anything else in there," she said, straightening up. "I mean, look at it."

"Can I feel it?" Sage asked. She nodded, and he gently pressed his hands to the protrusion. "It's a lot harder than I thought."

"That's what she said," Lyssa said, catching Sage's eye.

He nodded. "I walked right into that one."

She stared at his hands on her stomach, and he quickly removed them, turning to look out at the vista.

"So have you been seeing a doctor? Any...anything you want to share?" Sage asked.

She thought about the photo in her back pocket and shook her head. She wasn't quite ready to show proof that this thing—the bug— was real to Sage. Something about that final step made her nervous.

"You never told me what got you so spooked on '882," Sage said after a few minutes. "Everything okay?"

"I ran into Opli," Lyssa said, not going into details. "Like this."

"I see." Sage nodded. "Are you afraid he's going to spill it?"

"That's the thing. He's known that my name is Lyssa Peate for months and he hasn't done anything. And when I went digging into his past, I found someone on D-882 I thought was his mother. And that's...that's when he found me."

"Lyssa..." Sage groaned.

"I didn't get into any fights!" Lyssa said quickly. "I kept to the shadows and just…" She swallowed as the concern eased from his face. "But I wanted to find out for myself why he's so intent on destroying piracy. But besides the fact that he was born on D-882 and his mother is a drunk, I can't quite figure out the link."

Sage stared out over the ocean, deep in thought. "Have you tried going back and looking at the pirates he's taken down?"

She opened and closed her mouth. "No, I haven't."

"Want to go use that fancy new desk I put in for you?"

She was halfway to it when she stopped and turned around. "What do you mean, put in for me?"

"N-nothing," he said with a small blush.

***

The light danced over her face and she woke slowly, breathing in the salty air of the beach. She'd left the doors open, as she had the past three nights, because there was nothing better than sitting up and watching the blue waves crash against the white sand first thing in the morning.

She heard Sage banging around downstairs and smiled to herself. He'd surprised her with his cooking—her memory of his skills on Tauron ship was a lot of burnt and overcooked meat. Whatever he'd been doing in the three months since she'd seen him, she and her stomach appreciated it greatly.

She stretched and slipped on a jacket, padding down the stairs.

"Morning," he said with a grin.

"Morning," she replied, yawning.

"Do you want to eat before you get back to work?"

She couldn't help the grimace that crossed her face. She had been avoiding working on her Opli project, choosing instead to do some research on some pirates to send to Ganon.

"What?" Sage said, sitting across from her on the dining room table.

"I'm stuck," she said, pressing her cheek into her hand.

"You must be, if you're admitting it," he said, sipping his coffee. "Want me to help? What do you have so far?"

"Thirty pirates have bowed out for one reason or another since the break-in. I know, specifically, that Stenson, Hardrict, Fried, Bullock, and Needler were targeted by Opli, but I don't know of any of the others."

She listed the specific pirates and Sage wrote them on a piece of paper, placing stars next to each of the ones that Lyssa mentioned.

"I think we can safely knock out the guys who haven't been around for at least ten years," Sage said, drawing a line through three pirates.

"Why would we do that?"

"Because if Opli has a vendetta, I assume it was something that happened before he joined the Academy."

She shook her head, blushing at how obvious it was. "Sorry, I've got…I'm not as smart as I used to be apparently." She gestured to her stomach. "The bug, you know…"

Sage glanced up at her. "I'm not touching that one. But why don't we start with breaking these guys out into their webs?"

After a few minutes, they'd sorted the thirty into lists, finding that Insurgent had the most. Lyssa stared at the list and willed it to give up answers to her, but was coming up empty. She focused on the five pirates who had stars next to their names. Stenson and Bullock worked for Dissident, Hardrict for Contestant, Fried and Needler for Insurgent. None of them were particularly beloved by their runners, or no more than any other top pirate.

"Didn't…didn't Stenson work for Insurgent at one point?" Sage said. He pulled out his mini-computer and tapped out a message.

"Who are you talking to?"

"Harms." A pause. "Yeah, Harms said Stenson started out with Insurgent, but switched about seven years ago." He tapped out more and waited. "And Hardrict's only been his own pirate for a few years, but Harms can't remember for whom."

"Maybe if I go back to before he joined the web, I can search through some of his older transactions and work backwards," Lyssa thought aloud. "If all three of them worked for Insurgent, maybe Opli's beef is with him?"

"Sound reasoning," Sage said, leaning over her chair. "Why don't you get to work on that? All of this thinking's made me hungry."

Lyssa went to the office and sat down, leaning back into the comfortable leather chair and running her hands over the set-up. Besides the fact that Lyssa couldn't sit down for more than a few minutes before her hips started aching, the desk set up in the small office was perfection. Sage had even commissioned an extra few communication satellites to boost the connection signal so the searches to the pirate web and Universal Bank were lightning fast.

It was her brain that was slow. Even with three screens, she couldn't keep track of what she was thinking. Sage brought her breakfast and helped her a little bit, and then disappeared. She stared at the screen for what felt like a moment, and Sage was asking her if she wanted lunch.

"Lunch?" she asked. "Didn't we just have breakfast?"

"A few hours ago?" Sage smiled. "I'll take that as a no."

Lyssa leaned forward and searched on one pirate, but realized she'd been staring at the same name for over an hour. She sat back and looked out into the living room. Sage was nowhere to be found. She pushed herself up (now having figured out the trick) and left the office and the research.

She found Sage in one of the guest bedrooms, painting a wall. He heard her approach and smiled over his shoulder.

"So what did you find on Opli?"

"Who?"

Sage laughed. "You were right, pregnancy's done a number on your brain. Opli, the guy you're supposed to be searching for? The current threat to piracy?"

"I have more important things to worry about," she said, shocked by her honest admission. "What are you doing in here?"

"Trying to get all this painted."

"Where'd you learn how to paint?" Lyssa asked, standing in the hall so the smell wouldn't bother her.

"It's not that hard," Sage said, rolling the paint onto the wall.

"You're certainly doing a lot for this thing." Her hands were back on her stomach, their default position now, it seemed. "I mean, this is a huge house for just…you and the bug."

"I figured the crew would come visit. Harms, Vel, probably. Lizbeth," Sage said, not looking at her. "Want enough rooms for all of them."

"Does the crew know about this place? About what you've been up to?"

"Not yet," Sage said, turning pink. "But as soon as the baby arrives, I was going to tell them."

"Ganon said that you were going to give him your ship and crew…is that true?"

Sage's pink cheeks grew red and he busied himself with refilling the paint tray.

So he was planning on giving everything up—everything—for the bug. His crew, his career, his life on D-882 all for this little thing that wasn't even born yet. He'd made provisions for everyone to come to him instead of the other way around.

When the bug came, she really *would* have to say her goodbyes. Sage's life was about to be completely different and…she looked around…was there room for her in it? Even if there was, did she *want* to be in it? Could she bring herself to come here and sit on his couch and watch her own child—yes, *child*, she told herself—and pretend to feel nothing?

And if she chose the alternative…

"You okay?" Sage said. "Do you need to sit down? You look faint."

"I…need to take a walk and clear my head," she said quietly, taking a step back.

"Want me to go with you?"

"N-no, I'll be fine."

***

Rushing down the stairs two-by-two, she landed in cold, white sand. She kicked off her shoes as best she could and continued walking. She focused on the sand in front of her and the sea beside her until she could no longer see the house.

Panting from the exertion, she stood on the shoreline, letting the cool waves lap over her feet. The bug was thrashing wildly again, and Lyssa began to worry that her own nervousness was seeping into it.

"Please don't make this thing be like me," she whispered.

She pulled out the ultrasound photo from her back pocket and stared at it. The face on the ultrasound had burrowed far into her heart. She knew it better than her own now. The contour of the cheeks, the shape of the nose. The little fingers that she'd counted nearly every day to make sure all were accounted for.

Could she really stay?

"I'm sorry," she whispered. "But I can't..."

She wasn't completely stupid or emotionally stunted, no matter what Lizbeth might think. This house was meant for her, this island on this moon was chosen for her. That office had been built for her. Every single thing Sage had done over the past few months had been in pursuit of building a new life for the three of them.

She put her hand over her mouth. *Three of them.*

Sage always seemed to know just before she would change her mind about staying. But this was different than staying for another round of sex. This was staying *forever.*

Another kick from the bug. "Hey, I am not your punching bag!"

On the horizon, she saw both the gaseous planet and the sun moving lower in the sky. It was quite beautiful, and she could see herself being very happy there.

But how long would it last before the Great Creator pulled the rug out from under her?

And could she survive a fall from such a great height?

She returned to the house, but couldn't bring herself to face Sage. Lucky for her, the lower deck offered a step-down bench surrounding what she guessed was an outdoor fire. She climbed into the area and stuck one of the pillows behind her back, opting for sore hips instead of sore feet. The sky grew darker as night fell, and soon she could only hear the waves crashing on the shore.

Without warning, the structure in the middle of the benches burst into flames, and she screamed.

"Relax." Sage's amused voice was behind her. "It's just a fire pit. It's remote controlled."

He climbed down onto the benches next to her and handed her a cool glass of water, placing his own on the edge of the bench.

"Didn't mean to scare you," he said, staring at the fire. "I like to come out here at night."

She didn't disagree that the crackling fire could've put her at ease, but with him so close, she was anything but relaxed. Not with the thoughts churning in her head, and how the bug was moving within her.

His hand rested near hers and she wondered if he would take it. She could let herself believe for a minute that this house and this man and everything was hers. She missed the nights when she'd curl up next to him and fall asleep, when they'd banter back and forth.

With shaking hands, she pulled the ultrasound out of her back pocket.

"Is that..."

"Yeah," she said quietly. She handed it to him and waited.

"That's...that's..." He laughed, although his voice was suddenly thick. "Leveman's, she looks just like you."

"I don't know if it's a girl or a boy," she whispered, forcing herself to stare at the fire. "I didn't ask..."

She dared to glance over at Sage, holding her breath and her tongue. He stared at the photo with such unabashed emotion that she wondered if he needed privacy to process it.

"This is my kid. My baby."

She gripped the edges of the cushion, needing to get away before she said or did something that she'd regret. But she stayed where she was, unable to stop watching Sage absorb every detail of the photo the way she had over the past few weeks.

Finally, he turned to her. "Thank you for this. For taking care of her...or him." He looked at the photo again and nodded. "Yeah, I think she's a girl."

"That doesn't change your mind, does it?" she asked.

"Why would it?"

Why would it indeed? Sage was planning to give up his pirating ways, it wouldn't matter what the gender was. She had heard an earful growing up about being a girl in a pirate's world. Then again, Sage had always been Lyssa's biggest champion, and she was sure he'd be the same for... She sat up and refused to finish that train of thought.

"Can I keep this?" he asked.

"N..." He should keep it, she realized. After all, it was good for her to start separating her emotions from the bug. She needed to become unattached so when the day came to hand her over, she could.

The thought made her irrationally angry.

"Take it. I don't want it," she snapped. "I don't want this, and I don't want…I don't want this thing to even know I exist."

"Do you really mean that?"

"Yes."

"But that means once the baby is here, you won't ever see me again."

"That's fine, too," she said, even though it wasn't.

"Whatever you want," Sage said, looking down at the photo again. She could tell he was trying not to show how much she'd hurt him. And at the same time, the fact that he *wasn't* angry was infuriating. He was back to his old ways of appeasing her instead of fighting her, and it just made her angrier.

"Let's just… This is just a business arrangement," she continued stiffly. "I don't want you to think that it's—"

"No, I get it," Sage said. His brow furrowed. "Your mini's lighting up."

She picked the infernal device from beside her. "Why does Dorst call me at the most annoying times?" She answered it. "What?"

"Just wanted to remind you that your presentation on Leveman's Vortex is in two days," he said. "So you might want to consider getting here to do it." The call went dark.

"I am getting sick and tired of these phone calls ordering me around," Lyssa grumbled, sitting back.

"Do you want me to go with you?" Sage asked, trying to sound normal.

"No. You haven't been here so far, so why would I need you now?" With that, she pushed herself to stand and waddled towards her ship.

Unfortunately, when she tried to get up her ladder, she found she couldn't manage to find the right grip to climb. And Sage, damn him, already seemed to know that.

"It's going to be hard to fly your ship if you can't get up to the bridge, you know."

"I…" She grunted and pulled herself up the first rung. "I can do this."

"Lyssa, stop being so damned stubborn. Let me fly you back to the Academy."

"Why? You haven't wanted to be around at all. You've just been building this stupid house for the stupid kid and never called and—"

"I called you every single day," Sage said, a little angry. "Lyssa, you wanted space, so I gave it to you. Now you're telling me you didn't want space? You need to make up your damned mind and tell me what you want from me!"

She clenched her jaw and didn't answer. He slid his hands over her shoulders and pulled her away from the ladder. She leaned against him, and let him rest his hands on the swell of her stomach.

"Let me take you to the Academy," he whispered in her ear.

She was dangerously close to slipping off that ledge. Every instinct she'd built over the last twenty-three years told her to turn and tell him to leave, to push him away.

Instead, she whispered, "Okay."

CHAPTER THIRTEEN

Lyssa stood in front of the mirror and adjusted the white shirt that wasn't helping much. She had hoped when she put on her lab coat, there would be an optical illusion that would magically hide her bump. But it not only didn't fit around her, it made her stomach pop more.

"I don't think there's any way around it," Sage said, joining her in the bedroom. He was already dressed in his own DSE attire, sporting those silver frames and a sharp-button down shirt. "You're going to have to tell them."

"I don't have to tell them anything if I don't see them," Lyssa grunted, pulling on her glasses.

"How are you going to manage that and give a presentation?"

"I'll…figure it out," she said. "Did you get it?"

Sage pulled the black journal from his back pocket and handed it to her. "What is it?"

"It's…nothing," she said. "Just something I need." She hoped there was enough in there to last the full hour. Most of Sostas' journals were still in his laboratory beneath the Manor.

She followed Sage out of her bedroom to the back of her ship. He lowered her ramp and poked his head out, before turning back to her and giving the thumbs up. "All clear."

"Good, so if we see anyone—"

"Run away."

She nodded and stepped out into the Academy. Unlike D-882, she really hadn't missed this place all that much. Not the dock workers who paid her no mind, nor the sterile smell that permeated even the docking stations. She'd told Sage she *might* be able to fit in a quick lunch with Vel, but it all depended on whether Dorst was also hanging around.

They arrived at her laboratory without incident, though she was quick to slip inside since Dorst's lab was located down the hall. She plopped down at her computer and told Sage to keep watch. She hooked her mini-computer into the old machine on the desk and took a deep breath, struggling to find the train of though that would lead her to Leveman's Vortex, and what she could tell them.

"What is it?" Sage asked.

"I just never thought I'd ever have to talk about this stupid thing," she said, staring at the blank presentation in front of her. "That I could avoid and delay forever. Or that someone would figure out I'm a pirate before then."

"So you think they'd fire you if they found out about Razia?"

She shrugged. "I guess I always assumed they would. They're pretty strict about a lot of things. I don't think they'd let me bounty hunt and do planet excavations."

"Probably not." He looked out the doors again, then back at her. "So what is this presentation supposed to be about?"

"Leveman's Vortex."

"Sorry!" he said, hands raised in surrender. "I won't ask again."

"No, I mean, it's actually about Leveman's Vortex," Lyssa said with a small smile. "My f...Sostas...that was his thing. He studied it." She paused and looked at him. "Did I ever tell you anything about him?"

"I gather you aren't a fan."

She placed her hand on her stomach and flipped open the journal. "He wasn't a great person, let's just leave it at that. But I've been using his research as an excuse to bounty hunt, you know? It's easy to be gone for weeks at a time when everyone thinks you're lobbing satellites into a giant black hole."

Sage snorted. "Did you ever?"

"Did I ever what?"

"Continue his research?"

She stared at the screen, reliving memories of her trip with Pymus and Vel. That had been a truly life-changing experience for her, it had started her down the path of accepting the two halves of herself. There were times when she'd considered the entire episode to be a trick of the magnetic fields, or that she'd dreamed it. But afterward, she'd felt different, and that was real enough for her.

"I didn't," she said. "Because he was an ass."

***

Lyssa finished her presentation with only an hour to spare—just enough time for her and Sage to take the freight elevators and backstairs down to the auditorium wing of the station. Their quick movements and furtive glances reminded Lyssa of running from the U-POL when they were the most wanted criminals, right down to the way his fingers intertwined with hers as they moved.

Lyssa let them into the side wing of the stage, cramped already with extra podiums and presentation materials lining the walls. A dull roar of chatter echoed in from the auditorium. Lyssa crept over to the edge of the curtains lining the stage and looked out.

"Wow." From the sounds of the audience, it was packed with scientists. She hadn't realized so many people were interested in Leveman's Vortex.

"I wouldn't go out there," Sage said, leaning over her shoulder. "I hate public speaking."

"Since when have you ever spoken in public?"

"Exactly."

She stifled a small smile and turned back to the space. "So how am I going to get from here to there without showing off this thing?"

She and Sage scoured the backstage area for something that would hide herself. She picked up a piece of paper and held it sideways.

"Nah, too obvious," Sage said, glancing up from behind one of the podiums. He stood with a clipboard in his hand. "Try this." She held it sideways against her body and looked to him for approval. He gave her the thumbs up and she blew air out between her lips as she noticed the time.

"Guess I should get it over with, huh?"

"You'll do great," Sage said. "After all, compared to nearly having your brains blown out by your brother, talking in front of all those people should be easy, right?"

She snorted. "You don't know the half of it." She adjusted the clipboard against her body and straightened her shoulders. "Here goes nothing."

She walked out onto the stage, making sure that the clipboard was angled in front of her, but lazily enough so that no one would notice. She gauged the reaction of the crowd; from what she could see; no one was paying attention to her anyway. She stood in front of the podium and smirked. Perhaps this wouldn't be so bad after all.

"Leveman's Vortex," she began, showing a swirling galaxy behind her, "is a scientific phenomenon that the Academy has yet to explain. My f-father," she tried not to grimace at the word, "spent his career researching several theories about the phenomenon through repeated, measurable data collection."

She flipped to the first slide, showing a mockup of one of the satellites he'd built. She'd found the drawing in his notebook—one of several she had peppered into the presentation to make it look like she'd done the work. "Over the years, his primary focus was testing a hypothesis that the Vortex could, theoretically, allow a spaceship or other foreign body to fly directly into the center—"

A chorus of laughter echoed through the room, and she cleared her throat.

"Fly directly into the center. Obviously," she glared at the audience, "this would have huge ramifications for the religious community. However, after years of research and testing, we...I have found, conclusively, that it is impossible."

Another rumble of laughter. Lyssa quickly flipped through the rest of her slides, ignoring all of the fake information about angles and test criteria and other information she'd pulled out of her ass, and ended on the last slide.

"And that concludes my presentation. Any questions?"

"Dr. Peate, do you mean to tell us that your father is still alive?"

"No," she snapped. "Next question."

"Dr. Peate, are you trying to see the face of the Great Creator? Have you no respect for the scientific process?"

An arch flashed in her vision and she shuffled her papers. "My father was very interested in the phenomenon from a scientific perspective, that's all."

"But you've continued his work. Are you so delusional as to believe you can reach the Great Creator without due soul reflection?"

Again, the arch flashed in her mind and her hand ached to meet her stomach, where the bug was shifting. "I think that whatever you choose to believe is fine. I was simply finishing what he started."

"I think it's highly unprofessional to discuss religious matters in the context of science."

"But our science is founded on the principles of finding the truth, and the Great Creator is the truth," came a high-pitched voice from the back.

Lyssa knew that this very quickly would devolve, and she gathered her things. "Any further questions, please direct them to my supervisor, Dorst Peate." She unplugged her mini-computer and grasped the clipboard at her side as she scurried out of the lights into the waiting form of Sage and...Vel, she realized with a smile.

"Hey, you!" Vel said, pulling her into a hug. "That was some presentation."

"If I'd known that's all it took to get these bozos off my back, I'd have done this years ago," Lyssa said with a snort. She peered out into the auditorium where the loud arguing continued in the audience. "I should have known better than to mix science and religion. Recipe for disaster. What was Sostas thinking?"

"Well, I have to say, I'm pretty impressed," Sage interjected. "That's a side I've never seen of you. Lyssa the scientist."

"Might be the last time, too," Lyssa said.

"Are you thinking of calling it quits?" Vel asked.

"Maybe." She shrugged. "I'm hungry. Let's eat before Dorst finds out I didn't do a good job."

"Oh, I'm sure he's busy with Mother," Vel said lightly. "She's ordered the whole family to the Academy's finest dining, but I was able to sneak away for a bit to see your presentation."

Lyssa stiffened and her eyes widened. "She's *here*? What is she doing *here*?"

"Didn't Dorst tell you? I'm graduating today," Vel said.

She opened her mouth to snap then blinked. "Wait...you're graduating *today*? Why didn't you tell me? Did you tell me?" Her face darkened. "Damn it, Dorst! He planned all this, didn't he?"

"It's not really that big of a deal," Vel said with a laugh. "Me and five thousand of my closest friends walking across a stage for ten seconds. I really didn't think you'd be interested."

"If it's important to you, I'm interested," Lyssa said, and glared at the surprise on Vel's face. "Hey, I'm not *that* terrible of a person!"

"No, but..." His gaze fell to her stomach. "I'd have thought that you want to keep that under wraps."

"I came to this presentation, didn't I?" Lyssa barked. She paused and added, "I did a terrible job, but at least I showed up this time!"

Sage and Vel shared a glance and a shake of their heads.

"That you did, Lyss," Vel said.

***

Although Lyssa would have rather *not* put herself anywhere in proximity to her mother, she couldn't miss Vel's graduation. So it was with no small amount of trepidation (punctuated by the frantic movements of the bug), that Lyssa and Sage traversed the long hallway of auditoriums to the largest in the Academy.

"So if we see her, I'm leaving. Got it?" Lyssa said.

"Understood. Do you want me to throw my body in front of you to shield you?"

"This isn't funny. That woman is a monster."

"I know, I know," he said, placing his hands on her shoulders as he faced her. "But I would seriously throw my body in front of her bullets for you." The laughter in his eyes told a different story. "But like Vel said, there are going to be thousands of people here today. So take a deep breath, wipe that scowl off your face, and smile."

Since they were the last to secure tickets to the event, they had to climb a few flights of stairs. When they reached the top, Sage took Lyssa's hand before she could even process how far down the stage was. The podium and chairs were minuscule, and if not for the giant screen, Lyssa might've called it a loss even to be there.

Sage tugged at their joined fingers and led her to their seats. He helped her sit in the folding chair and then settled in himself, kicking his feet on top of the seat in front of them.

"Wake me up when it's Vel's turn," Sage said with a yawn.

She elbowed him to remove his feet when two finely dressed parents walked down the aisle and sat down in the chairs where his feet rested. He grumbled and put them back on the ground.

The auditorium filled with music—Lyssa guessed it might have been the official song of the Academy, but she'd never been interested enough to know—and the pomp and circumstance began. Once the graduates and faculty were seated in their appropriate places, the dean of the Academy stood and began his speech. He droned on and on about the importance of planetary sciences for the good of the UBU, and how Deep Space Explorers and their close cousin, Close Space Explorers, had cured diseases, solved an overpopulation problem, and contributed to the overall economy of the union.

"Not to mention driven countless species to extinction," Lyssa said to Sage, but he was napping quietly next to her. She moved to wake him, but the bug decided to start kicking her.

"Fine," she muttered, rubbing the spot where she could feel the legs moving around. "You're awake, at least, huh?"

The bug shifted, and Lyssa couldn't help but smile. She poked the bug, and the bug kicked back. They played this game through the first queuing of students to receive their diplomas. Sage awoke just as the "O" students lined up, yawning loudly and stretching. Lyssa placed her hand over her stomach to hide the bug's movements from him.

"Is it over yet?" Sage asked.

"Not yet," she said, squirming as the bug began to protest the lack of play. "Nearly to Vel."

An eternity later, Vellexore Peate's name was called, and Lyssa was surprised to hear a loud roar of cheers for him. His face reddened on the giant screen in front of them as he awkwardly waved to the crowd.

"Our little guy's all grown up," Sage said. "Reminds me of Sobal."

Lyssa didn't like the use of "our," but let it slide. "I wonder what he's going to do now that he's graduated. He was thinking about joining me."

"No offense, Lyss, but I told him not to," Sage said with a huge yawn.

She most assuredly took offense. "And why not?"

"Because Ganon would take better care of him. Give him more opportunities, let him fail a little bit, give him some serious shit," Sage said. "And Ganon's looking for a new bounty hunter anyway."

"But I don't want him to work for Ganon, I want him to work for *me*." She crossed her arms over her chest. "And why is he talking to everyone else about his career choices?"

She'd thought she and Vel had a good relationship, but finding out that he was seeking guidance from everyone *but* her was disheartening.

"Have you ever thought of calling him instead?" Sage asked. "Relationships are two-way streets. You aren't the center of everyone's universe, you know. You should try reaching out."

Lyssa muddled on his words, but Vel sent them a message saying he was out in the massive hallway next to the auditorium. Sage helped Lyssa stand, and they made their way out of the dizzying arena and waded through the throngs of cap-adorned graduates. Sage held onto Lyssa's hand so they wouldn't get separated, but also, she supposed, for moral support.

"There he is!" Sage said, pointing to a tall man towering over the rest.

Vel waved, a huge grin on his face.

"Congratulations, man." Sage finally released Lyssa's hand so he could shake Vel's.

Vel then turned to Lyssa and hugged her as best he could.

"I'm really proud of you," she said to him. He stepped back and knitted his brows together, his tassel falling into his face. She balanced on her tippy-toes and realigned it to the right side. "Seriously," she said, gripping his arms, no longer long and spindly. "I'm proud of you."

"Thanks Lyss," he said, pulling her in for another hug. "That means a lot. And I'm really glad you came."

Behind them, someone sucked in their breath in shocked surprise. She knew who it was without turning around, or perhaps because she smelled the familiar expensive perfume mixed with a pound of hairspray.

"M-mother!" Vel exclaimed, looking over Lyssa's shoulder.

Dread filled Lyssa and she wished more than anything that she didn't have to turn around. She was fairly sure her shape was unmistakable, especially when she heard the sharp, "Well, well, well, *this* is a surprise."

Lyssa refused to turn. "Congratulations, Vel. We gotta run. Bye—"

"Don't," Vel said. "Just…get it over with."

She pleaded with him silently to let her just disappear, but he spun her around to face the motley crew. Eleonora was resplendent in her finest green dress that still hadn't been tailored to hide her bulging waist. Her dyed-blonde hair was coifed and curled, and her makeup settled into the creases on her face. But the look of pure and utter disdain was as clear as in her younger days. Behind her stood Sera, dressed much less finely in a simple black dress and pearl earrings, and Dorst, who wore his normal DSE attire and whose eyes were nearly falling out of his head.

"Hullo, Mother," Lyssa mumbled.

Eleonora turned to Dorst with a sneer. "Dorst, *when* were you going to let me know your sister was with child?"

"I…didn't know…" he stammered. "Lyssa, why didn't you tell me?"

"Because it's *none* of your business," she snapped.

"Actually it is, because I could get in real trouble for letting you excavate without having a doctor's—"

"She didn't do any excavations, don't worry," Sage said, coming to stand next to her and Vel. In one fluid motion, Vel released her and Sage pulled her closer to him with an arm around her shoulder. "Lyssa, I told you that you needed to tell them."

Shocked and confused, Lyssa could do nothing but stutter aimlessly.

"Al, pleasure to see you again," Dorst said, but sounded a little less pleased than usual. "I can't believe you kept this from me. Lyssa, I am your supervisor—"

"And I am your mother." Eleonora's eyes flashed as she cut Dorst off with a wave of her hand. Lyssa tensed, wondering if Eleonora's rage would overpower her sense of decorum. She would waste no time eviscerating Lyssa in private, but it usually took more brandy to get her to lose face in public. "And you, getting pregnant before marriage. How dare you embarrass me?"

Lyssa's heart raced as Eleonora's evil smile blossomed further. Even though Lyssa didn't care about premarital sex, somehow, standing in front of her mother, she was self-conscious about her bump and her lack of ring and—

"Lyssa, did you forget your ring again?" Sage's voice rang out like a bell, shattering both Eleonora and Lyssa's stares. "Tell me you didn't lose it?"

"I..."

"And are you going to introduce me to your mother or what? You've told me so much about her." Without waiting for Lyssa's response, Sage strode forward and offered his hand to Eleonora, who scoffed at it. Sera, however, stepped forward and gently took Sage's hand.

"Sera," she said with a surprisingly genuine smile.

"Alejandro." He dropped her hand and looked back at Lyssa. "I married this one."

"You must be a saint," Sera replied.

Sage simply grinned.

"At least you've taken that much from Temple," Eleonora drawled. "Have you had a blessing for the child?"

"A what?" Lyssa said, exchanging a look with Sage.

"A blessing," Sera said, her tone a little less genial now. "A chance for the family to be introduced to your child and to ask the Great Creator to guide the child in the right direction."

Lyssa snorted. "No."

Sera's eyes flashed. "And why not?"

"Because that's stupid. The Great Creator doesn't give a rat's ass whether the family asks for His blessing or not."

"And you're an expert?"

Lyssa pursed her lips and glared at Sera.

"And so you would rather risk eternal damnation for your child than come spend an hour at the Manor to have a simple ceremony?" Sera said.

"Basically."

"Lyss." She didn't like the tone of Sage's voice. "Maybe we should consider it."

"Since when are you religious?" Lyssa blanched.

He shrugged. "I'd like to take every precaution necessary."

"Hey, why don't you guys come this weekend," Vel interjected. "Mother is throwing me a graduation party, why don't we celebrate your baby as well?"

If looks could kill, Vel would have been obliterated.

"I think that's a great idea," Sage said, wrapping his arm around Lyssa's shoulder as if it belonged there.

"Excellent!" Sera grinned brightly, almost unrecognizable from her normal dour expression. "I shall call back and make preparations for the ceremony."

As Sera turned away to make a call on her mini-computer, Lyssa glanced to her mother, who looked about as pleased with the plan as Lyssa did.

Instead of saying anything, though, she looked at Dorst, who stood a little away from the group. "Dorst, you look peaky. Have you been eating? Kasan, I haven't seen you home in two months. Is there something you wish to say to me, young man?" And off she went, remarking on every Peate child she laid eyes on (and some who weren't even hers) until her acerbic voice was drowned out by the general volume of conversation.

"I see where you get your charming personality from," Sage remarked with a sly smile.

"Remove your hand or I will cut it off."

"See?" But he removed his arm nonetheless.

"What in *Leveman's Vortex* did you just agree to?" she growled. "Do you even know what happened the last time I went there?"

"It's going to be different this time," Vel said. "And Sera's right, you do need to have a blessing."

"Of all people," she said, throwing a piercing look to Vel, "*you* should know how completely pointless a stupid ceremony is."

"Actually, of all people, I know how important it is," Vel replied. "I saw what happened when you don't have a good soul."

"I'm lost," Sage said, looking between the two of them.

"And what is a stupid ceremony going to prove?" Lyssa barked.

"It's a promise that you and Sage are committed to raising your child with good morals and in the teachings of Temple," Vel said.

"I don't need Temple to know how to be a good person, need I remind you—"

"Lyssa, *I* am asking you to do this," Sage said, cutting the two of them off. "I think I'm going to need all the help I can get to keep this kid on the right path. I mean, I'm a pirate." He shrugged. "Not exactly the most moral of professions."

"Tauron was a good person," Lyssa reminded him. "You don't need some stuffy priest in his morally superior ways to tell you what you already know."

"Please?" Sage said, taking her hands. "This one last thing."

"You have asked *a lot* of me so far—"

"And you know you have my undying appreciation," Sage said.

She stared at him for a moment, weighing her options. The idea of going back to the Manor was suffocating. But at the same time, the smallest part of her that wondered if her own bad soul would leech into the bug's. She'd already been feeding the bug all her nervous energy, what if she had done more damage than that? If there was a chance that Lyssa's own awfulness could ruin the kid…

"Fine." She sighed loudly. "I'll go."

CHAPTER FOURTEEN

Somewhere between the Academy and her mother's home planet of B-39837, Lyssa had come to her senses and realized what a horrible, terrible, not good idea it was to revisit such an awful place. She'd begged and argued with Sage from the bottom of her ship, even tried to climb up the ladder before Sage had barked at her to give it a rest. She'd plopped into her bed and refused to come out, even as Sage docked her ship and lowered her ramp.

"You have to leave some time," Sage said, leaning against the doorframe to her bedroom.

"Nope. I'll just stay here until you're done," she said from her spot on her bed.

"Aren't you the guest of honor for this thing?"

"I can't go in there."

"Two days, Lyss. One night. That's all," he said, coming to sit on the bed. "You can handle two days, can't you?"

As if to butter her up, he pulled one of her socked feet to him and rubbed it, digging his fingers into her swollen arches. She closed her eyes and frowned, though a little moan of pleasure escaped her lips.

"Besides, I have something for you," he said, standing and walking to his duffle bag. He dug around for a minute and then pulled out a small black box. He tossed it to her and then waited on the other side of the room.

She picked up the velvet box, and quirked her eyebrow. "What in Leveman's Vortex is this?" She gently opened the box and her eyes widened; a silver ring sat encased in more black velvet. The diamond was clean, but minuscule. Had Sage run out of money? "Are you serious? You went out and got a ring?"

"No, actually, I had it." He looked at the ground and stuffed his hands into his pocket. "It was my mom's."

Her sarcasm evaporated and she let out a small, "oh." His mother, Isabel Teon. She'd remembered the name and often wondered if she should look the woman up. Lyssa didn't even know if she or Sage's father were still alive.

"Don't lose it," he said with a grin.

"I won't," she said, slipping it onto her left ring finger. It was snug, but it fit well enough. She considered why he had his mother's ring on him—especially as the trip to the Manor was unexpected—but found herself not really wanting to know the answer to that question.

"Are you ready?"

"Not in the least bit," she said, scooting off the bed as gracefully as she could. He took her hand, and she felt the presence of the ring on it. "But I don't have much of a choice, do I?"

The last time she had been in the Manor, with Vel, it had been nothing but cheap shots, scowling faces, and, of course, the announcement that Eleonora wished Lyssa had never been born. But now, with Sage, she was experiencing it through his eyes. He pointed out every detail and carving of the pillars in the elaborate docking station, commenting on how often they must have to perform maintenance to keep it sparkling. They traversed the long covered hallway that opened into the main foyer of the giant house.

"And you said my house was big!" Sage said, craning his head to count the floors that rose around them. "How many rooms are in this place?"

"Too many to keep track of," Lyssa said. The entranceway to the large dining hall stood open in front of them, the long dining table already filling up with children.

"Wow." He whistled. "Look at all these people…" He looked to Lyssa. "All these are related to you?"

"Yup."

He grinned.

"What?"

"I feel like I'm going into the viper pit. One of you is bad enough. Look at all these Lyssas."

"They aren't all like me," she said. "Vel isn't like me. Dorst isn't like me." She paused. "I hope."

Sage didn't answer, but pointed to the long row of chairs that lined either side of the table. "Where do we sit?"

She spotted Heelin, her immediate older brother, at his chair and pulled Sage toward the middle of the table. "Oi, Heelin."

He scanned her momentarily and snorted. "What do you want?"

"Do you know if they made a place for us or not?" Lyssa said. "Or else, I'll just take Jukin's seat again."

"There will be no need for that." Sera had appeared across the table, looking much more comfortable in a simple green dress than she had at the Academy. She gestured to the two seats next to Heelin. "You and Alejandro will be here. Right where you belong."

Lyssa rolled her eyes, but Sage offered his thanks as they took their seats. Lyssa squirmed in the hard chair, trying to find a more comfortable spot and Sage reached over to take her hand.

"It's fine. We're fine," he said quietly.

"I'm not… Put your head down."

"What?"

"Head down!"

Sage ducked, and Lyssa cast a weary glance to the side of the room where a bearded man had stumbled in. His hair had grown out and hung limply around his face, as if he hadn't showered in a few days. But more than anything, she recognized the way he slouched and gazed out into the distance as if he had nothing left to live for. Jukin had truly fallen far from grace.

"Holy…" Sage hissed. "*You didn't tell me he was here.*"

"You're the one who wanted to come!" she barked back.

"He can't...he can't do anything," Sage said, exchanging a look with her. "Can he?"

"I don't even think he's on this planet anymore," Lyssa said, watching him chug the glass of brown liquid in front of him. The butler refreshed it as soon as it landed on the table.

"Serves him right, the bastard."

Lyssa wished she could agree with Sage, but all she felt was pity.

"Lyssa," Sage growled. "Don't tell me you're still...apologizing for him?"

"No." She shook her head. "Yes? Maybe a little?"

"Leveman's..."

***

After a surprisingly uneventful lunch, Lyssa and Sage found Vel, who offered to take Sage on a tour of the estate. Lyssa, having nothing else to do and not wanting to be alone, joined them, adding her commentary about how she'd climbed this tree, or how she'd hidden from her brothers under that statue as Vel talked about which ancestor each part of the gardens was dedicated to.

"I wonder what you were like as a little girl," Sage asked, his hand still entertwined with hers.

"You know what I was like."

"No, I mean a *little* girl. I need to know what I'm getting into."

"So you still think it's a girl, huh?" Vel asked from the other side of Lyssa. "I think so, too."

"Why do you say that?"

"You had morning sickness for a long time," Vel said with a shrug. "Sera says that means you're having a girl."

"That doesn't mean shit," Lyssa scoffed, but placed her free hand on her stomach regardless.

After the tour of the outside, Vel briefly explained the set up of the house: five stories with fifty rooms on the top three levels. Sera and Jukin, as the eldest girl and boy, were granted a large swath of the estate, and Sera would soon take over the entire Manor once the youngest daughter came of age.

"Normally, that means that everyone's gotta get out," Vel said, as

155

they walked by the expansive kitchen. "But Sera only has ten kids, and I don't think she wants this whole house to herself."

"But that's half the fun, kicking all the siblings out," Lyssa said. She stopped short, her gaze falling on a door at the end of the hall, with a glowing red keypad.

"What's behind the creepy locked door?" Sage asked Vel. "More children?"

"That's my father's lab," Vel said.

Lyssa let go of Sage's hand and walked up to the door. No matter how many years had gone by, this door looked the same as when she was a little girl. Her fingers danced along the keypad, the tone pattern eliciting a warm feeling in her chest. The lock clicked, and the door cracked open. With no small amount of trepidation, Lyssa pressed her hands against the door and pushed it.

She felt along the dark wall until she hit the light switch. The overheads illuminated a long staircase. She tossed a look back at Vel and Sage, and they followed her down into the dimly lit staircase.

She found another switch, and a light came on over the laboratory. Her breath left her as she took in every inch of the room before her. It was the same—exactly the same—as the last time she'd been there.

And that was just the tiniest bit disappointing.

"Wow," Vel said, passing her down the stairs and stepping into the laboratory.

Chalkboards lined the walls; she'd forgotten the way he used to stand in front of them and scribble out his thoughts, tracing lines to make parallels between observations. There were tables full of opened books and half-built machines, projects he'd started and then abandoned when he got distracted. A small table sat in the corner, where her own set of number game books lay.

"You just made a whole lot more sense," Sage said, walking to the chicken scratch of handwriting on the walls. He squinted at the writing then back to Lyssa. "Yeah. A whole lot more sense."

She didn't even have it in her to argue, especially as she approached Sostas' desk. It was exactly as she'd left it, with all his black, leather-bound journals stacked in a neat row.

"Are you all right?" Vel asked quietly.

"Yeah," she said, picking up one of the journals. "It's just... I guess I kind of figured that things might be a little different, you know?" She set the journal back on the table. "Maybe there'd be *one* thing out of place."

Vel wrapped an arm around her. "Yeah, me too."

She leaned into him and looked at Sage, who was thumbing through one of her childhood number books with a confused look on his face. "What in Leveman's are these?"

"It's a pattern," she said, leaving Vel and walking over. "You have to fill in the numbers to meet the pattern. Sostas used to give them to me to keep me busy."

"So much sense. *So much sense.*"

The door to the lab squeaked open and shadowy figures appeared at the top of the stairs. Lyssa tensed immediately, remembering an awfully vivid dream about this sort of thing.

"Sera!" Vel said with a smile. "And...Mother.'

"I can't believe this place is down here!" Sera said, a little breathlessly.

Eleonora seemed much less impressed as she glanced around the room. Lyssa was surprised to see her without any servants nipping at her heels. "If I'd known *you* had the code, I'd have asked for it years ago. We're running out of storage space for our wine cellar, and this would be perfect for it."

"You can't turn this place into a wine cellar, you..." Lyssa stopped her tirade when Sage's hand slipped into hers. She swallowed her angry barb and forced a smile onto her face. "It would be disrespectful to Sostas."

"And what did that man ever do to deserve respect?" Eleonora said, stepping into the laboratory and walking around. Lyssa clenched Sage's hand when Eleonora picked up one of Sostas' delicate satellites and tossed it back on the table.

"He was your husband, for one," Sera said under her breath.

"Hmph," Eleonora said. "He was a monster. Glad to be rid of him."

"Oh yeah?" Lyssa said, Sage's gentle tug on her hand stopped her from speaking more.

"This is not worth it," he said quietly. "She is not worth getting upset over."

Lyssa opened her mouth and closed it again. It was true, Eleonora wasn't really worth getting upset over. Yet, there was still the jittery feeling in Lyssa's chest as Eleonora walked around the laboratory. She didn't belong in Sostas' sacred space, the same way Pymus hadn't belonged in Leveman's Vortex.

"Why are you even down here? Shouldn't you be getting ready for your..." Eleonora snorted as she glanced at Lyssa's stomach. "Blessing?"

"I wanted to come," Vel said, stepping forward. "I thought...I wanted to know more about Sostas, Mother."

"Vel, don't—" Lyssa said.

"And why is that, hm? Do you consider yourself just like him?" Eleonora glanced around. "No, son, you are nothing like him. Unlike her." Her eyes landed on Lyssa, who returned the look with gusto.

"Better than being like you," Lyssa replied, but stopped when Sage tugged on her again.

"Stop," Sage said.

"It's important to me, Mother," Vel said. "After all, he's my father and—"

"You think so?" Eleonora said, her eyes glittering in amusement. Lyssa saw it; that deliciousness that came with destroying others. Eleonora drunk in the way Vel's face went slack, the way Sera's mouth fell open in surprise. Eleonora considered herself to be the grandmaster of things, slicing open her opponents with each flippant remark.

"What are you saying, Mother?" Vel said.

"Do the math," Eleonora seethed. "Your father was gone with you for months at at time. Barely even looked at me towards the end. What was I to do?"

Vel seemed to be processing the information slowly and painfully. He wore the same look that Sage had when Lyssa had dangled the news of the bug over him, and it sickened her.

"You stupid hypocritical *monster*," Lyssa screamed, feeling the strongest urge to simultaneously beat the shit out of her mother and wrap Vel in a protective cocoon. "So you couldn't keep your legs closed, the least you could do is keep your mouth shut. This was…you just…this is your *son* and that's how you treat him?"

"Perhaps he should've learned not to associate with the wrong sort of person," Eleonora said quietly. "Bad things seem to happen to people like that. You should consider who you married, Mr…whatever your name is." She gestured to Sage then turned and surveyed the room, plainly unconcerned that she had just dropped a bomb in the small laboratory. "I shall send the servants to clean out this mess and make room for my new wine cellar. Feel free to take…" Her gaze landed on the book in Sage's hands. "Whatever you wish." She turned with all the air of a woman in charge and walked back up the stairs.

Lyssa stepped forward to Vel, who hadn't moved since hearing the news.

"W-why don't I show you where the blessing is going to be tomorrow, Alejandro?" Sera said lightly.

"That'd be great," Sage said.

Their footsteps echoed up the stairwell, and the door creaked closed.

"Vel?" Lyssa asked after a moment. "What are you thinking?"

"I'm just calculating how long I wasted looking for Sostas, when my real father was probably working here at the Manor the whole time."

"Oh," Lyssa said with a shrug. "I don't think Mother would have dared sleep with a servant. It's probably some baron or…" When Vel's face didn't show any sign of happiness, she switched tactics. "I think you may be one of the few who are actually Sostas' kid."

"Why?"

"Because you've got his obsessive nature," Lyssa said. "For me, it's hunting pirates. For Jukin…" She closed her eyes and shook her head. "Same damned thing. Sera has her religion, Dorst his work. For you….it's finding out about your father. I mean, you've been talking about it for years. You don't get that kind of focus without…"

Vel didn't say anything.

"I'll take a DNA test if you want," Lyssa offered. "But I know when I look at you that you are Sostas' son."

"I don't know what you're afraid of, Lyss." He smiled. "You make a great mom."

"What?" she said, uncomfortably rubbing her stomach. "No, this is not about me."

"Seriously," Vel said, turning to look at her. "Any kid would be lucky to have you as a mother. I wish I had you for a mother. I suddenly hate mine…"

***

Vel assured Lyssa that he was fine, but needed some time alone. So she walked him to his room and made him promise that if he wanted to talk about anything, he would come find her. Not very hungry, she ignored the sound of dinner getting started in the dining room and plodded to her room. To her surprise, Sage was already there, lying on her bed with a pen in his mouth.

"I have no idea how to solve these puzzles," he said, looking up at her.

"It takes a strong mind," she said with a heavy sigh. Her former bed looked so inviting, especially after standing all day. She lay on her side next to Sage and let out a long breath.

"Vel okay?"

"I think? Maybe? He's doing that annoying thing you do when you pretend like everything's fine when it's not."

He made an amused sound. "At least he's not pulling a *you* where he just pushes people away when they're trying to be helpful."

"Well?" She grunted and rolled over. "Look at what I come from! My mother is a total bitch, and my father ignored everything that wasn't his work. It's not like I had the healthiest relationships with my parents."

"Just because your parents were a certain way doesn't mean you'll be that way, too."

Isabel Teon. "Yeah, so…what are your parents like?" Lyssa asked, picking at the bedspread.

"My parents?" Sage blinked and furrowed his brow. "Why?"

"I mean, you got to see the massive shitstorm that is my family, it's only fair that I know a little about yours…"

"Well, my mother was…amazing," Sage said, looking at his hands distractedly. "She was…she had this gorgeous long black hair. And she smelled—she always smelled amazing."

"And your dad?"

"Complete asshole. Drunk, most of the time. Whiskey, I think. Or something foul like that. He worked in a docking station on D-882. He was gone for most of the week, and then came back just smelling like the inside of a bottle. Usually find something wrong with something my mom said or did and knock her around—sometimes if she wasn't quick enough to hide me in the closet, he'd remember me and knock me around too."

Lyssa's curious smile faded to one of concern as he stared blankly at the ceiling.

"One night, my mom heard him rambling up the stairs of our small little apartment and she made me hide under the bed. For some reason, I think maybe he was home early or something. Maybe he'd gotten fired. I don't know. All I know is he came home and started beating her. She was screaming for help and nobody came….nobody ever did. And then she just stopped screaming. My old man disappeared after that. I never saw him again."

"Did the police come?" Lyssa whispered, almost afraid to speak. "Did he go to jail?"

He shrugged. "The U-POL on D-882 aren't really looking at the slums."

She remembered the apartment building where she'd found Opli's mother. That Sage came from a home like that, and still managed to be a good, kind person was nothing short of a miracle.

He let out a deep breath, punctuated by a soft laugh. "Wow."

"What?" Lyssa said.

"I've never told anyone that before." Sage shook his head, taking a few shaky breaths. "Not even Tauron."

"That's why you don't…you don't like to drink?"

"You know." Sage laughed softly. "The drinking just doesn't appeal to me. It smells disgusting, and I'm sure it tastes as bad. Not to mention the compete buffoon that everyone seems to turn into. But you know what I hate more?"

"What?" Lyssa asked.

He took a long, deep breath. "I can't watch you get hurt. I know it's stupid and completely irrational. I know you can take care of yourself. But..." He finally turned to look at her, the light reflecting in his wet green eyes. "I just can't stand to see you black and blue, Lyss." His voice cracked. "It's like...it's like I'm that little kid, and I can't stop it. I let him hurt my mother and..." He trailed off, swallowing hard. "You're the only thing I have left and I can't...I can't lose you."

She gently placed her hand on his cheek as one tear fell from his eye. She was overwhelmed with need, but this was different than passionate nights on D-882. She wanted to make his pain stop, to fix whatever had been broken in his childhood and make him whole again. To erase every single horrible word she'd ever said to him, and to make a safe space for him in her heart.

So in lieu of anything else, she closed the distance between them to brush her lips against his, short and sweet. He rested his hand behind her head and pressed his forehead to hers. She gently took his free hand and placed it on the swell of her stomach. He leaned down and pressed his lips to the top of her stomach and whispered something to the baby. Tears welled in her eyes, as they so often did these days, but she didn't cry, content to watch how much better he was, how furiously he wished to be not like his father.

His eyes lingered on her stomach, and she turned her head. "What's wrong?"

"You are so damned pregnant." His eyes drifted up to hers, and she saw a sparkle in them. "I did this."

She snorted before she could stop herself. "What?"

"This is mine." He kissed her stomach again. "I did this."

She sat back from him and quirked her eyebrow. "Way to ruin the moment."

"I didn't ruin shit," he said, pulling her sideways onto his lap. Before she could argue with him, he pressed his mouth to hers and, to Lyssa, it felt like coming home. "You're heavy," he murmured against her lips.

"Stop," she murmured back. "This is supposed to be serious."

He nipped her lip and sat back. "Serious, huh?"

She jumped; the bug kicked her.

"What's wrong?" Sage said.

She grinned and placed his hand where she'd felt the movement. "Someone's awake."

They waited for a few breaths, but the bug wasn't going to comply. She poked the other side, where the bug's head rested. "Hey, wake up," she whispered.

"Does that work?"

"Sometimes," she said, pushing on the baby harder.

"Stop," he said, alarmed. "You'll hurt her."

She stroked his face. "I won't. Trust me. Dr. Bianco says—"

"Dr. Bianco." He absentmindedly rubbed her stomach.

"I have another appointment in a few weeks," she said quietly. "Come with me?"

He leaned forward and captured her lips with a smile. She grabbed his head and pulled him back down on the bed with her. Immediately, she pushed him away, the pressure on her internal organs too much.

"What?" Sage said, concerned.

"I can't lie on my back anymore," she said, turning on her side. "This thing is getting annoying now."

Sage lay next to her and kissed her again. "I think it's awesome. I made you like this." He laughed and ran his hands around the circumference. "Yeah. I did this."

"Are you going to pee on me next? Claim your territory?" She felt something very different pressed against her leg and Sage moved his hips away from her.

"Sorry," he said, glancing down. "I know that's probably the last thing you want to do right now."

"Why do you say that?" she said, toying with a lock of his hair.

"You told me as much," he said. "You said, Sage—"

She grabbed the back of his head and kissed him roughly, the way she had before this thing came between them.

"Is it safe?" he whispered against her lips.

"Very."

"How…" He swallowed. "How do we do this?"

Lyssa stopped kissing him and sat back. Then she realized what he was asking and couldn't stop the giggle that burst forth. He joined in her laughter and soon they were both heaving, Lyssa grasping her stomach.

"Leveman's," Sage said, face-up on the ground with a smile on his face. "I haven't laughed like that in a while."

"Are you nervous?" she asked quietly.

"For sex?"

"For this."

"Scared out of my damned mind."

"And you still want it?"

"Right now, I want you," he said, pulling her closer.

It was the strangest sex they'd ever had, full of stops and starts and laughter and experimentation.

"Not on my back."

"Wait, hold on."

But it was the first time she wasn't just having sex, she was having fun.

"I don't like that either, no—wait, yes, yes, like that."

There was nothing else in the universe but him and her and the room and the feel of his hands on her body. She had jumped way off that ledge and was falling fast, but Sage was falling with her, like he had on that ill-advised space jump, and she was not afraid.

Her first climax was intense. Sage covered her mouth with his as she clenched around him, and he held her tenderly for a moment. He asked if she was all right (which she knew meant if she and the baby were all right), and she promised him they both were. Once he was satisfied no damage had occurred, he lay behind her gently and slid himself in her again and she exhaled from the pleasure and the tightness. He moved inside of her, his breath warm and ragged on her neck. Her hands grasped his and he pulled her tighter against him. He groaned in pleasure as he came, and she kissed his knuckles. After a moment, he laid his cheek on top of hers.

"Are you finished already?" she asked.

"Yeah." She loved the husky sound of his voice, but she didn't want this to end just yet. It was perfection and she wanted it to last as long as possible.

"You want to go again?" he asked, nuzzling into her neck.

She turned her head to look at him. His eyes were shiny and

clouded in his post-orgasmic glow, but there was something else there too.

Love.

This guy was absolutely, unequivocally, no-holds-barred in love with her.

A trickle of fear slid down her spine.

She wanted to get up and sleep somewhere else, but all the activity had evidently woken the baby and she kicked, hard, right where Sage's hand lay on her stomach.

"Ow." She winced.

"Shit," Sage whispered. "Shit, shit, shit. That was... She kicked. Shit, she kicked."

His wide-eyed excitement dissolved her fear and replaced it with amusement. Sage eagerly ran his hands over her stomach, poking and prodding the same way she did. She joined in with a smile.

"I'm sorry," she said after a few minutes of unsuccessful poking. "Looks like she's gone back to sleep." She paused, realizing she'd given the bug a gender. "I really don't know if it's a boy or girl."

"I kind of hope it's a girl," he said, resting his cheek on her stomach. He looked up at her. "Do you think she'll kick again?"

"We...we could always try waking her back up?" Lyssa said with a coy smile.

Sage grinned in the darkness and captured her lips with his.

CHAPTER FIFTEEN

Lyssa awoke the next morning as she did every morning, uncomfortable and feeling an incredible need to pee.

Except this morning, she woke up without clothes on, with nothing but a sheet and Sage's arms for cover.

As gracefully as a pregnant woman could, she slipped out of bed and rubbed her face, replaying the previous night in her head. She wasn't even sure how long she'd been asleep, for they'd spent most of the night trying to wake the baby—

The baby. She was now calling it *the baby*.

The kid had been too stubborn to comply, but they'd had fun regardless.

It had been *fun* with Sage. And some part of her could see them having fun after the baby came. Living in that beach house. Waking up to him every morning. Having him hold her the way he did when they drifted off to sleep: protectively, *lovingly*.

She gripped the sink, her heart racing. There was something so tempting about all of it, about losing herself to the protectiveness of him. To let herself believe that she could have that beautiful life of kids and Sage and bounty hunting and joy.

She was in free fall and it terrified her.

There was a commotion in her room, and she stepped out of the bathroom, nearly squealing when she saw Sera and Vel talking to Sage. She slammed the door behind her to cover her naked form and seethed.

"What are you doing here?"

She ripped a robe off the door and tied it around herself, stalking out into the bedroom and trying to salvage her dignity. Sera stood authoritatively in the doorway while Vel wore an amused smile as he glanced between the two of them.

"Stop smiling," she hissed at Vel before turning to Sera. "What do you want?"

"I'm here to take you to the Temple for your morning ritual before the blessing," Sera said.

"No."

"She's going," Sage said. "Just give us a second."

Sera nodded, and she and Vel left.

"I'm not going with her," Lyssa growled at the closed door. "She might sacrifice me or something."

"Stop being melodramatic," Sage said, yanking on his boxers. He crossed the room and pulled her into his arms like a lover would. And damn it all, she rested her head on his chest. "It won't be so bad."

"You know none of this matters, right?" she whispered against his skin.

"I'll take my chances," he said, kissing her nose.

When Lyssa emerged from her bedroom, she said nothing to Sera nor Vel, who still wore a smug smile. Sera led the way down the spiral staircase, through the already loud dining room, and out the front door to the Temple.

Sera continued in silence as they walked into the empty house of worship, the murals on the walls of all the religious parables she'd grown up learning. But they bypassed the center room and walked through the doors behind the pulpit. Lyssa had never been in this back room. It was, for lack of a better word, serene. White curtains hung in the full-length windows that overlooked the sparkling lake on the property. The panes were open, letting the cool breeze flow in.

"What is this?" Lyssa asked.

"Before every blessing, the godmother does the ceremonial washing of the mother-to-be," Sera explained, walking to a large gold tub and turning on the spigot.

"No."

"Oh, get over yourself, I changed your diapers," Sera snapped. "Besides, there's nothing I haven't seen many times before."

Her words triggered a memory and Lyssa began to panic slightly. "Wait, I don't want you to be the godmother. Someone else—"

"It's just a formality," Sera said, pouring in some salts and liquids into the bath. "The Great Creator will let me stand in for whomever you deem fit to raise your child."

Lyssa nearly tripped over her feet. She really didn't have a say about who would raise her child because it wasn't really her child. It was Sage's.

But after the night before, things felt different. She'd pictured herself sharing her life with him, and she knew from the look in his eye, from the house that he'd bought, from the way he'd been protecting her for years, that if she'd asked, he would gladly jump with her.

Sera's beady eyes and her nerves weakened her resolve, and she disrobed and stepped into the warm tub that smelled of flowers and mint. Sera gently poured the water over her head, making sure to keep the suds out of Lyssa's eyes, before she massaged Lyssa's scalp with soap.

"Feels good, hm?" Sera said as Lyssa leaned back.

"I suppose."

"You're a stubborn ass, Lyssandra Peate," Sera said with a slight smack on the shoulder. "I wonder how your husband puts up with you."

Husband—Sage. Lyssa felt the ring still resting against her finger and ran her thumb along the silver band. This was his mother's ring. The mother that he'd watched his father beat to death and never told anyone about. He'd obviously gone back for the ring.

Which he'd kept.

And given to Lyssa.

And she knew that if she never gave it back to him, he'd be just fine with it.

And she almost didn't want to.

"It'll be fine, Lyss," Sera said as she pulled Lyssa back and began scrubbing her face with something rough. "The ceremony will be about the baby, not about you. I made sure of it."

"I'm not worried about that," Lyssa replied.

"So are you worried about having the baby, then?" Sera said. "I promise you, it's not as scary as you'd think. You and Alejandro have a birth plan, yes?"

"What in Leveman's is that?" Lyssa blanched.

"Your plan for when the baby comes," Sera said. "Trust me, it helps. Though if you're anything like Jinjina, you might have a quick birth. Her last one lasted fifteen minutes from first contraction to delivery." Sera's face darkened. "Bitch."

"Er…" She didn't feel like discussing this with Sera. "Sure. Do you have one?"

"I did, but I don't plan on having any more children," she said. "I don't think anyone wishes to marry the matron of a manor with ten children."

Lyssa's eyes flew open. "What happened to your husband?"

Sera peered down at her with a peculiar sort of stare. "Lyssa, we've been divorced for years."

"W-what?"

"News doesn't travel, I guess."

Lyssa recalled a particularly biting repartee the last time she was home. She had the good conscience to feel bad about making a remark about Sera's husband.

"I realized a few years ago that I didn't want to end up like Mother," Sera said. "A loveless marriage, too many children to keep track of. You know she only had so many to keep up with her sister. *She* wanted to have the most. I think she only stopped because it would've been too obvious that she was sleeping with someone else after Father disappeared." Sera paused for a moment, her face contorted before shaking her head and finishing with, "I ended things with my husband. And I'm much happier for it."

Lyssa couldn't help but ask, "And how did Mother take it?"

Sera paused. "She doesn't know. Or doesn't care to know. She never asks about anyone outside her own selfish bubble."

A small knock on the door interrupted their conversation, and a nanny brought in a sniveling, red-faced child. Lyssa tensed, remembering how interruptions were handled in her childhood. But Sera rushed over to the nanny and swooped the child into her arms, comforting him quietly.

"What happened?" she asked.

The child proffered a finger that was red.

Sera took the finger and kissed it. "All better?" The child shook his head and latched himself onto Sera. She nodded to the nanny and walked back to Lyssa, picking up a towel and handing it over.

"It's entirely possible to choose not to be like them," Sera said as Lyssa dried herself off. "I decided I wasn't going to let my children grow up thinking that their mother hated them. And they have plenty of uncles and aunts to give them all the love they desire."

She put the now-quiet child on the ground, and he scampered over to the corner where a pile of books sat. He opened one up and began to read.

"You should come home more," Sera said, motioning for Lyssa to join her in front of an ornate gold vanity with a white pouf chair. "It'll be good for your child to grow up with family. And it'll be good for you, too."

"Why, so everyone can just remind me how much they hate me?"

Sera snorted, a very un-Sera-like sound as she picked up a brush and ran it through Lyssa's hair. "We don't hate you, Lyss. I confess, I thought you were an entitled little brat for many years, but…after what Mother said to you…"

"And you wonder why I never come here?"

"The thing is, Lyss, Mother doesn't have the power she once had. She's grown meaner and harsher as she's aged, and no one wishes to spend time with her. We don't have to bow down to get her affection, because we don't need it. Vel was the first, you know. After you left the last time, he stood up to her. We all thought she was going to kick him out for good, but he came back the next weekend. And he looked her straight in the eye and dared her to say anything."

Lyssa cracked a smile. She would have liked to have seen that.

"Now if only I could convince him to stop looking for Father, then maybe he could move on with his life," Sera finished, putting down the brush and picking up white ribbons.

"Dorst said the same thing," Lyssa said, watching Sera's fingers braid her hair deftly. "But he hasn't asked me about Sostas in years. I thought…I thought he'd moved on from it." She considered that he'd probably never ask again, now that there was the seed of doubt that Sostas wasn't his real father. What else might that change for him? She hated Eleonora even more.

"Probably because it's a sore subject, no?" Sera said. "Your temper is legendary."

"But if it bothers him that much, he should say something. And —" A vice-like pain grew from her lower back, crawling around to the center of her stomach. Lyssa grasped her stomach and hissed at the pain.

"Breathe, Lyss," Sera said, placing a comforting hand on her shoulder. "It's just a contraction."

"W-what?" She began to panic. "I'm not…it's not…"

"Shh, relax," Sera said. "Breathe in and out. Come on. It'll pass soon."

Lyssa did as instructed and the pain lessened, but the nervous feeling remained. "Does that mean—"

"Probably not. Sometimes you get mini-contractions starting in the eighth month." She paused, and her mouth twitched. "I've heard if you have sex, it can bring them on."

Lyssa's face turned bright red, and she looked forward.

"You should be careful after the baby arrives. I noticed I was most fertile—"

"Nope. No more of this conversation."

***

Sera dressed Lyssa in a white gown that tied with a silk ribbon around the back and accentuated her round stomach. Sera added some white ribbons to Lyssa's hair, and white slippers to Lyssa's feet just as there was a knock at the door. Sage poked his head in and smiled when he saw the two of them.

"You got her in a dress!" he said. "Did she fight you at all?"

"Barely," Sera said, running the brush through Lyssa's hair one final time. "I have to run and check with Helmsley to make sure everything is set." She patted Sage on the shoulder as he walked in, wearing a much-too-nice white button down shirt and black slacks.

"You look…" He couldn't suppress a grin, "pregnant."

"If you pee on me, they'll notice it."

Sage walked over to Lyssa and knelt in front of her. "Thank you for doing this for me. For all of this, coming home. Dealing with your mother and your siblings."

"It's not so bad," she said quietly. She ran her hands through his hair and smiled. "I just hope this ceremony doesn't last too long. I didn't bring my mini-computer and these things can get *so* boring."

Sage laughed and helped her stand. He led her out the doors and into the Temple, now full of her family. She noticed more looks than usual as she and Sage took their spot in the front pew. Sage slung an easy arm around her, drifting his fingers up and down her bare arms. She leaned into him, glancing around at the murals on the walls. Her eyes lingered on the fiery river that threaded around the room, the end state for all the religious tales depicted in the plaster. At the head of the room, she saw Helmsley, her childhood priest, conferring with Sera, who caught her eye and winked at her.

"I don't know why you hate her so much," Sage whispered. "She seems really nice."

"She's nicer than she used to be," Lyssa said.

"So are you." He pressed his lips to her cheek, and she felt the weight of his mother's ring around her finger.

Dorst came to sit beside Sage. "I know you'll be most upset to hear this, but Mother has taken ill this morning. She won't be able to attend your blessing."

"Oh no," Lyssa deadpanned.

"Such a shame," Vel said, sitting on the other side of Lyssa. They shared a grin, and Lyssa patted him on the leg. He took her free hand in his and squeezed it.

Sera took the seat normally reserved for the matriarch. She was much smaller and less imposing than when Eleonora took up the room, almost like a child playing dress up. But she nodded to Helmsley, and he turned to the congregation, holding out his hands to quiet them.

"Here we go," Lyssa whispered. Sage tucked her in tighter under his arm.

"Brothers and sisters, let us praise and thank the Great Creator, who took little children into His arms and blessed them. Praised now and forever."

A murmur of response came from the congregation. Sage shared a look with Lyssa, and she shrugged.

Helmsley led them in a prayer, then a song which Lyssa vaguely knew, but which Sage had a great time making up words to. When it was over, he whispered that he might have a future in songwriting, a comment she answered with an elbow to the ribs.

"Today, we will be celebrating the newest member of our growing family," Helmsley said.

Sera made a small motion from the front of the room and Vel pushed Lyssa a bit.

"That's your cue," Vel said.

Lyssa stood and walked the suddenly long distance up the three stairs to the raised platform where Helmsley and Sera stood. Sera took Lyssa's hand and gently spun her around to face the crowd who all wore...

Smiles.

Grins, happy faces. None of the loathing and hatred that she was used to. Even Jinjina, four months along with her next demon spawn, was beaming, between breaking up the spats of her two closest children. There was not one unfriendly face in this very unfriendly place.

"Er...what's the gender?" Helmsley said to Lyssa.

"Uh..." Lyssa blinked with a nervous look at Sage. "It's...I don't know."

"A surprise!" Helmsley said with a disgruntled look. "You *would* make this more difficult—"

"Helmsley!" Sera barked. "One more snide remark and you'll have to find a new family to minister to."

Helmsley swallowed and blushed, but turned to the congregation with a false happiness. "The scriptures say that children have the purest souls, welcomed through the Arch of Eron into the arms of the Great Creator without worry. They say, 'the Great Creator welcomed children, believed in their dignity, and held them up as a model for all who are seeking the Arch of Eron.'"

Lyssa shifted against Sera and caught Vel's eye. She knew all this first hand—Sostas had used her as a "good-soul-shield" when she was a child to allow him to experiment at the Arch.

"But children do need the help of grownups if they are to develop their individual gifts, and their moral, mental, and physical powers, and so keep to their pure path. Let us therefore ask for the Great Creator's blessing, so that we will devote ourselves to the upbringing of this child and so that…he or she will accept willingly the guidance he or she needs."

Lyssa glanced out and caught Sage's eye. He mouthed, "What is it?"

Lyssa shrugged with a grin, and he shook his head at her.

"And now we ask the father…there is a father, right?" Helmsley asked Sera who glared at him so fiercely Lyssa thought he might burst into flames. She turned to Sage and waved him up onto the platform.

"Stand behind her," Sera said, gently adjusting him and placing his hands next to Lyssa's on her stomach.

"Let us pray," Helmsley boomed. "Through his or her parents and the Temple, show this child the tenderness of Your own love; grant that those entrusted with his or her care will be tireless in watching over…him or her."

"You really don't know the gender?" Sage whispered.

"We can find out together at my next appointment," Lyssa replied, placing her hands on top of his and leaning into him.

"All-powerful Great Creator, You are the source of all blessings, the protector of infants, whose gift of children enriches and brightens a marriage. Look with favor on this child and, bring…him or her into Your own spiritual family, the Temple. Protect her from temptation and—"

"Hands off my sister, pirate."

Lyssa's gaze flew to the back of the Temple, where a bearded, baggy-eyed, possibly drunk Jukin stood, his trusty U-POL gun pointed at Lyssa and Sage.

"J-Jukin!" Dorst stood with a horrified look on his face. "What in Leveman's Great Vortex do you think you're doing?"

"That…that man…he…" Jukin snarled, stepping forward.

Before she could stop him, Sage pushed Lyssa to the side, into the waiting arms of Sera. "Put the gun down, Jukin," he said, too calmly for someone with a deranged former police officer pointing a gun at him.

"Sage!" Lyssa said, shoving Sera off.

"Lyssa, you don't know who this man is," Jukin said.

"I know exactly who he is!" Lyssa growled. "Put the Goddamned gun down."

"He's a pirate named Sage Teon!" Jukin said and a ripple of horrified gasps erupted from the congregation. "He is a dangerous and wanted criminal."

Lyssa couldn't believe her eyes nor her ears that he would recognize *Sage* and not her, even after all they'd gone through, but was more concerned with what Jukin might do.

"The Universal Police won't take care of this problem, but I damned well will," Jukin said, cocking the gun. Jinjina screamed and covered the eyes of her children.

"Jukin, don't do this here, not in front of everyone," Sage said.

"Then let's talk a walk," Jukin growled.

"Jukin, this is Lyssa's husband," Dorst said, placing a calming hand on Jukin's arm.

Jukin threw him off with such force, he went careening into the pew.

"Sage, don't you dare leave this room," Lyssa said as he took as step forward.

"It's okay, I can—"

"Don't you dare," she growled, pushing off Sera and standing between Jukin and Sage.

"Lyssa!" Sera exclaimed.

"Put the gun down, you stupid asshole," Lyssa said to Jukin. "You didn't shoot me then, you won't shoot me now."

"Lyssa, this has nothing to do with you."

"Look at me."

"What?" Jukin said, his eyes focused over her shoulder.

She balled her fists in anger. "I told you to look at me."

"Lyssa, don't," Sage said behind her.

"I don't have time for this," Jukin said, swaying slightly. "Get out of the way and let me—"

"*Look at me*!" she screamed, her voice echoing in the cavernous room. Jinjina's quiet sobs and Dorst's moans of pain faded away as Jukin's eyes flickered for a moment, then finally drew away from Sage to look at her.

"What am I looking at?" he snarled. "Aside from a sister who made a dumb mistake. Did you know that he's got another girlfriend? She's...."

He swallowed.

"That's right. For once in your stupid, self-absorbed life, take a good, long look at me," Lyssa whispered. "Because you sure as shit haven't been seeing me up until now."

"God in Leveman's Vortex," he whispered, the gun falling out of his limp hand.

"Not in your office. Not in the Presidential Palace when I saved your ass the first time," she breathed. "Not when I proclaimed in front of all of those cameras that you were innocent even though I knew, I knew, you were complicit. But I apologized for you, I made excuses. And what did you do?" She shook her head. "You arrested everyone and you made me the most wanted pirate in the universe."

He staggered back, his eyes wide.

"And not once, not once, did it ever occur to you who I really was," Lyssa said. "Not even when you were threatening to blow my brains out. Not when I told you to do it."

"It's you," Jukin whispered. "R-Razia..."

Jukin's face twisted in anguish, and he staggered back again, his hands coming to his face in horrified realization. She hoped he was reliving every single interaction they'd shared, every moment when he looked straight at her and didn't recognize his own flesh and blood.

"W-why would you do this to me?" Jukin growled. "Why would you betray me like this?"

"B...betray *you*?" Lyssa gasped. "Betray *you*? Do you not even remember when I was kidnapped? Do you not remember what you said to Tauron? You told him to go ahead and kill me!"

"I said no such thing!" Jukin gasped.

She snarled angrily. "You said, *be my guest*!"

"Because I knew the gun wasn't loaded!" Jukin barked back.

Her shoulders went slack as the world tilted. "You...what?"

"Pirates are awful, disgusting creatures, but I knew that gun wasn't loaded. There's no way he was planning on killing an eleven-year-old girl in cold blood."

"Then why...why didn't you...."

"The moment he called, I was scrambling to mount a rescue attempt. I had ships, I had men, but...he dropped you off."

Lyssa couldn't believe her ears.

"Why do you think I chose Tauron to capture?" Jukin said. "He *threatened my family*."

"You...you went after Tauron because of me?"

"McDougall didn't want me to go after any pirates," Jukin snarled. "Said whatever I did was on my own head, and I took it. He needed to pay for what he did to you—"

"*He took care of me*!" Lyssa bellowed, unable to breathe. "Leveman's, Jukin—he was the only person who ever gave a shit about me!"

"He had a gun to your head, Lyssa!" Jukin seethed. "How could you have possibly ever wanted to join a crew like that?"

"I don't know. Maybe because I thought *my brother left me to die on a pirate ship!*" She ran a hand through her hair, feeling the white ribbons Sera had placed there. "And if you cared so Goddamned much, why didn't you ever call? Why didn't you even check to see if I wasn't completely screwed up from the whole episode?"

"I asked after you, but everyone said you were fine, not bothered at all by it," Jukin said, falling into the pew to sit. "How was I to know you were—"

A rumbling interrupted their conversation and a shadow crossed over the light streaming through the window.

"And that is *our* cue," Sage said, gripping Lyssa's hand and pulling her down the aisle. She wordlessly glanced around at all the faces in the room. From happy, smiling, loving—now angry, disgusted. Hurt. She glanced at the mural on the wall, the river of fire. Nothing good ever lasted for her, did it?

"C'mon." Vel was on her other side, pushing her forward. He made sure to kick the gun far away from Jukin's grip.

"Oh yeah. Hey asshole," Sage said, stopping in front of Jukin. Before Lyssa could stop him, Sage reared back and decked Jukin in the mouth. "That's for ruining my child's blessing."

Jukin sprawled back on the pew but didn't move to follow them, and neither did anyone else. Lyssa felt their stares on her back as she and Sage hurried out into the bright sunlight of the early morning.

She stopped short when she saw Sage's ship parked on the grassy green of her mother's estate.

"You called your crew?" she said, ripping her hand out of his.

"Yeah, I did," Sage said. "They've been orbiting the planet ever since I found out your nutso brother was here."

"They don't know!" Lyssa said. "They can't know—"

"Does it really matter? We need to get out of here, *now*," Sage said, glancing back into the Temple. "Before he gets any more ideas."

"Holy shit!" Ganon called, running up to them with the rest of the crew in tow.

"Lyssa's pregnant!" Sobal gasped.

"C'mon guys, let's get out of here," Sage said, clapping them on the back. "We'll open a bottle of champagne. We still got some in there?"

Lyssa dug in her feet. "I *told* you not to tell anyone."

"Lyssa, what did you want me to do?" Sage said. "Let him shoot you and my kid?"

"You didn't have to call *them*—"

"I made a choice and I'm not sorry for it," he growled, stepping forward. "Because I love you and I won't let anything happen to you."

Everything went deathly quiet.

"What did you say?" Lyssa whispered, something buzzing in her ear.

"I said…" He straightened his shoulders. "I said I love you."

She took a step back.

"I love you and our child and I won't let anything ever happen to either of you. I will protect you from—"

"I don't want your protection!" Lyssa barked, her heart beating wildly. "*I don't love you.*"

Her words hung in the air. Even with the sound of the engines roaring and the growing crowd of siblings pouring out of the Temple behind her, she heard them echo around her head.

"You…" Sage whispered, stricken.

"I don't love you," she said, that malicious, evil voice inside her taking over. "I don't know what you thought this was, but…nothing's changed. I'm going to have this baby then give it to you. And I don't want to see you again. Ever."

Sage's eyes widened, and she hated herself more than ever. Her inner voice was screaming at her to make it right, to fix what she had broken. But she couldn't make her mouth open to form the words.

"Really?" Sage said after a lifetime. "You don't love me?" He laughed and she was suddenly frightened. There was nothing familiar about him anymore. "Tell me, do you honestly believe that? Really? Or are you too much of a fucking coward to accept reality?"

She swallowed.

"I mean, I've done everything for you. I would have worshipped the ground you walked on, and yet…you still won't let yourself believe that this," he pointed between them as she had done, "this is *real.* This is *happening.*" His eyes hardened. "Well, it was happening. But not anymore.

"I'm *done* with your bullshit. I'm done with your little tantrums. I'm done with your excuses about how fucked up your family is. I'm done with you expecting everyone to come running whenever you throw a fucking hissy-fit like a five-year-old. I'm done expecting that you will ever change because you have proven to me, time and again, that you are incapable of seeing outside your own Goddamn bubble.

"You're so afraid of anyone getting close to you—fuck, you're afraid of your own Goddamn child! You think everyone's going to leave the way your father did." He laughed at the irony. "And now, you're finally going to get your wish. I'm fucking gone." He marched up to her and held out his hand. "Give it back."

"What?" she said, wishing she sounded more angry than hurt.

"The ring. Give it back."

Pain sliced through her chest and she took a step back. Without a word, she slipped the silver band off her finger and placed it in the palm of his hand.

He spun on his heels and stormed onto his ship.

Lyssa stood, stunned, as he disappeared up the ramp. She moved to walk forward, but Ganon held up a hand.

"I don't think so, sweetheart," he said, his voice full of poison and venom. "I'm just glad that he finally saw you for the horrible human being you are because I, for one, am *tired* of seeing you treat him like shit."

"Fine, I don't like you anyway!" Lyssa snarled back. She turned on her heel to face Vel, who looked angry.

"Are you serious?" he said. "After all that he's done for you over the years, you're just—"

"Don't tell me you're on his side?" Lyssa snapped. "That's just classic *you*. Maybe, for once, you could care about *me* instead of—"

"Wait up!" Vel called to Ganon. "I am suddenly tired of her bullshit. too. She's too much like my mother."

Lyssa's mouth fell open.

"You wanna come with us?" Ganon asked, both eyebrows raised. "What about your scientist thing?"

Vel turned to look at Lyssa and shook his head. "Let's see what piracy is like, huh?"

She stood, open mouthed, as he climbed onboard, welcomed like an old friend. Ganon paused once more to rudely gesture at Lyssa before the ramp closed. A few seconds later, the ship blasted off and disappeared into the bright blue sky.

"So…what was *that* about?" Dorst asked behind her.

She turned and realized that the entire family had witnessed everything. Dorst was aghast, as was Heelin next to him. Sera stood with her hands over her mouth, wide-eyed and unsure. Lyssa's gaze danced over the rest of the faces in the crowd.

"You're a p-pirate?" Heelin said, blinking wildly. "Not only a pirate, but *her*? How did I not see this before? You dropped me off at the prison? How could I be so stupid?"

"And Al is a pirate, too," Dorst said, running his hands through his hair. "And I liked him so much for you."

"I can't say I'm surprised."

The collective attention turned to the left. Because the Great Creator was not finished yet, Eleonora had witnessed the entire exchange. Her look of pure joy at Lyssa's suffering was almost too much to bear.

"Mother, now is not the time," Sera snapped, stepping forward. "Lyssa, let's get you back inside and talk about this, all right—"

"I have always known you were rotten and here is the proof," Eleonora continued, cutting off Sera. "You vile, disgusting creature. I can only hope that your child choses a different path from you, but it may be too late, what with parents who are obviously morally corrupt. You've obviously been a terrible influence on poor Vel, that child is now doomed to Plethegon because of you. I hope you're happy, Lyssandra!"

Lyssa stared at her mother, wondering why she wasn't getting angrier. But she felt numb, her heart already smashed to smithereens. There was nothing her mother could say to her now that would hurt any more than she did already.

"I'm...I'm gonna go now," Lyssa announced quietly.

CHAPTER SIXTEEN

Lyssa sat against a shady tree, mind blank, eyes fixed on the yellow grass that stretched as far as the eye could see, the occasional wind rippling across it as if it were a living thing. She'd been on this planet for a few rotations, however long that equated to in Universal Time. The first few days had run by in a blur as she relived every moment of the disastrous trip to the Manor.

Sera had tried to talk with her, as did Dorst, but Lyssa didn't feel like talking. She'd realized just how big she had become when she tried to climb her ladder. After realizing that it was impossible, she'd had to fly her ship from her mini-computer, a real feat considering she had a tenth of the capabilities on her remote control than on her dashboard on the level above her. But she'd figured it out with minimal damage to her ship and her mother's exquisite docking station.

Once out in open space, she set a course for the farthest planet she could find.

She couldn't stop seeing Sage's face, hearing the words he'd spat at her. He truly hated her now, and she deserved it. She could see the fall coming from miles away, she'd known that it was going to end badly.

Yet, she'd jumped anyway. She'd been right about one thing: it hurt worse to have allowed herself to believe only to have it taken away from her.

Her mini-computer by her side, she reached down to turn it on, telling herself she only wanted to check the time but even she couldn't believe her own lies anymore. She wanted to know if anyone still cared about her.

As her mini to booted up, she glanced out on the plains, wondering if she should feel trepidation or nerves or something other than numbness. She lifted the device again and blinked—fifteen missed calls.

She cracked a smile.

But none from Sage. Or Lizbeth. Or Vel.

Five from Dorst, that was predictable. Three from Bianco's office —Lyssa winced; she'd missed an appointment. Four from Dissident.

She scrutinized the list, checking three times that she hadn't missed a call from Sage, Lizbeth, or Vel and swallowed the hurt that they hadn't.

"I'm done with you expecting everyone to come running whenever you throw a fucking hissy-fit like a five-year-old."

She closed her eyes and the baby kicked, keeping her from falling too far into misery. "I hear you, Bug. I hear you."

She assumed that Dissident was calling to inform her that she'd been kicked out of his web. It didn't devastate her as much as it did the first few times. She almost didn't care at this point.

She switched to the pirate web application and furrowed her brow.

	25) Peate, Lyssandra
Wanted for	Engagement in piracy, bounty hunting, kidnapping, aggravated assault, resisting arrest, jailbreak, attempted murder of a police officer
Reward	32,548,456
Known Alias	Razia
Known Accomplices	Tauron Ball, Sage Teon
Pirate Web Affiliation	Dissident

Two things jumped out at her immediately. The first was that seeing her own name where Razia's had been wasn't as strange as she'd thought. Much like when she'd given her Leveman's Vortex presentation, she had been preparing herself for these things for so long that it seemed a natural progression. Or perhaps her brain was still frazzled from pregnancy.

The second was that she was not only still listed in Dissident's web, but she wasn't on probation.

Curiosity getting the better of her, she dialed his number.

"Uh. It's you. Girlie, when I call you, you answer, understand?"

"Why am I still in your web?" Lyssa asked.

"Why wouldn't you be? I ain't got nobody left but you! Leveman's knows you broke Teon." He snorted. "Do me a favor, if you plan on sleeping with any other pirates, make sure you don't get knocked up."

"And you don't care that Jukin—"

"The only thing I care about right now is that you get your ass in gear and find me some pirates!" Dissident barked. "And why haven't you solved my Opli problem, hm? I thought you were the best bounty hunter? Maybe I'll get that brother of yours to take your place!"

She breathed a long sigh. "I'll get right on it."

"Good, because I'm tired of your bullshit!"

"So's everybody, it would seem."

Truth be told, Lyssa hadn't thought about Opli once since she and Sage had figured that he was targeting pirates specifically, and whatever Dissident might say, she wasn't really in the mood to continue her investigation without him. Her focus now was on the number of days until her next appointment with Bianco, and the number of days since her fight with Sage.

If the good doctor had noticed anything amiss with her patient, she didn't mention it. But she did remind Lyssa that the mother's health was as important as the baby's, which only made Lyssa feel guiltier about her constant anguish.

Spurred by Bianco's reminder, Lyssa began half-hearted attempts at apologizing. She started with Vel, but he didn't answer his mini-computer, nor the messages she sent to him. Then again, based on what she was seeing on the pirate web, he was busy as Ganon's brand new bounty hunter, and had been getting all sorts of attention. She might have been jealous, if she didn't miss him so badly.

Lizbeth was the same, not answering her mini-computer nor messages. When Lyssa went to the Intelligence Agency after an appointment with Bianco, the security guard told her "Ms. Carter was not accepting meetings at the moment."

Harms, at least, took her call, but the conversation didn't go as planned.

"You're Jukin's *sister*?" he spat. "All this time, and you never told me? You also never told me that you're *pregnant*?" He sat back. "And then Sage shows up at my door, looking like someone *died*, and now I can't get him to leave. And now I have your little brother showing up and acting like he knows me. How long has *he* been around?"

Lyssa chewed her lip. "Which of those do you want me to address first?"

"None of them," Harms said. "Because I think it's time you find another informant. I'm not quite sure I want to talk to you anymore. Not sure I feel like dealing with all your complaining. Especially considering you don't even trust me enough to tell me the truth about yourself."

Something buzzed in her ear. Harms had been angry with her before, but this was a new level.

"I thought we were friends, Razia. I thought that after all these years, after everything we've been through, one day you would have trusted me enough to tell me. But no, I had to find out from the news. Not even the pirate news, the *regular* news!"

"Harms, I'm sorry—"

"It's too late, whatever your name is," Harms growled, and the line went dark.

Lyssa decided against calling anyone else. She spent the days between her appointments with Bianco buying lots of food she didn't eat and beverages that she didn't drink. She even bought a bottle of whiskey, just to see if anyone would show up and yell her for it. The only thing her flurry of transactions served to do was attract a couple low-level pirates who hadn't yet heard. They took one look at her, bowed their heads in apology, and left.

After the second appointment with Bianco, she waited in the food court of the transport station with her fourth cup of coffee she'd purchased that day (the other three sat untouched in front of her), and watched the screen of her mini-computer like a hawk.

Her brow furrowed; she felt a presence behind her. A smile grew on her face and a rush of relief washed through her. It had only been a matter of time before he got over himself and—

"Pregnancy suits you, Lyssa."

Her face froze in the half-smile. Opli's voice, not Sage's. His heels clacked on the linoleum as he circled the table, loudly scraping a chair out and sitting down as if invited. He surveyed her with his usual smug superiority. "Yes, indeed. You look almost docile. When are you due?"

"Right after I murder you."

"Oh, I didn't do anything," Opli said, drumming his hands on the table. "At least, not to you. I'm not the one who spilled your secret." He paused and his gaze dropped to her stomach. "Either of them."

She narrowed her eyes. "And why was that? Did I not rank high enough on your pirate hit list?"

"Everything is about worth to you, isn't it?" Opli laughed and looked around the food court. "This may come as a surprise to you, but you weren't part of the plan."

"P-plan?"

"I had a very specific set of people I needed to destroy," Opli said. "You already know about my mother, but what you don't know is how she got that way. My father owned a small pharmacy on '882, and the majority of his customers dealt in the illegal kind of drugs. His primary supplier was Jeam Bullock. When the Piracy Act was passed, suddenly Bullock no longer dealt in pills and left my father thousands of credits in debt. When my father couldn't pay his rent, his landlord—you know him as Insurgent—sent some of his goons to punish him. Only Fried, Hardrict, and Stenson didn't just break his legs, they broke his back." He paused, disappointment in his eyes. "My mother couldn't handle it, so she turned to drinking. My father died from infection a few years ago in a terribly managed hospital—owned, in part, by Waslow Needler and his brother."

Lyssa couldn't help the words that came out. "I'm sorry."

"When the Piracy Act happened, it's like…nobody was answerable for their crimes anymore. People had done heinous things and simply walked away." Opli's face reverted to the sadistic smile that suited him so. "But those who harmed me no longer got away with it. They have paid—and are paying—for their crimes."

She swallowed, counting off the pirates who'd had disappeared in the past few months. "So many more pirates have retired though…"

"You give me too much credit," Opli said. "I was only responsible for the pirates I've mentioned. The rest simply got spooked after Jukin's epic failure of an arrest."

"But you're…you're supposed to…" Lyssa shook her head. "So what now? Are you just going to continue digging up dirt on people?"

"Don't you see? I've won. I have destroyed the very people who destroyed my life. So it's over."

She blinked. "Over? What about me? What about Sage?"

"That's the problem with you, Lyssa, you work and work and work and don't see the big picture. When you get one victory, you simply focus on what the *next* problem is, or your *next* conquest. And in all of that time, you neglect the people who love you.' She glanced up and realized Opli was looking away from her. "Even when they are right in front of your face."

"What are you talking about?"

"Do you think you're the only person your brother ignored? I told him to let it go, that once you'd testified, he had nothing to do with the assassination. He could move on and focus on something else. But no. No, he had to go storming into that damned Pirate Ball, guns blazing." He looked at Lyssa. "He even put a gun to your head and couldn't pull his head out of his ass long enough to notice who he was threatening."

"He knows now."

"He does, and so does the rest of piracy," Opli said. "Funny, wasn't as big a bombshell as you thought, hm? All that trouble to keep your identities separate and you find that nobody *actually* cares about you?"

Lyssa rubbed her stomach. "So what now? Are you going to just walk away from all this?"

"From my paycheck? Absolutely not," Opli said with a shake of his head. "I have an alcoholic mother to take care of. But yes, my vendetta against the pirates is over." His mouth curled into a smile. "The only villain left, my dear, is you."

***

In all of her years of living, Lyssa never thought that she'd consider the Planetary and System Science Academy a safe haven. She'd spent nearly all of her teenage years trying to get *away* from this place. But after everyone had basically given up on her, she was thankful that something, at least, still wanted her.

She wasn't sure what she planned to accomplish on this visit, though she was fairly sure it would be her last one. She carried a black bag over her shoulder, intent on trying to salvage the one bridge that didn't seem completely burned up. When she walked into the busy laboratory, the conversations ceased as every eye was plastered on her. Murmurings and whispers followed her as she trudged the short distance to the back of the lab and found Dorst at his desk.

"L-Lyssa," Dorst said, shocked. "I didn't expect to see you here."

She nodded, unsure of what to say.

"Are you all right?" he asked.

"Do you care?"

"Of course I care, you're my sister," Dorst said.

Lyssa remembered all the calls that had gone unanswered to Vel. "I'm afraid that doesn't count for much anymore."

"What Al, Sage…whatever his name said to you—"

"Was deserved."

"It wasn't deserved," Dorst said with a kind smile. "I'm glad to see you."

Dorst would never know how much Lyssa appreciated those words at that moment.

"Glad because I have *tons* of paperwork for you to fill out." Dorst said, reaching into his desk and pulling out a thick folder.

"Are those my firing papers?"

"Firing?" Dorst shook his head. "Maternity leave papers. When you're due, who your doctor is, backpay and all that—"

"You mean I'm not fired?" Lyssa asked, shock replacing the numb devastation that had taken hold of her the past few weeks.

"Surprisingly…no. You aren't. As much as they've looked, and trust me, they've looked, there actually isn't any rule that explicitly forbids piracy," Dorst said. "Now they're a little pissed that you've hidden a pregnancy from them. And to be frank, so am I."

She picked up the bag and tossed it on his desk. "Take these. As an apology."

"What's this?" he said, picking up one of the carbon analyzer sensors.

"S…Father made them," she said. "Or he designed them and I had them rebuilt. They record the molecular signature of plants and…" She trailed off. "Anyway, I wanted you to have them."

"Why?"

"Because you haven't been awful. And I thought you might want to patent them so you could get a bigger lab."

"Just tell me this…Father wasn't a pirate, was he?" Dorst asked, glancing up.

She snorted. "No."

"And…" He sighed heavily. "And you really don't know where he is?"

She rubbed her stomach absentmindedly. After a long while, she realized Dorst was still waiting for an answer. "Dorst, I haven't seen him since I was eleven years old. Like I've been *saying*."

"And you've never looked for him? You mean, you're a woman who looks for people for a living and you've never once checked any of his bank accounts?"

"It was pretty clear he never wanted to see me again."

"But Father loved you—"

"That's bullshit. That man only loved one thing—his stupid experiments. I was just a means to the end."

"Why do you say that?"

"Because," Lyssa swallowed, unsure if she wanted to tell Dorst the truth. "Because why wouldn't I say that?"

"Why do you think he chose you for his assistant?"

"Because Mother didn't care if he killed me in the process," Lyssa snapped. "Least valuable kid over here."

"Oh Lyssa," Dorst said with a sigh. "You have no idea how much he fought for you."

"What are you talking about?"

"You were so smart, and so bored. Even as a little girl, you were always getting into trouble, stealing books from me and Jukin. Missing your sewing classes. We'd find you up some tree."

Lyssa didn't look at him.

"Mother, of course, wasn't interested in letting you attend preparatory classes with the other boys. She thought it indecent for a Serann woman to be alone on planets, and was convinced she could discipline the rebel out of you. She and Father had a major falling out over it when, one day, he left with you in tow."

"I don't remember any of that."

"You were so young, Lyss, just a baby. But after that, Father started telling everyone you were his assistant."

"Yeah, I was his assistant all right," Lyssa said darkly. "I was just his stupid pawn so he could experiment at Leveman's Vortex."

"Whatever he did with you as his assistant, he only did to protect you, to do right by you. He wasn't the best father, but his heart was in the right place."

"I wish I could believe that," Lyssa whispered.

"You'll find when you become a parent that nobody is perfect," Dorst said, sitting back. "Leveman's knows, my son—"

"Wait, you have a son?" Lyssa finally noticed the gold band on his hand. "When did you get married?"

Dorst smiled and shook his head. "My point is, when you become a parent, you'll discover that nobody has all the answers. When you're a kid, you think adults have it all figured out, and that they just… know everything." He smiled. "But as you grow up, you realize that the very things you hated your parents for are some of the behaviors you share."

"I'm nothing like Sostas—"

"Lyssa, you've been my employee for almost a year and you've just now noticed that I'm married with a son—your nephew, I might add. You don't know the names of most, if not all of our siblings. And from

what I can tell, you have been too wrapped up in your own little...
illegal endeavors to be bothered with anything else unless it pops up
screaming at you. And that is exactly how I remember Father to be,"
Dorst finished. "You are *just* like him."

She looked at the ground; Dorst wasn't the first person to say that
to her.

"The one thing I've learned is that you can't choose your genetics,
but you can choose what you do with them. You know, I came from
the very same parents you did, and I'm perfectly normal." His face
shifted. "Even with a father who ignored me and a mother who was
nothing if not overly critical of me almost my entire life."

She looked at her hands and let his words sink in, even though she
didn't want to. Sage was trying to tell her the same thing. He *was*
different than his father, because he chose to be. But she wasn't sure
she could be.

"I'm going to give you a little bit of unsolicited advice. Try and
find him. Use all of those skills I've been reading about. I think you'll
be able to find some peace and maybe move on." He paused. "You
need to move on. Even if you decide to give up that child to Al—Sage,
whatever his name is. You as a person are harboring a lot of guilt for
something that you are not responsible for. You need closure for
yourself. Go use that Universal Bank alias thing that I keep hearing
about."

Lyssa knew, deep down, that she didn't need to scour the
Universal Bank to find Sostas. She just needed a complex algorithm to
calculate angle of entry.

CHAPTER SEVENTEEN

Leveman's Vortex swirled in front of her as she thumbed the black leather journal nervously. The baby had been kicking nonstop, stirred up by Lyssa's own anxiety.

"I know, I know," she hissed at her belly. "I don't want to go either. It's so stupid of me to even think about going."

The baby kicked again.

"Seriously, this is so stupid." She leaned back in her chair. "Didn't we yell at Vel for this exact same dumb idea?" She let the grimace cross her face. Vel, who wasn't speaking to her. Then she shook her head. "I *know* he's not there. Remember? We went there with Pymus." She paused. "Well, you weren't there. But I was. And there was no one else."

She chewed her lip and the baby moved again.

"Who needs to have closure anyway?" she asked. "And there's no guarantee I'm going to get closure. And…"

The baby kicked, hard, and she winced.

"You really want to go? I mean, it's gonna be dangerous."

No response from the bulge.

"Sage would kill…" Sage wasn't actually talking to her right now. Nobody was talking to her because she'd done a damned good job of destroying every relationship she'd ever had. No matter what Dorst might say, she knew where she'd learned she was worthless and not deserving of happiness.

The baby kicked again, and she sighed.

"I mean, this is stupidity," she said, pulling up the application she used to calculate the angle of entry. "Pure madness." She adjusted the calculation to mark an entry instead of an exit.

Then she waited.

"Kick once if you think this is a good idea."

The bug kicked.

"*Aaah*," she said, jumpstarting her ships engines and speeding toward the whiteness ahead of her.

Almost immediately, her hands on the joystick felt heavier. Everything felt heavier. Bits and pieces of space debris clouded the window, but disintegrated from the sheer force of the vortex. The green on her dashboard flickered red for a moment then displayed an odd error. She placed a hand on her stomach, and the gravitational forces pushed and pulled on her as she sped towards the center. She was heavy and then light as air then heavy again, and she began to worry—had she made a terrible mistake? Had she just put her child's life in danger in the pursuit of some misguided search for her probably-dead father? Was it—

Then nothingness.

The instruments on her dashboard displayed completely different readings from each other. The space outside her ship was pure white, blinding, but at the same time not. She pushed herself out of her chair and waddled back to the edge of her ship. She noted that she was not dead and she was definitely still pregnant as she struggled to lower herself down her back ladder. That, at least, was good news.

She pressed the button on the back of her ship and lowered her ramp, gazing out into the white landscape. She rubbed her belly nervously and looked around for a sign of anyone. Pymus, even, might be welcome.

"Okay, Bug," she said, standing on the edge of the ramp. "Last time I was here, I hallucinated something terrible the moment I set foot on this place. I can't… This is so stupid. He's not here, obviously."

She looked out again, squinting for the ship she so desperately wanted to see. "I mean, it ended up working out in the end. I had a good run as Lyssa and Razia, but…" She hopped on one foot, then the other. "I've been a shitty person lately, and I'm pretty sure that if I take that step, we're both headed for a fiery doom."

She closed her eyes and walked back onto her ship, then returned to the edge of the ramp. "This was so stupid to even come here. He's not here and…" She sucked in a deep breath. "Okay, kiddo. We're going to do it. Nice and quick. If the world blows up, we hop right back on the ship and get out of here. And if we die, this was *your* idea, okay?"

She paused.

"Okay, this was my idea. But you goaded me into it."

Another pause.

"Why am I talking to myself?"

With her eyes closed, she lifted her foot and placed it on the ground. When she didn't hear the booms and thunders of the world disintegrating, she cracked open her eye. The world remained as white and pristine as before. She looked to her left and to her right, and everything was just empty.

"Huh…" She began to laugh. "Okay, I am officially confused, Great Creator."

"Lyssa."

Ice shot down her spine.

That voice was so familiar—gravelly, heart-rending, emotionally-charged.

Emotions welled up from somewhere deep and hidden, and she fought to keep them down where they belonged. She wasn't going to turn around, she wasn't going to give him the satisfaction of knowing that she'd returned to find him.

"Lyssa."

"I can't believe you," she hissed to the whiteness in front of her. "You stupid son of a bitch."

"Lyssa, turn around."

"No."

The hand slid over her shoulder, and it felt exactly the same, except she was much bigger than the last time he'd touched her. She rotated slowly, wishing she'd never even ventured there in the first place. She knew now that he had left her to...

Her mind went blank when her eyes landed on him. He wasn't as tall as she remembered, but his face was burned into her brain. The eyes, the beard, the hair. His nose. His shirt, his pants. Even down to his shoes. He was everything she remembered he would be—exactly as she remembered him to be.

Except he was smiling. He rarely did that.

"Hey, kiddo."

"Don't you '*hey, kiddo*' me!" she snarled, suddenly furious again. "You are the worst piece of shit I've ever... How could you... You left me to fend for myself...and you never... You've been here...and...." She trailed off, emotions threatening to broach the surface again. "You are the worst human being—"

"I'm dead, Lyssa."

Again, her mind went blank. "D-dead?"

"A miscalculation on my part, it would seem," he said, sounding like he had added too much sugar to his coffee. "I was so used to calculating the gravitational weight of two aboard my ship, that when I suddenly had one..." He sighed, and smiled warmly.

"D...dead..." Lyssa was still wrapping her head around this new concept. She suddenly realized that she *had* always considered him alive, that she had never actually believed—really believed—that he could have actually *died*.

"I never expected to be gone for more than a week, kiddo," Sostas said.

"B-but why didn't you bring me with you?" Lyssa felt eleven again. "You left me—"

"Coming here was too dangerous," Sostas said before giving her a sideways look that was suddenly so familiar. "I might add that you took a risk in bringing your daughter here."

Lyssa didn't even register that comment, she was still too tied up in coming to terms with the fact that Sostas was really dead. "You told me that I had screwed everything up, you said—"

"I never said that, Lyssa. You never listen, do you?"

The barb, even gently given, hurt.

"It was too dangerous for you to come with me anymore. I wasn't a very good father to you, and you were better off without me."

"So you think abandoning me was…" Her mouth dropped and she took a step back. Something thudded in her chest, as if the world had just turned over again.

She was planning to do the same thing to her kid that Sostas had done to her.

For the exact same reason.

She let this new knowledge settle in the deep recesses of her mind. It wasn't that Sostas didn't love her, it was *because* he loved her that he left her. Dorst was right. Sostas had no more idea how to be a good parent than she did. But she had a choice—she could be like him or she could choose to be better.

She could be better.

"I have to go," she whispered, taking a step back. "I have to go fix this. I don't want her to end up like me…"

She looked up and realized she was all alone. Perhaps it had been nothing but another hallucination, but it felt as real as the first one He'd given her.

She eyed the distance where she knew the Arch of Eron stood, the silvery veil floating in the distance. And for once, she had no desire to seek it out. She knew, very acutely, what kind of a soul she was. Wayward, a little lost, and definitely one that made a lot of wrong choices for the right reasons. But she was a good person, worthy of love and happiness.

She just hoped it wasn't too late to get it back.

***

Lyssa's surety of herself faded the closer she came to D-882, but she didn't waver or second guess her decision to return. For once, when she slid her Lyssa Peate C-card, all the close-in parking stations popped up on the screen and she laughed to herself. Now that everyone knew Lyssa Peate was Razia, she would receive all the benefits

196

of being a top pirate.

Lucky for her, because she was definitely achier since she'd left the heavy pressure of Leveman's Vortex. The bug had been pretty active, and she was eager to see Dr. Bianco at her next appointment to make sure everything was still fine. But this time, she expected to bring Sage with her.

She had absolutely no idea how she was planning to get Sage to forgive her, or even talk to her, but she was hoping for a burst of inspiration.

Popping out of the lift, she nearly scrambled back in. Twenty pirates stood in the street, all gaping at her with open mouths. They must have assembled when she made the parking deck purchase. She'd somehow not connected the dots that she still might be a wanted pirate. Or, perhaps, people just wanted to see her pregnant.

"You're so *fat!*" There was Fiege, the leader of the gang.

She ignored them and walked with her head held high across the street into the familiar bar. She hadn't been there in months, not since she was four months along, and it felt good to walk back in the front door.

Harms was exactly where she'd hoped he be, and she was glad to see him a little surprised to see her. He eyed her up and down and sat back.

"So who are you hunting today?" he asked with a ghost of a smile on his face. "An obstetrician?"

"Go get him," Lyssa said. "Please."

"Your friend has been trying to get him out of bed for a week," Harms said, slowly getting up out of the booth.

"Which friend?"

"The girl."

"Lizbeth's here. Good, I need to talk to her, too." Lyssa tried to squeeze herself into the booth, but found she didn't fit. Instead, she pulled up a chair from the table next to the booth and sat down.

"I don't think he wants to talk to you, Raz," Harms said. "He's pretty beat up."

"I know, and...just..." She clenched her jaw. "Just ask him if he's willing to listen for a...for a minute."

Harms nodded and left through a back door. His apartment was a few stories above his bar, and she hoped—prayed—that Sage would come down. Her back was aching and she breathed through some low-intensity cramps, which she'd been having since leaving the Vortex. Bianco had said she'd start having them in her last month, and it made her even more eager to get back to S-864.

Thee bar was quickly filling up with pirates, she began to question the sanity of talking to him in front of a crowd. And a crowd it was—she groaned when Relleck and Linro Lee took a front row seat next to her.

"Looking good, Razia," Relleck said. "Say, I've never slept with a pregnant chick before. You think it's any different?"

"Why don't you ask Teon?" Lee said with a snicker.

"Oi, knock it off before I knock you out." Ganon was now a party to her embarrassment, but she was glad to see Vel show up beside him. She waved at him, but Vel gave her such a dirty glare that she retracted her hands and placed them back on her belly, turning her eyes to the door and waiting.

After an eternity, she heard footsteps coming through the door and frowned when Lizbeth came out, looking livid. She walked right up to Lyssa, intent on striking her, and Lyssa cowered back.

"*I told you to be careful with him!*" Lizbeth seethed.

"I know, I know, I'm trying to make it right," Lyssa said. "Just… please go get him?"

"She doesn't need to."

Lyssa turned to see Sage standing in the door. He had dark circles under his eyes, and his hair was greasy. But she felt that same angry fire radiating off him as he took her in. He glared at Lizbeth and said, "You said she was here with the baby."

"I didn't lie," Lizbeth said, gesturing to Lyssa's stomach.

"I asked her to get you," Lyssa said, pushing herself out of the chair. She didn't get a good grip on the chair and fell back down. With a glare to the room, she pushed herself upright and sighed. "Look, we need to talk."

"Are you still pregnant? Then I have nothing to say to you." He didn't even bother looking at her.

"Sage, please," she whispered, not even embarrassed to be standing here, swollen bellied, begging Sage to listen to her, in front of probably the entire pirate population.

Yep, she spotted Dissident and Contestant wander in, pushing their way to the front of the now crowded bar.

"I told you that I was done, and I meant it," Sage said. "You and your self-centered, egotistical....*Ugh*!" He threw his hands up. "I can't even look at you anymore, I'm so done with you."

"You're right."

"Yes, I know I'm—"

"I am the worst kind of person." Another tear fell down her cheek, followed by another, as the dam she had spent so many years shoring up burst. A loud, barking sob shook her body as the release reverberated through her. He turned, eyes wide, but she buried her face into her hands as her shoulders shook.

"Are you crying?"

He was concerned and a little bit confused. She tried to speak, but only choked. Labored sobs came out as she placed her head in her hand, trying in vain to get a hold of herself. Once the dam had broken, the emotions flooded out like a river. She took heaving breaths, but that only served to make it worse.

His hand came to her cheek, brushing away a tear. "Why are you crying?"

"Because I can't..." she sniffled.

"Lyss, I—" His face softened. "I shouldn't have said—"

"You were right though." She lifted her eyes to meet his.

"Lyssa, I didn't mean—"

"I know what I say is wrong. I know I'm mean and hateful..." Her lip began to tremble. "And I know that I am, and I can't...I am so scared I can't change." She took a long breath in. "I've spent so long blaming everyone else...everything that's ever happened to me...for the way that I am. Because... because that was easier than admitting..." She took another shaky breath. "Easier than admitting I'm... I'm responsible for the way I am."

"Lyssa, I—"

"I spent my entire life thinking I was damaged in some way," she whispered. "Everything bad that ever happened to me… my father leaving, Tauron's death… I always knew it was because of me… Because in my soul… it's less painful not to try than to be hurt again because I will *always* get hurt…" She sniffed and more tears fell. "Because I thought I didn't deserve to be happy."

"Yes, you do," he said, brushing away her tears with his thumb.

"I know," she said with a smile. "I finally figured it out. And I just… I want to fix this. I don't want my kid to grow up thinking that she's not loved. Because I do… I love her." She laughed a little when his eyes flashed in happiness. "I love this kid more than anything. And I… and I love you, too. I want us to be a family, and I want—"

Sage took her cheeks in his hands and kissed her gently. She might have heard a little whooping from the crowd, but she didn't register it. She pressed her forehead to his and let more tears fall freely down her cheeks.

"So help me, I'm dragging your ass to therapy," he said. "Because you *so* need it."

She opened her mouth to retort something to him when a wave of pressure rolled through her and her hands flew to her stomach. "Ow."

"O…ow?" Sage's eyes widened. "Ow?"

Her hands clasped around his arms to support her as the pressure turned into pain and the need to push. "*Ow!*"

She sunk to her knees, bracing herself through the pain. Someone beside her was coaching her to breathe and two hands clasped hers. When the pain released, she took deep gasping breaths.

"Shit," Lyssa whispered, looking up into the eyes of Vel and Lizbeth, who had taken hold of her hands.

"Are you ready for this?" Lizbeth said with a grin.

Lyssa violently shook her head.

"It's okay," Vel said, glancing at his mini-computer. "This can take hours and—"

Another tightening started in the back of her body and moved forward. She clenched her fists and breathed through it, feeling like it was worse than the first.

"Wait a second." Sage stood behind her. "That's too close together."

"Sera said…sometimes they come quicker," Lyssa whispered, trying to remain calm between the contractions. "Call Sera, call Sera. Call…" She gritted her teeth. "Sera."

"*Yes?*" Sera's voice echoed on Vel's mini-computer. *"Is she going into labor?"*

"Yes!" Lyssa cried as the contraction pulsed.

"How close together?" Sera asked.

"Too close," Sage said. "Maybe a few minutes?"

"Damn," Sera said. *"Okay, can you find her a bed or somewhere to lie down?"*

"I have a backroom?" Harms offered, appearing at her side.

"No, no, no!" Lyssa barked, clutching Sage as he helped her up. "I am not having this baby in a pirate bar!"

"But it's the best pirate bar in the city?" Harms said with a laugh.

"And I don't think you have much of a choice, Lyss," Vel said. "To the backroom!"

Sage and Vel half-carried her into the back and helped her up on a table, with her protesting the whole time. "This is bullshit. I am not having a baby in here. It's gross and filthy. What if something goes wrong, what if—" She clenched her jaw as another contraction pressed down on her.

"Stop bitching and breathe." Sage sat behind her and she leaned into him. Sera's voice barked directions to Vel and Lizbeth, and Vel's mini-computer was pointed straight between her legs.

"Yes, that looks about right, looks like you've been blessed with a quick labor. Jinjina's last was fifteen minutes."

"Blessed is not the word I would use," Sage grunted, grabbing onto Lyssa's hand. "Okay, what do we do?"

"You are going to have to keep Lyssa calm, okay? Vel, I want you to hold the mini-computer steady. Lizbeth, you're going to have to catch the baby."

"This is not what I signed up for when I became your best friend, by the way," Lizbeth said with a wink. She handed the mini-computer to Vel, who held it steady.

Lyssa was aware that she was breathing, and that every few minutes, contractions occurred, but the number of times began to blur together until she heard Sera say, *"Lyssa, I am going to need you to push now, all right? Two big pushes and this will be over."*

"Did you hear that?" Sage said in her ear.

Lyssa grunted and grasped his hand tighter. "I don't think I can do this."

"Yes, you can."

"Push!"

Someone was screaming, perhaps it was her. Everything was hazy now, even though she could hear loud noises and see Lizbeth telling her to push. Vel was to her left, one hand holding the mini-computer, the other clasping hers. Sera's face was on the mini-computer, smiling and nodding. And Sage was behind her, where he'd always been.

"Push!"

Then she heard it. The wailing.

Her eyes flew open as a small, pink squirming thing with a loud squeal appeared in Lizbeth's arms.

"It's a girl..." Lizbeth choked out as she placed the baby with a shot of wet, black hair in Lyssa's arms. The room grew quiet except for the squalling coming from the little face taking big gulping breaths.

Lyssa had never seen anything so... There were no words. She had literally no words to describe the range of emotions coursing through her as she held her little girl in her arms.

Her little girl.

Her daughter.

Lyssa gently stroked her baby's cheek, and realized her own were wet. She took the tiny hand in hers and smiled. All the fear, the worry that Lyssa would never be able to love her own daughter, was gone. The idea that Lyssa would ever *leave* was laughable. She'd never let this beautiful kid out of her sight. Nothing else in the entire universe was as important to Lyssa as this little girl, and she was going to make sure her daughter knew it every day.

"Hi there," Lyssa murmured.

"She's perfect," Sage whispered, his chin resting on her shoulder. "Leveman's... She's so perfect." His hand came up to cup the baby's head and gently brush away the goo there. "We did good, Lyss."

"We did," she said with a small laugh.

A loud sob broke the bubble between them, and Lyssa finally remembered that Vel and Lizbeth were still in the room. Lizbeth's face was beet red as she sobbed what could only be described as ugly tears, and while Vel seemed to be a bit more dignified in his emotion, he was barely holding it together.

"Congratulations," Vel said, brushing hair out of Lyssa's face. "That was impressive."

"More impressive than taking down Dal Jamus?" Lyssa asked.

"Yeah," Vel said with a laugh. "Much more impressive."

Lyssa looked down at her daughter and grinned. "I have to say, I cook a pretty beautiful baby."

"Lyssa, that's vulgar."

"Oh, I forgot about you," Lyssa said, looking at the face of her sister in the mini-computer screen. To her surprise, Sera's face was also wet and twisted with happy emotion.

"I am so proud of you," Sera said. *"Now come home. I want to see my new niece as soon as possible."*

"Thank you," Lyssa said. Then, smiling, she added, "And I will." Sera nodded and ended the call.

"But really, you do cook a really nice baby," Lizbeth said, coming to stand on the other side of Lyssa. Lizbeth leaned down to press a kiss to Lyssa's head and Lyssa leaned into it.

"Thank you, too. I couldn't have done this without you," Lyssa whispered.

"What are best friends for but getting up in your business?" Lizbeth said with a laugh. She brushed a hand over the baby's face. "What's her name?"

"I... don't have one," Lyssa said, panicking. She'd been calling her 'bug' for so long that she'd never even considered an actual name. "Sage?"

"Er..."

"You didn't name her?" Lyssa blanched.

"Well, I did, but..." Sage hesitated. "I didn't think you'd like it."

"What, is it like Taurona or something stupid?"

"R-Ragen," he said. "Little bit of you, and a little bit of me." The cheek she could see turned a darker shade of red. "I mean, Ragen

Lyssandra. If you want."

"Wait a second," Lyssa said. "What if it was a boy?"

"Sage. Obviously."

She barked laughter. "What happened to, little bit of you, little bit of me?" Sage shrugged and she rolled her eyes. "I can't believe I just had a baby with you." But as she said it, she smiled. "I can't believe I just had a baby with you." She gazed at her daughter again, seeing so much of herself and at the same time, so much of Sage. "You know, I hate my full name. How about Isabel for a middle name? I think that sounds better, you know?"

"Isabel?" Vel said, sharing a look with Lizbeth. "Where'd that name come from?"

"It was my mom's," Sage murmured quietly. "That sounds great, Lyss."

"Aw, you big softy," Lizbeth said, patting Lyssa on the leg.

There was a knock at the door. Harms poked his head in, eyes closed. "Is everyone decent? I want to see my godchild."

"Uh, he's not the godfather," Vel said, giving Sage and Lyssa a look.

"We'll figure all that out later," Lyssa said as Lizbeth tossed a blanket over her lower half.

But it wasn't just Harms, it was Harms, Ganon, Sobal, Keal, Nalton, Dissident, Relleck, Linro Lee—

"*Lizbeth*!" Lyssa barked, holding her baby closer. "Crowd control, please!"

Lizbeth nodded and turned to the growing crowd in the back room, counting off five and shooing the rest out the door. She took special care to kick Relleck out, making sure he knew he wasn't welcome back in at anytime. She allowed Ganon, Sobal, and Harms to remain, and they crowded around Lyssa with wide grins on their faces.

"You really pushed that out of you?" Sobal asked, wide-eyed.

Ganon scoffed. "Can't take this kid anywhere, you know?"

"She's beautiful, Raz… Lyssa…whatever in Leveman's I call you now," Harms said. "Are you going to continue bounty hunting?"

She arched her brow at him. "Um. Obviously."

"I expected you would," Harms said with a hearty laugh. "Just give it a few months, okay? Vel can uphold the family name."

"Yeah about that," Lyssa said, glaring at Vel. "Time to quit Ganon's crew and come work for me."

"Lyss," Vel said, sharing a look with Ganon. "I mean… I love you, but… I kind of want to see what it's like on a real pirate ship, you know? I mean, you had Tauron." He looked down at the baby in her arms. "Besides, you're going to be pretty busy, right?"

She followed his gaze and looked into the bright eyes staring back at her. She could give up bounty hunting for a bit if it meant she could stare at this beautiful creature all day. Without taking her eyes away from the baby, she reached out her free hand to grab Ganon by the shirt and yank him down to her level, saying sweetly, "If anything happens to my brother, I swear to Leveman's Vortex that I will destroy your manhood."

Ganon laughed, but she heard the requisite amount of fear. "I promise I'll take good care of him."

She let him go and returned her hand to her baby, who was starting to squirm and writhe. She realized, very suddenly, that she had a living, breathing thing in her arms that she was responsible for.

"What do we do now?" she whispered to Sage. "Do I… do I feed it or something?"

"How about we find you two a hospital and get checked out?" Sage said. "Then we'll figure it out from there."

"But I would take the backdoor," Harms said. "Because it's packed out there. It's a good thing Jukin's out of commission. He'd have his pick of the top pirates."

"See?" Ganon said proudly. "What I'd tell you—most famous kid in piracy!"

CHAPTER EIGHTEEN

Lyssa Peate, bounty hunter, new mother, all-around kickass human being, strutted down the orange dusty streets of D-882 with a smug smile on her face. Next to her, wearing their two-month-old daughter, was her...Sage. Her Sage, that was how she decided to define him. Not as if she'd given much thought to their status during weeks of sleepless nights, breastfeeding, diaper changes, and near constant visits from Lizbeth, Vel, Ganon and his crew, and even a week-long stay from Harms.

Before she'd known it, Ragen was at her two-month checkup and the calls started from Dissident, reminding her that she was supposed to be his top bounty hunter and she needed to get her ass in gear and capture some pirates, as long as she stopped in and let him hold the baby for a bit (she'd agreed to the first part, but not the second).

For this trip to D-882, she had her eyes set on Dalton Burk, one of the last few pirates remaining of the old guard in Contestant's web. She'd found some very old research on him that was still good after nearly two years, and was hoping to nab a quick win.

She glanced over to Sage, who had one hand in hers, and the other scrolling through his mini-computer, with Ragen tied tightly to his chest. There was something so incredibly sexy about Sage when he was fathering. She was particularly grateful when Bianco gave her the go-ahead to start working out again, among other things. Sleepless nights had resulted in their fair share of blow-up arguments between the two of them, and it was nice to be able to make up with him in all the fun ways. Things weren't perfect, and yet they were. She found herself too busy enjoying her life to worry when it would come to an end.

Lyssa peered between the folds of the wrap to make sure her baby was still sleeping. Sage was typing a message to someone.

"Who are you talking to?" Lyssa said to Sage.

"Sera. She wants to know if you still want her to come visit next week or if you'd like to come to the Manor for a few days."

Lyssa considered the proposition. Faced with the unknown territory of motherhood, Lyssa'd found herself in near constant contact with Sera, who had been a wealth of information. After the fifth call during one particularly sleepless night during the first few days, Sera had offered to come spend a week and help out. It went so well that Lyssa had asked her to come back more often.

She had also found out during this visit that Mrs. Dr. Sostas Peate had "decided" to move into one of her many guest houses (far, far away from the Manor) and that Jukin had been volun-told to live with her to ensure she was well taken care of in her old age. The two of them were rarely seen around the Manor anymore, except by expressed invitation from the new matriarch, Sera. True to her word, she'd allowed everyone else to stay in the Manor if they chose to, even moving Lyssa's room to a larger suite with an attached nursery.

"Lyss?" Sage asked. "What do you think? Manor or our house?"

"Oh, why not? Let's go spend a few days there," Lyssa said with a small shrug. "I told Sera I'd clean out Sostas' office anyway."

"Would you like me to invite Vel—?"

"He can get sucked," Lyssa said with a growl.

"You know changing runners wasn't his decision. Contestant offered Ganon a better deal. I can't blame him for taking it."

"But now he could hunt *me*. His big sister."

"You know he'd never go after you." Sage's mouth twitched.

"Would you go after them?"

She didn't answer. "Maybe I'll go find me a different runner then."

"I think you should," Sage said, grasping the tiny feet at his waist. "Insurgent could use a decent bounty hunter. He's hurting. None of his new pirates are worth anything."

Lyssa surveyed him curiously. "For a retired pirate, you know an awful lot about what's going on in the universe."

He shrugged. "Who knows, maybe Ragen and I will go into business for ourselves. Daddy and Daughter Pirate Informants."

"She's going to be a bounty hunter, thank you very much."

"Of course she is."

"And speaking of that, what in Leveman's is with Dalton Burk right now?" Lyssa grumbled. "The whole way to '882, he's active. Now that I'm here, he decides to be quiet?"

"Well, he's probably asleep, don't you think?"

"People do that still?"

"Wouldn't know. I have a newborn."

She smiled and glanced down at the baby on his chest. "She looks so cute, doesn't she?" Lyssa reached her hand in and grasped Ragen's tiny hand, kissing it gently.

"Hey, Lyss, your mini's lighting up."

"Finally!" Lyssa said, as the alert popped up on her mini-computer. "Burk is on the move. Gotta run."

Sage grabbed her hand before she got two steps and she bounced back to him, pressing a short, sweet kiss to his lips and then one to Ragen's forehead before dashing away.

"Don't forget to duck!" Sage called after her.

She tossed him a rude gesture before sprinting down the street.

It took her just under an hour to find and capture Dalton Burk, who was more interested in hearing about her baby than realizing he'd just been captured. Lyssa filled him in on life with a newborn as she handcuffed him and pushed him onto her floating canvas. She walked out of the bar and grinned when she saw Sage and Ragen waiting on a nearby bench.

"Nice work," Sage said, looking up to see her bounty on the ground. "And nice shiner."

"Didn't duck fast enough," Lyssa said, more interested in the baby. "Did she miss me?"

"She definitely missed you," Sage said patiently. "Even though she's two months old, and she was asleep the whole time, she definitely missed you."

Lyssa nodded and bit her lip.

Sage, again, sounded very patient. "Would you like to hold her while I take your bounty?"

Her first reaction was to blanch, to throw a hissy fit that he *dared* insinuate that she needed help, and to try to balance the baby and the bounty in her hand.

"Remember what the therapist said."

"*Shut up!*" Lyssa barked, hoping that Burk didn't hear.

"Well?"

She thrust the cords of her floating canvas at him. "Please?"

Sage grinned at her proudly and transferred the small, warm baby into her arms. It felt like a piece of her had been returned, and she beamed down at their daughter. She was starting to look a little like Sage (although Sage said he thought she looked like Lyssa), and Lyssa hoped she had all of his sunny qualities and none of her self-doubt. Then again, Sage had said he hoped Ragen had Lyssa's intelligence and good heart.

"Hey there, Dalton," Sage said to the man bound below them. "How's it going?"

"Been better, Sage, been better," he grumbled. "Say, girlie…I mean, which confounded name do you want me to call you?"

"Lyssa is fine." She smiled as Ragen's tiny hand clasped around her finger.

"Yeah, so which of my aliases did you catch me with?"

"Oh…" She thought for a second, rocking slowly. "All of them?"

"Even George Yertza?"

"Yep."

"Damn. It's a good thing you had that baby."

"Oh yeah, why's that?" she snapped.

"'Cause there'd be no pirates left in our web!" Burk laughed. "How about you pick on some of the other webs for once?

Contestant's furious… he says, why in Leveman's Vortex did I take on her damned brother if she's just going to pick off all my pirates? I tell ya, girlie, Dissident sure got lucky that you fell into his lap."

She caught Sage's smile and tried not to beam too brightly. "You hear that, Ragen? Your mommy is one of the *best* bounty hunters in the whole universe. And someday, you'll be the *best* bounty hunter… And I will be so proud. Not like your stupid Uncle Vel, with whom Mommy is *fighting* forever and ever…"

ACKNØWLEDGEMENTS

This is the chronological end to Lyssa's story. Never in my wildest dreams would I have ever expected to have gotten this far, to have done the things that I've done, to have had the creativity and focus to have put on paper the four books of this series. And I have you, the reader, to thank for that. You guys keep buyin' em, I keep writing 'em. I hope that Razia's journey has been as fulfilling for you as it's been for me these past fifteen years. Ugly tears all around.

My beta readers are the wind beneath my wings. Julia, Christina, Bexter, Kristin and, of course, Mom, thanks for taking this journey with me once again and providing me your thoughtful and awesome feedback.

Extra special thanks to Valerie, for helping me make Lyssa's pregnancy truthful, and Adelyn, for the cuddles that got me in the mood to write about the beebees.

Danielle, you are a magical unicorn. I'm so thrilled that I found you and even more thrilled that you helped me get this beautiful story up to snuff.

ALSØ BY THE AUTHØR

The Lexie Carrigan Chronicles

Lexie Carrigan thought she was weird enough until her family drops a bomb on her—she's magical. Now the girl who's never made waves is blowing up her nightstand and no one seems to want to help her. That is, until a kind gentleman shows up with all the answers. But Lexie finds out being magical is the least weird thing about her.

Spells and Sorcery is the first book in the Lexie Carrigan Chronicles, and is available now in eBook, Paperback, Audiobook, and Hardcover.

DEMON SPRING TRILOGY

Three years ago, Jack Grenard's wife was brutally murdered by demons. Now, along with his partner Cam Macarro, he's trying to rebuild his life in Atlanta. But on a routine investigation, they find a demon who saves instead of kills. They must discover who she is before Demon Spring, the quadrennial breach between the human world and demon realm, when all hell—literally—breaks loose.

The Demon Spring Trilogy is the first urban fantasy from S. Usher Evans and will be released in 2018 in eBook, Paperback, and Hardcover.

ALSØ BY THE AUTHØR

empath

Lauren Dailey is in break-up hell, but if you ask her she's doing just great. She hears a mysterious voice promising an easy escape from her problems and finds herself in a brand new world where she has the power to feel what others are feeling. Just one problem—there's a dragon in the mountains that happens to eat Empaths. And it might be the source of the mysterious voice tempting her deeper into her own darkness.

Empath is a stand-alone fantasy that is available now in eBook, Paperback, and Hardcover.

THE MADION WAR TRILOGY

He's a prince, she's a pilot, they're at war. But when they are marooned on a deserted island hundreds of miles from either nation, they must set aside their differences and work together if they want to survive.

The Madion War Trilogy is available in eBook, paperback, and hardcover. Download the first book, The Island, for free on all eBookstores.

ABØUT THE AUTHØR

S. Usher Evans was born and raised in Pensacola, Florida. After a decade of fighting bureaucratic battles as an IT consultant in Washington, DC, she suffered a massive quarter-life-crisis. She decided fighting dragons was more fun than writing policy, so she moved back to Pensacola to write books full-time. She currently resides with her two dogs, Zoe and Mr. Biscuit, and frequently can be found plotting on the beach.

Visit S. Usher Evans online at:
http://www.susherevans.com/

Twitter: www.twitter.com/susherevans
Facebook: www.facebook.com/susherevans
Instagram: www.instagram.com/susherevans